Disaster Girl

To Brian + Lisa—
So glad that we're re-connecting in 2021. Love you guys!
Michelle
(Dayton)

Disaster Girl

Michelle Dayton

Disaster Girl

Tule Publishing First Printing, May 2021

The Tule Publishing, Inc.

Second Publication by Tule Publishing 2021

Cover design by Erin Dameron-Hill

ISBN: 978-1-953647-82-5

Chapter One

"WHO WANTS DINNER?" I shouted, banging on Roz's door. My seventy-two-year-old next-door neighbor had been hobbling on the stairs when she went out for her copy of the *Trib* this morning. Like me, she rarely cooked. Unlike me, she hadn't quite mastered the variety of Chicago's food delivery apps. If her bad ankle was acting up again, she was probably scowling into her fridge right now.

But in my hands I held the answer to any hungry woman's dream. Spicy fried chicken sandwiches, along with sides of mac and cheese and peach cobbler for dessert. All courtesy of the Roost restaurant, conveniently located three blocks from our apartment building. Possibly I did their takeout a little too often; the guys who worked there had taken to yelling my usual order, "Extra pickles," in unison whenever I walked in.

Roz's door swung open, and she peered up at me through an enormous pair of cat-eye glasses. She looked down at the bags and up at my face. "Is this a bribe so I don't mention the revolving door of dick coming out of your apartment?"

My lips quivered, and I barely managed to hold a straight face. Roz's need to enter every single conversation with some sort of shocking statement or question was a quirk I adored.

"Not at all!" I answered. "I'd love your commentary on the amount of dick around here. And please, don't limit it to my apartment. I'd love your thoughts on the whole building."

Her nostrils flared, a sure sign she was amused. She raised an eyebrow and looked at the bags again. "Is there cobbler in there?"

I waved one of them under her nose. "Of course."

She sniffed. "Then I'll restrain myself to one more remark." She waggled the raised eyebrow. "That young guy you brought home the other night looked like a poor man's version of Channing Tatum."

I burst out laughing. Scott—I think that was his name—the guy I'd brought home from my favorite neighborhood pub on Friday night, *did* vaguely resemble Magic Mike. He hadn't exactly rocked my world in the bedroom, but he was cheerful and friendly and he knew the steps to the dance as well as I did. Drinks, laughs, sex, good-bye. A wonderful Friday night had by all. Easy-peasy lemon squeezy.

Roz snatched one of the bags out of my hands. "As self-control isn't really one of your strengths, I suppose I should take this before you eat it all yourself."

"I love you too, Roz." When I was a senior citizen, I wanted to be just like her: a single, sassy, foul-mouthed, city-living workaholic who did whatever she wanted. Actually, minus forty years, I was basically her already. Well, plus the revolving door of dick.

She grinned at me and gestured inside her apartment. "You want to come in? I was just about to open a Bordeaux and start on season two of *Outlander*."

Ooh, tempting. Roz was a wine snob and always had good bottles on hand. Plus, there was nothing more hilarious in the world than listening to her thoughts about kilted Scotsmen drinking whiskey, fighting, and indulging in Starz-channel sex.

But I hung out with Roz all the time, and I knew how easily we could make one bottle turn into two, and two episodes into four. I shook my head. "No thanks. Early night for me." I had a 9:00 a.m. presentation to a new client in the morning, and my boss had stressed the importance of the meeting multiple times, which wasn't like him. I wasn't worried though. I'd done my homework and I was completely prepared. Weekend Tess might revel in unpredictable spontaneity, but Workweek Tess always had her shit together.

Roz's eyes twinkled. "Early to sleep, eh? I guess that makes sense. You're definitely dressed for bed."

I opened my mouth wide and put my hand over my heart in mock offense. As alike as we were in other ways, Roz was old-school in matters of one's appearance. She'd barely left her apartment today but she was wearing tailored slacks, a perfectly ironed cardigan, and a face full of makeup. Along with my black leggings and thigh-high boots, I was wearing a thin T-shirt I'd slept in the night before. With no bra. It said: "Feelings are boring. Kissing is awesome." My hair was in an untidy ponytail and my eyes were smudged with last night's liner.

"I'm surprised Kat let you wear that to brunch," she said.

"Ha-ha. Good night," I answered, my smile fading a bit.

Unintentionally, Roz had scored a point.

Roz winked. "Thanks for dinner." She slammed the door without another word.

In my own apartment, I threw the bag of food on the coffee table and unearthed my remote from the pile of books and blankets on my couch. Before I turned on the TV, I pulled out my phone and looked at the text message from my sister I'd received first thing this morning.

I can't make brunch today.

I frowned down at the screen, just like I'd done when it first popped up. It was an unusually short message for Kat, and it was pretty weird for her to cancel on our standing tradition without explaining why. Year-round, rain or shine, we met at the same diner at noon every Sunday.

Dinner could wait another minute. Biting my lip, I tapped the Facebook app on my phone.

Technically, I'm not even on Facebook. I took a mouthy stand against it more than a dozen years ago to everyone who'd listen. "Why do I want to see people I secretly hate posting filtered photos of how fake-great their lives are?" That kind of thing.

But then I kind of wanted to see those stupid photos. And when Kat got old enough to have her own page, I figured it was only responsible that I be able to monitor her online activity. So I did what any intelligent, semi-sneaky person would do in such a situation. I created a fake profile using a stock photo I found of a generically cute girl jogging. Then I sent out friend requests to everyone I knew. People are more careful now, but for a while it was all about how many friends you had, so no one turned me down.

I navigated to Kat's page…and inhaled so sharply the sound bounced off the walls in my quiet living room.

Well, at least I knew why Kat canceled on me. She'd had other brunch plans.

The photo was shocking enough. But her comment underneath broke my heart.

I stood and started to pace. My beloved small apartment suddenly felt claustrophobic, like it was going to collapse and smother me. I needed air; I needed a drink; I needed a distraction from the memories that now threatened to ruin my night.

"YOU CAN'T EAT that in here, Tess." My friend Micki, the bartender and owner of Fizz, glared at me as I perched on my regular stool and spread my enviable supper in front of me on the bar. "We have a kitchen, you know."

I took a huge bite of the sandwich and rolled my eyes back in my head. So, so good. I chewed slowly, enjoying Micki's scowl. "Yeah, but your food sucks."

The other regulars hollered in agreement and raised their beers at me. "Cheers to that." I smiled at them and kept eating. Micki wouldn't do anything other than glower. In addition to being friends, I was also one of her most valuable customers.

As the calories hit my bloodstream, I blew out a long breath. I was feeling incrementally better after the short walk to the bar and hearing the crunching sound the dried leaves on the sidewalk made as I stomped on them with my boots.

It was a good move, to get out of the apartment and into the company of others. As my therapist liked to say, *"Nothing positive comes from stewing in guilt about old mistakes."*

Micki huffed. "Give me a damn biscuit, at least." I generously handed her half of my extra. She popped it in her mouth, wiped a few crumbs from her coat of bright red lipstick. As always, her classic makeup was the perfect contrast to her edgy black faux hawk. "You want a bourbon?"

Normally, yes. All Friday or Saturday night long. But I had that presentation in the morning. "Since it's a school night," I said. "Just one."

"I saw you in here on Friday," Joe called over, waggling his eyebrows at me. No surprise there. Joe practically lived at Fizz. I didn't think I'd ever been there when his ass wasn't parked in the stool closest to the waitress stand. "Made a new friend, eh?"

The other guys laughed, and I flicked my eyes to the ceiling. They loved giving me flack about the Magic Mikes in my life. "You finally gonna keep this one?" Joe yelled.

I swallowed some bourbon and cocked an eyebrow. Joe knew I couldn't stand the double standard about men and women and casual sex. "You gonna keep that girl with the nose ring you took home last week?"

Joe snorted. "No," he admitted. He looked up at me again, eyes twinkling. "You didn't get locked out again, did you?"

The rest of the guys at the bar hooted. The Lockout Incident was one of their favorite Tess stories. I'd been a little overserved one night last winter and hooked up with a guy just as drunk as I was. When we got back to my apartment, I couldn't find my keys in my purse. Never one to give up, I concocted a brilliant plan to climb on the roof of the building's entryway and lower myself through a skylight. My inebriated new friend agreed to let me climb on his shoulders to try to reach the roof. I'd grasped the snowy gutter for a glorious twenty seconds before the guy lost his balance, sending us both into the bushes. We'd reappeared at Fizz twenty minutes after we left, covered in snow, leaves, and bruises. At which point, we ordered a round for the entire bar. The Fizz guys' favorite part was that I'd had my keys in my coat pocket all along.

Now, as they made fun of me, I just shrugged and took another bite of the spicy chicken sandwich. I never minded their good-natured, big-brother-like ribbing. And hell, I had plenty of silly stories to keep them entertained. Per usual, Joe immediately teed up another one. "At least you weren't in a dancing mood on Friday. Remember when you climbed up on the bar to do the Whip/Nae Nae and kicked Micki in the face?" He mimed wiping a tear. "That one gets me every time." Behind the bar, Micki shook her head, less amused. She'd sported a nasty-looking shiner for weeks.

"Let her eat in peace." Not surprisingly, the request came from Toby, the youngest and most recent addition to Fizz's ragtag team of regulars. When he'd started coming to the bar last year, he'd watched every move I made. Hung on every word that came out of my mouth. It was extremely flattering, especially because he had a dimpled chin and was built like Thor. But I stayed far, far away. He practically had "I want a girlfriend" written in neon on his forehead. Toby was a total sweetheart, and despite whatever his hormones were telling him, the last thing he needed was a romp with me. I would have trampled the poor guy.

I took my time finishing my dinner, occasionally forcing a laugh to one of Micki's jokes or an eye-roll to one of Joe's pronouncements or a smile to one of Toby's earnest remarks. But I couldn't get Kat's Facebook post out of my mind.

I wasn't the only one staring at my phone. Usually the guys were more focused on their beers or the Sunday Night Football game showing on the flat-screen TVs, but tonight they were huddled over their phones while gossiping in low voices like a bunch of gangsters at a racetrack.

"What are you looking at?" I finally demanded, my curiosity getting the better of me.

Joe gave me a semi-sheepish look, while Toby flushed downright crimson. Clearly, it was something dirty. They'd show me anyway. I'd established my "one of the guys" cred a long time ago.

Joe shrugged. "There's this dude. Calls himself the FSG. About six months ago, he started an amateur sex tape site. He releases new ones every month. It's kind of a clearinghouse. He buys sex tapes from anyone who sends them in, and he releases at least one of his own every month too. You can sign up for his newsletter and he sends you teasers and announcements."

"Pervert," I said without heat, already losing interest.

Micki brought Joe another pint. "So guys are into porn. What else is new?"

Joe held up his phone and gave it a little shake. "Actually, this is a little different. From a marketing standpoint, the way he's released the videos has been kind of brilliant."

Micki and I both let out a long-suffering sigh. Joe was doing a marketing degree program at one of the city colleges, and he *loved* to talk about it.

Undeterred, he went on. "He's done a regional rollout. Six months ago, he released his California girls videos. Five months ago, his New York City files. Four months ago, the ladies of Texas. So there's all this localized interest; his site gets a brand-new boost every month. It's all over social media."

Toby put his elbows on the bar and leaned forward. "Don't sound impressed! He's a total creep! The videos are disgusting. I haven't watched them, of course—"

"Of course!" Joe and Micki said sarcastically in unison.

Toby glared at them. "He says on the site that all of the videos were created consensually, but even if that's true, I'll bet you a million bucks that the women aren't cool with him putting the videos on the internet."

I frowned. "That *is* really shitty. What's the FSG stand for?"

The guys groaned. Joe shook his head. "On his site, he says it can stand for 'Fucking Sex Ghost' because no one knows his real identity. But he personally prefers Fucking Sex God."

I gagged and lurched forward, like I was throwing up in my mouth. "It's truly hard to comprehend that level of douchebaggery."

"He's releasing a set of Chicago videos in less than a month. Right at midnight on Halloween," Joe said. "In the past, he's dropped ten or twelve per city." He wiggled his phone in the air again. "We were just wondering if we'd recognize any of the Chicago girls."

"Don't support him!" Toby protested. "Don't pay to watch stuff on his site. He's a criminal."

"I'm not going to pay for anything," Joe assured him. "But I did sign up for the free newsletter. I guess he puts stills from the videos in it, enough so you can see who'll feature in the upcoming release. Those pics are being sent out any minute now!" He rubbed his hands together maniacally.

My stomach started to hurt in sympathy for those poor girls. "Don't be such an asshole," I snapped. "That kind of thing can be a life-ruiner for women."

Joe lifted a shoulder. "Then they shouldn't have been so stupid to make a sex tape in the first place."

What?! I aimed my patented death stare at him and pointed a fingernail in his smug face. "You're seriously victim-blaming here? You're saying that if a woman chooses to be sexually adventurous and makes a recording, then all bets are off? That she shouldn't be allowed to decide what happens with that recording?"

"Don't get in a snit, Tessie. Christ." Joe sniffed.

My eyes flared. He knew I hated it when he called me Tessie. Although it was better than "Hair, Boobs, and Boots," his old nickname for me. "But it's perfect!" he'd protested slyly when I'd told him to knock it off. "It's your signature look." He wasn't exactly wrong, but I'd dumped a pint of Guinness over his head the last time he'd said it. Which meant I was kind of stuck with Tessie.

Now, he held up a mollifying hand, a physical gesture

that said "calm down." Which, as everyone knows, was a surefire way to transform irritation into full anger. "I'm not sayin' it's right for this dickwad to put the videos on the internet without the girls' permission. I'm just sayin' that it's not smart to make one in the first place. *I'd* never do anything so dumb."

"Reeallly," I drawled, throwing back the rest of my bourbon. As if I'd rung a bell, Micki appeared with the bottle of Knob Creek and a questioning eyebrow.

I ignored her because I was about to go on a roll. "Really, Joe? So if the hottest woman you'd ever seen, a Selena Gomez lookalike, took you home and said that her number-one turn-on would be to make a sex tape with you...you wouldn't do it?"

A minute of silence passed as Toby, Micki, and I stared him down. Joe's stubborn face eventually melted into a conciliatory smile. "Well, maybe in that one very particular scenario."

Toby and Micki laughed, but I wasn't quite ready to let him off the hook. "Women are allowed to define any scenario they want," I announced.

"Yeah, yeah," Joe conceded. "They—you—can do what you want, I know that. Get off your feminist high horse. I guess what I really mean, then, is that they just shoulda been more careful about what happened to the videos."

The TV above the bar returned from commercial to Sunday Night Football. Joe, Toby, and the rest of the guys erupted in cheers as the Bears' defense intercepted a Viking pass. Micki left us to serve a bunch of meatheads howling for Bud Light.

I tapped my empty bourbon glass against the bar, listening to the ice clink. I argued with Joe about something just about every time I came to Fizz, but it was usually just for fun. We both enjoyed sparring.

Tonight I was truly vexed.

"Try to be more deliberate with your emotions," my therapist always suggested. *"When you're feeling upset, really try to understand why."*

Maybe I was just transferring my hurt about Kat into anger at Joe's comments about the internet's latest sleazy celebrity. Anger was so much easier to deal with than hurt.

Kat wouldn't mention her special little brunch to me. I'd pretend I didn't know about it...and we'd move on. And the hurt would fade.

Sighing, I dug in my purse for my credit card, put it on the bar, and went over my Sunday night checklist: my Monday morning alarm—ringtone assigned to the fabulous '90s song "Bitch" by Meredith Brooks—was set and ready. I'd picked up my dry cleaning yesterday, so I had all my favorite pencil skirts to choose from. There'd be plenty of time to review my presentation notes on the "L" ride downtown in the morning.

Yep, I was good to go for the week. If Micki would get her butt back over here to take my card so I could pay for my drink and leave. I raised my head to call for her—

Wait, why was everyone looking at me?

Still partially hunched over their phones, Joe and Toby were doing a comical sort of down-and-up move with their heads. Their eyes flicked down to the screen of Joe's phone and then back up at me. Down, up. Down, up. Down, up.

Behind the bar, Micki was twisting a rag around her hands and staring at me with brows drawn together over stricken eyes.

"What?" I snapped. This wasn't a prank or a group sympathy card reaction. This was a "You'll never hold your head up in Fizz again" full-blown stare of horror.

Chapter Two

THE THREE OF them remained uncharacteristically silent. Micki's lips were tight with her cheeks slightly puffed out, like she was holding her breath. Joe picked up his fresh pint and downed half of it in a single gulp.

"WHAT?" I said again. "Tell me."

Toby jumped to his feet so fast his barstool crashed to the floor behind him. "Uh, sorry about that. I, uh, need to get home." He yanked the stool upright with one hand and grabbed his wallet and phone off the bar with the other. "See y'all later." He purposely avoided my confused gaze as he headed out.

Micki and Joe were still frozen in place. I stood on the rungs of my stool. "What is wrong with you guys?"

Joe turned to Micki. "Rock, paper, scissors? Loser shows her?"

She nodded quickly, and they each shook their fists three times before flourishing a symbol. Joe's fist-rock crushed Micki's finger-scissors, and he let out a loud whoop. "Thank Christ! I'm gonna take a leak." He hopped off his stool and headed to the men's restrooms.

Micki threw her head back and briefly closed her eyes. "Let's go to my office for a minute."

She motioned for one of the waitresses to cover the bar, and I followed her to the dark back area. Usually Micki only let me into her precious office if she needed my help with something, like distributing copies of the NCAA bracket for the bar pool or figuring out how to get her nightly specials marketed online in new ways.

In her tiny office she brought up a browser window on the old desktop computer and slowly typed a URL into the address bar. Before hitting Enter, she turned to face me. She didn't make eye contact though. Her gaze went to the floor, the walls, the ceiling. "Joe noticed it first. I think because of that summer when you wore a lot of backless shirts."

"Huh?" I asked, utterly confused. True, backless shirts were very in style a few years back, and I'd embraced it. Not the most flattering look I'd ever worn, but why would Micki be discussing my poor wardrobe choices now?

She cleared her throat. "That's how Joe remembered your tattoo, I mean. You already know how much I like the anchor on your back."

"Yeah..." It was one of the nicest compliments she'd ever given me, actually, since I'd drawn the design myself. Micki was a bit of an ink aficionado. Her forearms were completely covered in intricate art. But again, what did this have to do with anything?

Micki ran her hands along the close-cropped sides of her head, still avoiding my eyes. "That FSG sex tape site Joe and Toby were talking about..."

A sick shiver started at the base of my spine and crawled up until the hairs on the back of my neck rose. *No. No way.* "Micki. What?"

She hit enter and a webpage loaded quickly. "This is a teaser image, a still from one of his personal Chicago conquests. Joe got a link to it from the newsletter."

A banner continuously scrolled across the bottom of the screen in a font you might see on a TV commercial for a monster truck show: "Check out my Windy City Good Time!!!" And then there was a countdown timer. "25 Days, 3 Hours, 48 Minutes." The seconds were clicking by too fast for me to focus.

I leaned forward, praying my eyes were lying to me about the image on the screen. It was of a woman sitting on a bed with her back to the camera, looking out of a dark window at the lights of nearby skyscrapers. The woman had strawberry-blond hair that hung in ringlets past her shoulder blades, and she was topless. She had a small tattoo of an anchor at the bottom of her back.

Abruptly, I lost all of the air in my lungs. I saw stars and swayed on my feet.

"Jeez, sit down before you topple over." I let Micki shove me into her rickety office chair even though I didn't physically want to be closer to the screen.

"I hoped we were wrong." Micki shoved her hands along the sides of her head again. "The hair and the tattoo were giveaways, but the girl in the picture is skinnier than you, so we weren't one hundred percent sure."

Glaring, I gave her a poke on the hip. "We were all skinnier in our twenties, Micki." I looked at the screen and shuddered. "This was *years* ago."

Five years, to be exact. A one-night stand. A handsome stranger I met in a bar. An impulsive decision. A short and wholly forgettable encounter I hadn't even thought about in ages.

My brain whirred and chugged, unable to process. How was this possible? I'd made *one* recording in my life and it was with a semi-famous sleazebag? The FSG was fairly new to internet stardom. Had that predator been stockpiling sex tapes for years?

In my head, I heard Joe's declaration that the girls should have been more careful about where their videos ended up. I sat up straighter in my chair. I *had* been careful. I met Micki's sympathetic gaze. "But I deleted the recording. I know I did."

I cringed, hearing my plaintive voice. Oh, the irony. I specialized in data recovery for a fucking living. I should know, better than anyone, that nothing is ever gone. Yes, I very distinctly remembered hitting the delete key on the guy's laptop keyboard. But that asshole could have had cloud backups running every minute. It wouldn't matter that I deleted the video off his hard drive if the file had just been synced to a server somewhere.

I put my head between my knees. There was a very good chance I was about to vomit on Micki's floor.

That night had been so long ago, and my brain was too panicked for the memories to become clear. "Do you know anything about the FSG videos that are already posted? Are they explicit?"

Micki hesitated. I could almost see her debating whether to ease in or rip off the Band-Aid. "Yeah. It's amateur porn." She went for the rip. "It shows everything." Her voice lowered. "Tess, this guy, this FSG—he has a huge mailing list. The hype for his Chicago release is blowing up everywhere. Joe is not the only customer I've heard talking about it this week."

Tens of thousands of people. Maybe more. All of whom could simply click twice to see a video of me getting... Oh God, I *was* going to be sick. I lunged out of the chair and through the office door, almost knocking Joe over as he came out of the restroom. Luckily, the women's room was right there, and I made it to a toilet stall before my dinner came up.

I looked in the mirror while washing my shaking hands. My eyes were huge and dark in my white face. If my coworkers or my sister saw that video, my life would be over. I was unapologetic about my active sex life; I liked men and felt no shame about it. But enjoying sex and knowing the people in your life had watched a video of you having sex—a video I never agreed to share—were very different things!

Oh God. Oh God. This couldn't be happening. I hadn't felt this sick and horrified in years.

"Tessie?" Joe rapped on the door. "You OK?"

"No," I shouted.

"Well, don't lose it," he yelled back. "Maybe you can get it taken down. Sue his ass or something. You have, like, twenty-five days before the video goes live."

Twenty-five days.

"THE INTERESTING THING about global deduplication is..." My boss droned on and on as our potential new clients struggled not to yawn. We were fifteen minutes into our Monday morning meeting, and he was already off the rails.

Nothing, Paul! I wanted to scream at him. *There is nothing interesting about global deduplication!* There was no way we should be this deep in the weeds at an introductory meeting. The clients didn't want technical jargon. This early in the process, they simply expected a sales pitch.

I flicked my eyes from Paul's face to the clock on the wall. Even that tiny movement was a mistake. *Ow. Ow. Ow.* Everything throbbed. The hangover headache was so bad I could feel my pulse in my nose, and I was definitely sweating bourbon out of my pores. Drinking too much on a Sunday night was a huge Tess no-no, but exceptions could be made when one learned they were about to star in a porno—

No. I could *not* think about that right now. *Compartmentalize, Tess.* I'd promised myself. Just get through today and then I'd figure something out. I always did. At this moment I needed to focus on work.

As Paul continued to use words like *data compression technology*, the three young execs across the conference table gave up on him and began to jab at their phones. I respected my boss, I truly did, but these initial client meetings were not his strength. Paul was excellent at actually delivering our technology solutions, but he was not a schmoozy kind of guy. Why our sales team couldn't handle these pitches on their own was beyond me. Those guys were just plain lazy.

Companies hired our disaster recovery solutions firm to make sure that if their business was ever hit by a disaster—an earthquake or a hurricane or unexpected power outage—all of their IT and business processes would keep working seamlessly.

I'd worked here for six years, steadily shoving my way up. Paul was the best boss I'd ever had; he meandered around with an absentminded-professor vibe, but he was wonderful at seeing big-picture solutions and at mentoring people. A mentor was a valuable thing, so I'd made sure I was his number-one go-to person.

The dude directly across the table from me began to play a game on his phone. I could tell because the *Fortnite* music wasn't muted all the way. Wearing expensive jeans, trendy sneakers, and button-down shirts tailored to be worn untucked, these guys were from a company called Away-Ho, a newish tech-travel business that claimed to be a perfect mix of Expedia and Airbnb. This year, Away-Ho was first on *Crain's Chicago Business* magazine's list of fastest-growing companies.

Our target clients weren't the huge guys. We didn't go after Fortune 500 companies. No, we went after companies that were just past the start-up phase, the ones that didn't get bought by Google and who didn't crash and burn when their first round of VC funding disappeared. We went after companies that were just starting to put their big boy pants on. There were hundreds of companies in Chicago in that position, and I wanted them all.

Just as I was about to cut Paul off and put the Away-Ho bros out of their misery, the door to the conference room opened. To my shock, Jack Sorenson, the CEO of our company, let himself in and took a seat at the far end of the room. If Paul was surprised to see his boss, he didn't look it. He simply interrupted his own monologue to say, "Jack's just here to observe." I didn't share his nonchalance. I hadn't been in many meetings with our CEO.

I sat ramrod straight in my chair. Under the table, I began to twist the thin silver ring I wore on the longest finger of my right hand. It was the only ring I ever wore, and I'd bought it for myself. I saved it to wear on days when I had big meetings or presentations. I even kept it in my purse instead of a jewelry box on the off chance I'd need to slip it on in surprise stressful situations. In high school I learned that my hands shake when I'm nervous or tense—and I didn't like people noticing that sign of weakness. When I twisted my silver ring, the shaking stopped.

I stared at Paul, willing him to start wowing our potential new account—and our CEO. Instead, oblivious to my wide-eyed plea, he said, "Where was I? Oh yes. Most data stored on disk today has at least some statistical redundancy..."

Damn it. I didn't want Jack Sorenson to see Paul floundering. Paul was absolutely amazing at his job; this was not representative at all. Everyone on the technology side of the company loved him. He shouldn't be forced to do this sales crap; he wasn't good at it.

Wait a minute. I was in the room and *I* was good at it. Enough was enough.

I cut off my boss, sweetly and with a modest smile. "Paul, I think what you're discussing would be essential for us to talk about with Away-Ho's DBA team, but maybe we should go a bit higher level for now since this is our introductory meeting. What do you think, Chad?"

Surprised, the *Fortnite* player put his phone on the table.

"Huh? Uh, yeah, OK. Whatev."

Eloquent. "Wonderful, thank you so much." I'd been silent for much of the meeting thus far, so all three guys looked at me with interest. After watching them the last twenty minutes, I was pretty sure what they'd respond to. I just hoped it wouldn't come across as unprofessional to Paul and Jack.

I plunked my elbows on the table, leaned forward, and put my chin in my palms. "I think we all know the world is going to hell, right?"

They blinked, laughed a little. "Climate change, pandemics, the threat of war, mass shootings, et cetera. I hope I don't offend you when I say that lately...shit is getting a little real." Fortnite Chad laughed louder and nodded.

I continued. "Every single company in existence right now has some sort of disaster recovery plan or is scrambling to put one together. That's good. But *your* disaster recovery solution should be as individualized to Away-Ho as it can be. Too many DR solutions try a one-size-fits-all approach." I widened my eyes for emphasis. "We don't. Our team is focused on learning the nuances of *your* business and designing a custom, scalable, cost-efficient solution for *you*."

I hadn't said anything of substance, but I had their focus back and they were nodding. Good. "Let me show you some testimonials from other companies your size."

THE SALES TEAM finally reappeared to retrieve the Away-Ho contingent and take them out to an overpriced lunch. I shook hands with them and exchanged business cards, relieved the meeting was over. I was ready to escape to my office and chug a bottle of water. I needed to fight through this hangover and figure out a way to get my video off the Fucking Sex Ghost site.

Paul and Jack Sorenson remained seated at the conference room table. As I was about to excuse myself, Paul gestured for me to sit back down. "Stick around a minute, Tess." Jack closed the door and took the seat right next to me this time.

Oh crap. Maybe they hated the way I'd handled things. I glanced over at Paul. He never swore, and I'd noticed his lips thinning when I'd done so with a client in the past. "Hope you didn't mind that I stepped in or the way I approached them." I swallowed and fell back on one of my favorite handling-Paul themes. "You know millennials," I scoffed, cheerfully throwing my own generation under the bus. "They just need that drama to actually pay attention."

He shook his head in disgust. "Indeed. So juvenile, isn't it?" He turned to Jack. "Didn't I tell you? Tess handles herself perfectly in meetings with new clients."

A rush of heat hit my cheeks. This was unexpected. Paul was always good at handing out praise when earned, but a shout-out straight to the CEO was pretty special.

"You were right," Sorenson said. "And your replacement is going to need to hold their own when dealing with some of these forceful young tech guys."

Wait, what? "Your replacement?" I blurted, looking at Paul. "You're leaving?"

He smiled at me, the wrinkles around his eyes growing

deep. "Retiring. At the end of January."

That was only four months away. I blinked a few times, disoriented. This place wouldn't be the same without Paul. Whoever stepped in to replace him would have huge shoes to fill.

As both Paul and Sorenson waited for me to catch up, I cursed my hungover and slow-moving brain. "Are—are you considering *me* for Paul's role?"

Sorenson lifted one shoulder. "I'd prefer to promote internally rather than hiring from the outside. Paul has nominated you as the person he'd feel most comfortable taking the reins."

I didn't know whether to cry over the lump in my throat or scream for joy. I did sit on my hands so I wouldn't do a huge fist pump in the air. I met Paul's kind eyes. "Thank you." This was incredible. If I moved into Paul's role, it would be a career-changer. A big jump in salary, a VP title, and an office with a window.

"But," Sorenson went on, a clear note of warning in his voice, "I don't know you as well, Tess, and I need to feel confident in your abilities before offering the promotion."

"Of course." Bring it on. Whatever he needed to see or hear from me, I would show him. I forced myself to make eye contact and speak calmly. "I'd be thrilled for a chance at this opportunity, and am happy to formally interview—"

Sorenson waved a hand. "You're a good talker, Tess. Even I know that. I don't think an interview is what would make me feel comfortable." He folded his hands on top of the table. "What I need to know is if you can handle the tough stuff, the truly tricky situations."

Tricky situations, eh? *Like figuring out how to get a sex tape off the internet?* I quickly stuffed the panic back in its designated compartment.

I nodded at Sorenson as if I understood but snuck a questioning glance at Paul. Tricky situations? What was that supposed to mean? I handled sensitive and complicated circumstances all the time. We planned for—and reacted to—actual disasters, for God's sake. Wasn't that the tough stuff?

Paul understood my confusion. "Jack wants to be sure that the new VP can instill confidence in difficult clients."

"Naturally," I responded, still unsure what that meant in practical terms for me getting the promotion.

"Let me be blunt—and a touch politically incorrect," Jack said. "These young tech guys come through the door with a lot of ego. Piss and vinegar, we used to say." I smiled at the older expression. I knew what he meant. The Away-Ho guys had been a little rude but in a quiet way. A lot of the execs we met with brought more attitude with them. They swaggered in, daring us to impress them.

"Our sales team does a good job bringing in clients," he continued, "but the technology team is what gets contracts signed." I nodded in total agreement. Our products and service were top-notch. Jack sighed. "I think these young execs look at Paul and see an established man with a long career… He's immediately trustworthy. He reminds them of their fathers."

He lifted his eyebrows and tilted his head apologetically. "You would be a very different person to have in the role. I'm not trying to be an asshole, but you have to agree that it'd be a very different first impression."

I knew he was just trying to be honest, but the implication that I would somehow be seen as less trustworthy because I was a thirtysomething woman…it stung. I stifled my irritation. "I understand your hesitation," I said. "But I'm very confident I can represent the technology team and assure new clients that we're the right solution for them."

"I agree," Paul said firmly.

Jack moved his head from side to side. "Well, I'm going to give you a chance to prove it, Tess."

Challenge accepted. Eyes flashing, I leaned forward in my chair. "How?"

Jack gestured at the empty seats across the conference room table. "Away-Ho. I want them. You can't buy the kind of press they get. If we land them, it'll bring six or seven other clients through the door—and that's a conservative estimate."

My brow furrowed. Away-Ho? Those guys weren't the kind of alphas he was worried about. Why would they be such a challenge?

Jack grinned, following the direction of my thoughts. "Those fellas weren't the decision-makers. They were just a scouting team. Their CEO is a guy named Zack Morris, and he'll personally be deciding which firm they go with."

Zack Morris? The theme song from *Saved by the Bell* popped into my head. I ignored it. "So this Zack Morris is…demanding?"

Jack snorted. "He's a hyper-aggressive little shit, actually."

I had to laugh. "Sounds like fun."

He pushed his chair away from the table. "It won't be easy. He's turned down two of our competitors already. But Away-Ho is the consummate example of the clients we need to bring on board to meet our goals. It has brand-name recognition, a strong projected forecast—and, unfortunately, a difficult leader."

Sorenson stood and shrugged. "Those are your marching orders, Tess. Keep up everything you're doing for Paul—and land us Away-Ho. I'll be watching you."

Chapter Three

"I CAN'T BELIEVE you're leaving," I whispered to Paul as we walked down the hall. Paul drove me nuts at least half the time, but that's just what bosses did.

He winked. "Don't push me out the door quite yet. I still have four months."

As we approached his office, he reverted to his usual absentminded-professor mode and frowned down at his smartphone. "I installed some sort of update last night and now nothing is working correctly."

I arranged my features into one of concern, but inside I was chanting: *Please don't ask me to fix your phone. Please don't ask me to fix your phone.* That could be half my morning.

Thank God he just said, "Don't suppose you know if the timing of the Cubs playoff games has been announced yet?"

Of course I did. The first reason Paul started to prefer me above all his other project managers was that I *always* knew the sports scores, stats, and gossip around his insanely wide scope of favorite teams. I considered it another job skill, like being really proficient at Excel Pivot Tables or something.

"Sure thing. Game one is on Friday at 6:00 p.m. Game

two is on Saturday at 7:05 p.m." I wanted to roll my eyes at the way the facts tripped off my tongue. I was his own personal version of Siri or Alexa. "They haven't announced the pitching lineups yet," I said before he could ask.

He smiled at me and opened the door to his office. "What would I do without you? Good job this morning, Tess."

Whew. I'd made it through my colossal hangover. The headache was still fighting back against the four Advil I'd taken, but at least I had no other in-person meetings today. I could shut the door to my office and massage my temples during my afternoon conference calls. Maybe I'd start my research into the FSG and find a lawyer to make him take my video off his site. Actually, no—I needed to keep everything about my personal situation completely away from the office. I'd tackle that tonight.

Instead, I'd research Away-Ho and Zack Morris. I needed to knock my first meeting with him out of the park. A frisson of excitement and panic danced up my spine. I'd hate Jack Sorenson's scrutiny, but it would be worth it if he made me a VP. I shook my head, still a little dazed from the conversation. I couldn't wait until I felt better and could process this news properly.

My cell rang as soon as I dropped into my chair. It was Kat. I hesitated, unsure if I wanted to answer, as I was still a little raw over the whole Facebook thing. Of course, she didn't know I'd seen the picture or what she'd written in response to Daniel.

I almost let it go to voice mail. But my twenty-five-year-old sister was my favorite person in the entire world, and it was unusual for her to call me in the middle of a workday, so I answered. "Hey."

"Happy Monday, Disaster Girl." She sounded strangely giddy for a weekday morning. I ignored the nickname. She loved it because of my technical expertise and because of the odd misadventures I'd waded through during some crazy weekends. I just thought it sounded like the worst superhero ever.

"What's up?" I squeezed the bridge of my nose. How much Advil was too much to take in a four-hour period? I've always thought it cruel that alcohol and ibuprofen—the thing that makes your head feel better after overindulging in alcohol—are both harmful to your liver.

"I have big news." Car horns and wind joined her voice on the line. That was strange.

"Are you not at the office?" I asked.

Kat worked at one of Chicago's hottest digital marketing firms. I had very little idea what she did day to day, even though she'd explained it to me a thousand times: "You know how when you go look at a dress online at Nordstrom and then that same dress is in an ad on every website you go to after that? That's what I do." I hated that. One time—ONE TIME—I'd worried that my hair was thinning so I'd looked up a few things. For months, wig advertisements had followed me around online. I didn't want the internet thinking I was bald.

"I took a walk," she said. "I couldn't tell you my big news from my cubicle."

My stomach started to hurt. "What is it?"

"I got a job offer, Tess. A big one! To be an account

manager! At Starcross!" She squealed. "Oh my God. I can't believe it."

I read a lot of novels, but I'd never understood the expression "my heart plummeted" until now. I had heard of Starcross. It wasn't located in Chicago.

I forced myself to sound excited. "What? Kat! Holy shit! That's amazing. Wow! Congratulations. You totally deserve it, of course!" I closed my eyes. "Remind me. Starcross is in..."

"San Francisco!" she shrieked. "Can you believe it? I've always wanted to live in San Francisco!"

I joined her cheering, encouragement spilling from my lips while a heavy weight of some toxic feeling settled on my chest and the rest of me went completely rigid. My brain detached itself from my body's emotional cocktail and examined each ingredient critically: *What was Tess feeling?*

1. Pride. Kat was brilliant and wonderful and deserved everything she wanted.
2. Sadness. Good God, I would miss her.
3. Jealousy. Yep, that ugly little bugger was definitely here too. There'd been a time I wanted to live in California, back when I'd been accepted to Stanford. Of course, there was no question of me actually going. Kat was so young back then. I'm sure I didn't even mention it to her.

"When do they want you to start?" I interrupted.

She paused because the "L" train was screeching overhead. "In a month. I'll give my two-week notice today, and after I'm finished at work I'll have two weeks to focus on packing and the move. Oh my God, you have to help me find an apartment, Tess! Real estate is so crazy out there. Oh wow, what do you think Mom will say?" And, she was off and running again.

I leaned back in my chair and put my free hand over my eyes, blocking out as much as I could. I drew long breaths of air through my nose and blew them out slowly through my lips.

AT HOME THAT night, I pulled out my laptop and booted it up, emotionally preparing myself to dive into the FSG fiasco. Micki sat on my couch with her legs crossed and a glass of Merlot in hand. "Don't worry, Tess. We'll figure this out."

Roz popped through my open door and handed over a Xanax and a glass of Alka-Seltzer. She'd seen me clomping down the hall, a half weary, half terrified look on my face, and promptly decided that her presence was needed.

After I swallowed her gifts, she squeezed my shoulder. "Mohawk is right," she said, jabbing at Micki. "There's a plan for everything, and there's nothing new under the sun. Whatever's going on, I'm sure I've been there."

Micki snorted into her wineglass. Maybe it was because Roz's nickname never failed to give her the giggles, or maybe it was because she couldn't imagine Roz ever having been exactly *here*. Although, hell, with Roz, who knew? Maybe there were sex tapes of her all over the internet.

Sighing, I summarized the FSG situation. As unflappable as ever, Roz's only visible reaction was to narrow her eyes slightly behind her cat-eye glasses before nodding, sagely. "Got it. Let's dive in, shall we?"

Whether it was the ladies' support or the Xanax, I did finally feel calm enough to navigate back to the site Micki had showed me the night before. I was going to need as much information as I could find to figure a way out of this.

The FSG's home page featured a large photograph of the man himself. He was an extraordinarily handsome blond man with a finger to his lips, in some kind of supposed-to-be-sexy shush.

The moment I saw his picture, I remembered him. I remembered it all.

"Oh God." My stomach acid began an epic duel with the Alka-Seltzer.

"He's annoyingly good-looking," Micki said after we'd gazed at his face in silence for a few seconds.

"Hmm." Roz cocked her head. "Good-looking but smarmy. Who does he remind me of? Someone famous?"

I flinched, remembering some of the first words I'd exchanged with him five years ago. We were at a little hot spot downtown, a trendy tiki bar in the lobby of a fancy boutique hotel. My friends from work had just left, and I'd been sitting alone at the bar, wondering if I should call Kat to meet me. She'd insisted she wasn't angry anymore, but that didn't mean she wasn't still resentful. Debating the trajectory of my evening, I didn't even notice him until he sat down next to me and offered to buy me a drink.

My jaw had dropped, comically, when I looked straight at him. He had wavy, thick hair, bright white teeth, and an honest-to-goodness movie star face. I'd resisted the urge to look over my shoulder to confirm he was actually talking to me.

"What's your name?" I'd asked, taking a sip of the expensive cocktail he'd bought me.

He'd smirked. *"Call me Westley."*

"He looks like the actor from *The Princess Bride*," I said to Roz. "It's actually his whole schtick. Said he was a failed actor and told me to call him Westley, for God's sake." I put my face in my hands and moaned. "So fucking cheesy. Why did I even keep talking to him after that?"

Micki laughed. "Uh, because he's gorgeous? Do you know how many times a night I see a girl give a pass to a cheeseball with a pretty face? Besides, who wouldn't want to be hit on by Buttercup's true love?"

Roz made me lay out the rest of our meet-cute, word for word. She grabbed a pen and pad of paper from my coffee table and started jotting notes. "A failed actor," she muttered. "Figures. Probably an egomaniac with no talent. Would explain how he'd eventually turn to this," she said, gesturing at the site. She raised her eyes to me, pen poised above the paper. "Now, how did you get from pick-up lines at the bar to sexy time?"

I closed my eyes tightly, said through gritted teeth, "We were only talking for about ten minutes when he suddenly leaned closer to me."

His gaze had skimmed up my legs and lingered on my chest. *"So listen, pretty girl. I'm only in town until tomorrow morning, and I have a room upstairs. I'm looking for a good time tonight. Are you it?"*

"That's fast," Micki commented sagely. Her years of bartending had made her a guru of the pick-up scene. "Generally, there's a little more flirtation or banter or basic conversation before the 'come home with me' request."

"He didn't even ask my name," I admitted. "But at the time, I'd thought if we both knew where the evening was headed, why not get there faster? Why not just appreciate his flat-out honesty? I sure as hell wasn't looking for anything beyond a fun one-night fling myself. And he was one of the most physically perfect men I'd ever seen in real life. Why not just run with it?"

"I hear you," Roz said, shrugging. "Sometimes it's best to skip the verbal foreplay. Or any foreplay. Sometimes you just want efficiency!" I purposely did not look at Micki because I knew she was two seconds from spitting red wine all over my sofa in a scream of laughter.

I stood and took a lap around the couch. The memories were clear now, but that night still seemed like a very long time ago. A much younger and slightly different Tess. "I wouldn't go home with someone *that* quickly now," I said. "Now I'm more discerning about a guy's personality. Now I have a strict 'no assholes' policy. But back then I was more...inexperienced." I paused and they nodded. I didn't need to go into it; they knew all about Daniel and everything that happened.

Roz nodded briskly, scribbling away. "So you're in the hotel room with 'Westley.' How did the idea of making a video come up?"

I flicked my eyes to the ceiling, making sure I remembered the exact sequence of events. "I was looking out the window at the skyline when I heard a snapping noise. When

I turned around, I saw that Westley had used his laptop to take a photo of me."

"You're beautiful silhouetted against the city lights like that."

"Don't take pictures of people without asking. It's rude."

"Sorry." He raised his eyebrows. *"Can I take a few more?"*

"I asked him if pictures were what he was into. He gave me an expression that tried to be innocent but failed. No wonder he didn't make it as an actor."

"You don't have to put on a whole silly act," I'd said. *"If naked photos are your thing, just say so. I won't judge."*

I truly wouldn't have. Who was I to say what was right or wrong when it came to turn-ons? Everyone had their own kink. As long as actions were consensual, I had no problem with different sexual tastes. I'd still been discovering what I liked myself.

Westley had taken a deep breath, looking like a man about to roll the dice at a craps table. *"So, what if I told you that naked photos aren't exactly my thing. Videos are."*

Micki and Roz were both leaning forward, eyes rapt and lips parted. I couldn't help but laugh a little. "I know, right? After he took the photos, I shouldn't have been surprised. But still. You just never know where life in the city is going to take you."

"Are you asking me to make a sex tape?"

"You'd be incredible. And you can delete it right after we watch."

That was really all it took; I hadn't needed a lot of convincing. Because... "I'd thought maybe I'd like it." One of the reasons I enjoyed sex so much was that it could pull me completely out of the labyrinth of my head for a time. There were few moments in life where the distraction was so complete. Good sex could be an immediate renewal…a satiating physical release that was also a mood re-setter, a reorientation of wherever your mind was before.

"I wondered if being filmed would add a layer of intensity to the sexual experience," I elaborated. I didn't mind saying it aloud. Micki and Roz were the two least-judgmental people I'd ever met.

"But I never wanted anyone else to see it," I said loudly. "I saw nothing wrong with making a recording for our own viewing, but for me, privacy and pleasure go hand in hand. I told him we had to delete the file immediately after we watched it."

He'd nodded quickly. *"Of course. You're in control, baby."*

Micki cringed, Roz flipped a page in the notebook and continued to write furiously in jagged handwriting, and I paced faster.

"Fuck, I was stupid."

Micki made a protesting sound, and I looked her in the eye.

"NOT stupid to make a sex tape. That's not what I'm mad at myself about. I'm mad that I made a sex tape with *him.*" I jabbed my extended middle finger into Westley's slightly older face on my laptop screen. "I'm infuriated with myself because I thought he was just sort of a harmless, self-involved dude…not a freakin' predator!" My voice dropped. "And I'm mad that I was so naïve to believe that I'd deleted it."

Roz cleared her throat. "Yes, we'll need to talk about how

you deleted it. But first, not to be crude—"

I burst out laughing in spite of myself. Roz positively lived to be crude. Her eyes sparkled at me, practically outshining the rhinestones on her cat-eyes. "Let's hear about the sex. And did you actually watch the video when you were done?"

I nodded, nose wrinkled. "Yeah." I let out a harsh laugh. "I'd wanted to see what I looked like in a moment of pure abandon or distraction or pleasure. Unfortunately, what I actually saw was just a video of myself looking bored."

Side by side, we'd watched ourselves on his laptop. Westley had been fixated on the screen, nodding and emitting little grunts of approval every time his video-self flipped me into a new pretzel pose. Despite my rather loud comments about what I usually liked and what actually worked for me, he had insisted on maneuvering me into a series of different positions like we were working our way through some sort of porn checklist.

"I remember feeling uneasy as we watched it," I said, feeling the same jitters on my spine. "He was clearly no stranger to making videos. He made eye contact with the camera almost the entire time. He flirted with it and flexed to it and thrust toward it. I remember thinking that performing for a video means you're not performing for your partner." I let out an ironic huff. "My takeaway from the evening was that sex tapes were definitely not my thing. Possibly if my partner hadn't been a giant ass, I would have felt differently." But as he and I had finished watching, my fingers had itched to delete, delete, delete.

Finally, on the screen, Westley had pulled away from me,

slapped my ass, and said, *"Now that was a good time!"* I hadn't liked it when he'd done it, and I'd hated watching it on the screen.

"I grabbed the laptop, hit escape to stop the video, and deleted it. Same with the photo. Then I emptied the recycle bin."

"That was quick." Westley had pouted.

"You're telling me," I'd volleyed back.

"I practically ran out of the room." I'd thrown my dress and shoes on while he lay naked and smirking in the bed.

I looked at Micki and Roz, my lips twisted. "By the time I left, he didn't look the tiniest bit handsome to me anymore. He looked less like *The Princess Bride* hero and a lot more like a bad guy from an '80s movie...one of those blond villains with an air of smug superiority."

"Ooh!" Micki piped. "Like James Spader from *Pretty in Pink*?"

Not to be outdone, Roz added, "Or Johnny from *The Karate Kid*?"

I had to chuckle. "Exactly. Like a smoosh of those two."

Micki shuddered. "Awful."

Roz consulted her notes. "So that's all? No other contact with him?"

"No," I said emphatically. "On my way home that night, I stopped for a burrito. Kat met me with some of her sorority sisters, and I treated them all to late-night eats. By the time I went to bed that night, Westley was already a faint memory."

I glared at his face on the laptop again. "Which makes this all so surreal." My hands went to fists in my lap. I wanted to punch his face and break that exquisitely shaped nose. How dare he?

Beneath the glamour shot, there was a link that said, "Watch my mission statement!" Reluctantly, I clicked on it.

Beaming, he said, "Welcome, new fan of the Ghost!" His voice, I recalled now, had been one of the least attractive things about him. It was thin and reedy, weak. An odd contrast to the strong features of his face. "I'm thrilled to welcome you to my site. Over the past decade or so, I've banged a lotta women. Created a lot of good content. At first it was for my own personal, private viewing." He let out a greasy chuckle.

Then he flattened his expression into one of mock concern and rested his head on a manicured hand. "But you know what? Men have had to put up with a lot over the last several years." He rolled his eyes. "The #metoo movement? Please. Fuck that. Time's Up?" He snorted. "I'll tell you what it's time for—time for me to show you a lot of women just plain begging for it."

"Oh my God," Micki murmured. Roz quivered, probably with fury.

"Why keep my collection to myself?" he continued, waving his arms expansively. "Why not share?" He leaned closer, becoming larger. "In fact, let's all share! If you have a sex tape you'd like the Ghost to feature, let's make a deal! I'll give you a nice chunk of cash for any video that meets the guidelines explained in the clearinghouse portion of the site." He leaned even closer to the camera lens and his tone became mocking. "And by guidelines, I mean the chick has to be sort of hot, OK?"

He paused and raised his eyebrows as though listening to

a question from the audience. "Don't have a sex tape yet, but you're interested in making and selling one? A lot of my bros ask me how I get so many chicks to make a video in the first place. Visit my FAQ section for some tried-and-true methods."

The Alka-Seltzer gave up; it simply couldn't match the amount of acid rolling in my stomach. Shaking with rage, I watched as Westley went on to explain that a visitor to his site could choose one video for $1.99, but he really encouraged a "site pass" in which members paid an annual fee of $89.99 and got loads of fresh content every month.

His current release was a set of "the easy girls from New Orleans." Crossing my arms over my chest, I considered entering my PayPal info and watching the first video just to know what I was facing. But I couldn't do it. "I can't pay that asshole money or watch another woman get taken advantage of."

"You don't need to," Roz assured me. "We have enough to go to a lawyer as it is. And I think that's your next best step, Tess. Maybe the right kind of lawyer can do a sort of cease and desist to get your video taken down from the site."

It took us only about ten minutes of poking around Chicago's legal community to find Natasha Long, Esq, an attorney who specialized in the horrible acronym that was now going to rule my life: NCP—nonconsensual pornography, the "distribution of sexually graphic images of individuals without their consent."

Roz put the cap of the pen back on with a loud click. "I'll type up my notes tonight and email them to you. You should send them to the attorney ASAP."

I put my hand on her tough little shoulder, finally starting to feel like myself again. “Thanks.”

Micki laughed, low and long. “That son of a bitch sure messed with the wrong girl.”

I grinned at her, appreciating the sentiment. “Oh yeah?”

She snorted. “Uh, I’ve never really wondered if you were a fight-or-flight kind of girl, Tess. You know I consider you an unofficial bouncer at the bar.”

Now I laughed too. No, I wasn’t a “flight” kind of girl when it came to conflict. Sometimes I flat-out looked for a fight. In this one, I’d use my nails and teeth.

Twenty-four days.

Chapter Four

AFTER A PLEADING phone call and receiving Roz's carefully crafted Damn-Westley-to-Hell file, Natasha Long agreed to take me on as a client. But she couldn't fit me into her schedule until Friday. Which meant that four of my precious days disappeared into the air. I tried to block it all from my mind by staying busy. At work, I handled my own projects, covered for someone on maternity leave, became an internet stalker of everything Away-Ho, and even volunteered to fix Paul's phone. After work, I bullied Kat into letting me review her new hire paperwork and did a four-day juice cleanse to detox. (I made it through two days and considered this a huge victory.)

On Friday morning, I told Paul I'd be out all afternoon to get a tooth pulled at the dentist. He said, "Of course. That explains why your cheeks were looking swollen."

Oh Paul. *That's just my face.*

Natasha Long's firm had a suite of offices on Wacker Drive that overlooked the Chicago River. Her assistant seated me in a conference room, where I watched tour boats and architectural cruises navigate the smooth water and take advantage of the unusually warm October day.

"Ms. Greene? I'm Natasha." She was about five foot two

and had a gray crew cut. Her eyebrows were each plucked into an interesting diagonal shape that made her face look constantly angry. I immediately liked her. She looked like the kind of woman who could beat perverts like Westley to death with a yellow legal pad and not even break a sweat.

"Call me Tess," I said, and she sat across from me at the table.

She opened a manila file containing a printout of everything I'd sent her. She'd made notes in green ink in the margins.

"First of all," she said, looking up at me over the rim of her reading glasses, "I just want to express how sorry I am that this happened to you. Make no mistake—I, and Illinois state law, consider this to be a form of sexual assault."

I looked down at the table, disconcerted to feel a lump form in my throat. I hadn't expected sympathy. I'd prepared myself for more of a "we'll help you, but you got yourself into this mess" sort of attitude.

"Thank you," I said after a moment of silence.

She looked down at the file and back up at me. "However, I'm not going to sugarcoat this, Tess. There's not a lot we can do for you."

I blinked. There was nothing they could do for a form of sexual assault? She correctly interpreted the look of confusion on my face. "You're not the first woman to try and take legal action against this so-called Sex Ghost. I haven't personally represented any other victims of his—probably because he hasn't hit Chicago yet—but he's become well known in NCP legal circles over the last couple of months."

She reviewed her file. "A woman in California tried to

take legal action against the Ghost six months ago. California also has a strict NCP law, and she had a very sympathetic case. Like you, she had consensual sex and made a recording with this man after meeting him in the bar. Also like you, she claimed she never gave him consent to post the video online. To make things worse for this poor girl, one of her ex-boyfriends spotted her on the Sex Ghost site and then linked to it from his Facebook page and tagged her. So, not only was there a sex tape of her online, but everyone in her life found out about it. Scenarios like that are why NCP is often called 'revenge porn.'"

I clenched my fists, my fingernails digging into my palms. "That's my worst nightmare right now. Why do you think nothing can be done?" My voice was rising in volume and octave.

She held up a hand and began to tick off reasons on her fingers. "First, we don't know the Sex Ghost's true identity, so we don't even have a legal name. We can work on that by having one of our investigators reach out to the hotel you made the recording in to try to figure out how he checked in, but five years was a long time ago, and sometimes they don't keep data back that far." I bit the inside of my lip. I wasn't even sure I remembered the exact date.

Natasha was still talking: "...that bore no fruit in the California case. He appeared to be using false identification. Second, even if we did find him, he could easily claim that you gave him verbal consent to post the video of the sexual act, and it could devolve into a he-said, she-said kind of deal."

Dazed, I opened my mouth to protest, but she wasn't

finished. "Third—and perhaps most important—we researched his site. Like many of the more than 3,000 sites dedicated to NCP, it's hosted overseas and is therefore not subject to our laws. We can certainly communicate with them and try to have them take down the material, but I'll be honest with you in that it's not usually very effective."

The air in the room suddenly seemed much thinner. This was it? I had no options? I put my forehead on the smooth glass table.

I felt the exact same way I did when I was fifteen, came home sick from school in the middle of the day, and found my mom crying in her bedroom instead of at work. Like the world as I understood it had morphed into a slightly different and much worse place.

"Sorry," I gasped. "I just expected better news."

Natasha stood and walked away from the table for a minute before I heard a plunk next to my head. I lifted my face. She'd poured me a glass of water. "Thanks," I mumbled.

"I printed out some resources for you," she said, placing a stack of papers next to the water glass. I scanned them quickly: an FAQ for US victims of nonconsensual pornography, instructions on how to report nude images posted without consent from social media platforms and search engines, and online support groups for victims of NCP.

Holy hell, there was even a specific Facebook group for victims of the FSG.

She'd also printed an editorial from the *New York Post* written by one of the Ghost's Big Apple conquests. I scanned her words, flinching. *"How can it be that we've taken down powerful Hollywood producers and celebrity chefs and members of Congress, but we can't find and stop one asshole with a camera and a website who's ruining a dozen lives a month?"*

Bile rose from my stomach and burned the back of my throat. I hadn't expected the lawyer to provide an instantaneous solution, but I sure as hell thought there would be some sort of strategy or a fight or a process. Not this resignation to victimhood.

She sat down again. "I truly wish there was more we could do. If you want to foot the expense, we'll certainly take the actions I mentioned. You may want to take the next month to prepare the people in your life. Although, if you're lucky, maybe no one will identify you."

I snorted. If Joe was on the Sex Ghost's mailing list, I was sure other people I knew were too. Not all of them were as nice. Probably quite a few would get a kick out of mailing a link around. Chicago wasn't always a big city. Once it got put up on social media, I was toast.

I made a mental note to review the morality clause in my company's employment agreement. If I remembered correctly, it was fairly strict. After all, no one would want to hire a disaster recovery firm whose employees themselves were walking disasters. Forget the VP promotion; if this came out, they'd have grounds to get rid of me altogether. Even if they miraculously didn't fire me, I'd never command the same respect.

Natasha Long walked me to the elevator bank. I asked her to please take any and all possible actions. Try to find out who Westley really was. Try to get the site to pull my video. At this point, I was willing to sign over my entire 401k to make this happen.

"What is it you do for a living, Tess?" she asked, pressing the elevator button.

I shook off my daze, tried to act like a professional. "I, uh, specialize in disaster recovery for companies' IT infrastructure."

She laughed. "Well, a lot of those international sites we were talking about don't have anything like that. Maybe you should pray for a disaster to hit their server farm or something."

"Huh?"

She shrugged. "Maybe we'll get lucky and their servers will get ruined in a hurricane or taken down by a rogue hacker or something."

The elevator doors opened, and I rushed in without saying good-bye. Her words were ringing in my ears.

A hacker...

I WENT STRAIGHT from the lawyer's office building back to my own. Hopefully, Paul had ducked out earlier in the afternoon, per his normal Friday routine. If not, I was just going to shove some toilet paper in my mouth, puff out my cheeks, and pretend I had come back to work after dental surgery.

I dumped my coat and purse in my office and made a beeline for Developer's Corner, our little nickname for the set of cubicles where our most hardcore programmers spent their days. Lucky me, my purple-haired quarry was in her cube, typing away with huge headphones on her tiny ears.

"Abigail." She ignored me, her fingers flying over her keyboard. I squinted at her screen, trying to figure out what she was doing. She was one of those people who inverted the colors on all her applications so that her screen was always black and the text was always green or purple. Even when she was doing something as simple as her timesheet, it looked like she was typing in a mainframe terminal. I rolled my eyes. "We're not living in *The Matrix*, you know."

"God, you're old," she said, confirming my suspicion that she wasn't even listening to anything in those massive headphones. "That movie came out when I was practically in utero."

My lips twitched in spite of the awful day. Abigail and I weren't friends exactly. But we were almost always work allies. Technically, she reported to Paul, but she brought all her work problems to me, and I handled her assignments. We didn't have a ton in common. She never seemed to have much of a social life, and I was fairly sure she raced home most nights to watch retro, treasured episodes of *Buffy the Vampire Slayer* and *Battlestar Galactica*. But she was intensely smart and deadpan-funny. If I wanted to hang out with work-people after work (which I didn't), she'd be at the top of a list of one.

"I need a favor," I said. Understatement of the century. "A personal one. Completely unrelated to work and highly confidential."

That piqued her interest. She slid off her headphones and followed me when I gestured to a nearby conference room. The fluorescent lights made her skin look translucent under her vibrant magenta hair. Despite—or maybe because of—her aggressive blue eyeliner, she looked about fourteen years old. "What's the favor?"

I took a deep breath and closed my eyes. This was going to hurt. I hated, HATED, sharing my debacle with anyone at work, but I'd saved Abigail from getting fired last year, so I knew she wouldn't gossip. "A long time ago I went home with a stranger who turned out to be a real asshole. We made a video of us having sex—which I thought got deleted—but he kept it, and he's going to post it on the internet in less than a month on a site hosted overseas. I need someone to hack into it and delete the video."

Silence. I popped one lid open. Abigail's light green eyes were wide, and her mouth had fallen open. I huffed. "Can you do it?"

She cleared her throat. "I doubt it. It's not really my strength."

Humiliated, I nodded and stood. "OK. Thanks anyway. Obviously, if you could keep this qui—"

"I know someone who could though," she said slowly. "He's pretty incredible at that sort of thing."

I sat back down. "Who is it?"

"A guy I met through a coding meetup group a few years ago." She pursed her lips and furrowed her brow. "He's brilliant." Her eyes brightened. "He got fired from his job last year. He probably needs money. You could pay him."

I chewed on my lip. Brilliant sounded good, but I also needed someone discreet. If I had to work with a stranger, I'd prefer someone professional who would treat it like any other sort of business transaction. "Is he a grown-up? Or is he one of those antisocial unemployed guys who lives in his parents' basement?"

Abigail smirked. "Kind of picky for a desperate woman, aren't you?" Her face turned serious. "He's a good guy, Tess. Practically a Boy Scout. He doesn't do illegal stuff just for kicks." She shrugged. "He's the only one I can recommend. You want me to text him?"

She was right; I was desperate. It was either this or put an ad on Craigslist and watch the crazies come out of the woodwork. "Yeah." I put a hand to my upset stomach. Between the lawyer and Abigail and now a stranger, my secret was spreading already. "Don't put anything about why I need him in the text, OK?"

I was meeting Kat for an early dinner on Saturday night before she went out to the suburbs to spend the night with Mom. Maybe Abigail's hacker friend could join me afterward. "See if he can meet me on Saturday night to talk about it. The Gage. Eight-ish?"

She pulled her phone out of her pocket and went to work with both thumbs.

Chapter Five

THE WAITER STOPPED by our table yet again. "Sure I can't get you ladies anything else?" His eyes lingered on Kat.

She beamed up at him, activating the dimples in both cheeks. "We're great. Thanks so much." He walked away slowly, looking at her over his shoulder.

"Stop dazzling him or he'll never bring the check," I ordered. I snuck a glance at my phone. It was 7:45. I needed Kat to get out of here before Abigail's hacker nerd showed up.

Kat laughed, which is one of my favorite sounds in the world. It's a super-husky trill that doesn't match her doll-like exterior. Kat and I don't look anything alike. She took after my mother with her straight dark hair, blue eyes, and petite physique. Fair skin is the only thing we have in common. "Why don't you come with me out to Mom's?" she asked. "We can stay up late watching movies and take her to brunch in the morning."

Like my mother would want me horning in on their special time. "I can't," I said with a mock pout.

Kat's smile faded. She hated the tension between my mother and me. I hated that she noticed it and felt put in the middle. "I'm only here for another couple of weeks," she said softly.

Ouch, a direct hit. It would have worked, too, if I hadn't already had such an important meeting. "Well," I said lightly, evading. Time for a little fib. "I didn't know about your move when I said yes to a date."

Kat raised a skeptical eyebrow. "You have a date to-night?"

Offended, I crossed my arms over my chest. "Is that so hard to believe?"

"A real date?" she asked. "With a man?"

I glared at her. "I haven't switched teams in the last cou-ple of weeks. So yes."

Kat has never been able to tell when I'm lying. Her an-noyed face dissolved into one of curiosity. "What's he like? You haven't really dated anyone since that Jerry guy last year, and he was...ah..."

"An idiot," I supplied. Oh, Jerry. He never got my jokes. He'd never read a book or gone to a museum by choice. But I'd kept him around for a couple of months because he was broad-shouldered, considerate in bed, laughed a lot, and liked to go out for beers. Plus he was super handy for all the sports trivia I needed for Paul.

"No," she said. "He was really nice. He just wasn't the right person for you." Her face darkened. "But I know that's not really your thing anymore. Dating the right person, I mean."

I froze. So did she...as though the bitter words leaving her mouth surprised her as much as they did me. Her special little brunch last Sunday must have spun her up about the past more than usual. Because, here's the thing:

Kat and I talk every day. Multiple times a day. And yet, even though I know she had a sesame seed stuck in her teeth all day yesterday, even though I know this new job is approximately step thirty-seven on her plan for world domination, even though I know she starts to snore at 1:30 a.m. every night (except for nights she drinks wine, then the snoring starts immediately upon sleep)…and even though she knows I eat pickles on every type of sandwich, even though she knows the brand of concealer I use to cover the Mars-sized pimple I get on the first day of my period every month, even though she knows that I secretly wish our dad would have left us a series of video diary entries before he died for us to watch on birthdays like the tear-jerking premise of a cheesy movie…

Even though Kat and I know each other to the bone…even though I'd step in front of a train for her, there are two things we don't talk about.

Daniel is one of them.

The silence between us stretched to a full minute. Kat looked down at the tablecloth and gave a tiny shake of her head. When she looked back up at me, there was a glimmer of an apology on her face. She cleared her throat. "So, who's the guy tonight? How'd you meet?"

The waiter *finally* showed up with the check, and I threw my credit card at him before he could even put it on the table. "I'll tell you about it tomorrow," I said. "You should get going. It's dark, and at this rate you won't even make it to Glenview before 9:00."

Kat rolled her eyes. "Oh no, however shall I deal with

driving in the dark? Perhaps by using this fancy new technology called headlights?"

"You don't want Mom to worry," I countered.

"Fine." Kat stood and came over to hug me. "But I want full details on the date next time we talk."

"Of course." No problem. I'd come up with some sort of hilarious dating fiasco to entertain her. I certainly had enough real-life experiences to draw from.

With Kat gone and the check paid, I left the restaurant area and made my way to the trendy bar. It was a lot busier than I'd expected it to be this early in the night. I'd thought it would be easy to find Abigail's friend in an empty bar, but now I realized I should have asked for his contact information.

I squeezed onto the one open stool and looked around. Abigail hadn't said much about her hacker friend's appearance except that he was tall, skinny, and always wore jeans and a hoodie.

I checked out every guy at the bar, but nope. No Unabomber. I sent Abigail a text: *Your friend is late. Can you send me his number? Do you have a pic of him, btw? It's crowded in here.*

Ten minutes later, Abigail hadn't responded and no guy had approached me. I glanced down at my outfit. How had Abigail described me? Originally, I'd thought to wear a white, loose-fitting sort of peasant blouse with my jeans and boots. Maybe if I looked demure and innocent, he'd be more inclined to want to help. But then I figured that admitting I'd gone to a hotel room with a total stranger and made a sex tape would pretty much take the ingénue act off the table. So I'd worn what I normally wear when I go out on a Saturday night: a low-cut halter top. If my offer of a thousand bucks wasn't enough to convince him, maybe my boobs would help.

The guy in the navy suit sitting next to me at the bar had certainly looked over at them several times. In fact, right this moment he was downright staring. Amused, I gazed straight at his face until he raised his eyes and noticed.

He flushed and grinned at the same time. Behind his black-framed glasses, his eyes crinkled at the corners. "Sorry."

I gave him a cheeky smile. "Don't be. I wouldn't put them out there if I didn't want people to look."

He snorted into his cocktail. "Are you always so candid?"

"Only to strangers," I said truthfully. He laughed and finished his drink. It looked like a Manhattan, and I coveted it. Kat was driving so we'd had only one glass of wine with dinner, and I was ready for something a bit stronger. But I was saving that treat for whenever I finished making arrangements with Abigail's contact.

He noticed me looking longingly at his glass. "I'd offer to buy you a drink, but I'm meeting with a colleague in a few minutes, and I don't want him to bust me flirting."

That explained the suit. The Gage was popular with investment bankers in the Loop, and high finance didn't break on Saturdays.

"Are we flirting?" I flirted back. "So far you've just stared at my boobs and *not* bought me a drink. I don't think you really brought your A game tonight."

He turned on his stool to face me. "Oh, I brought it. I'm just very choosy about who I use it on."

I scanned his tight hair, fresh shave, and crisp, blue tie.

"Hmm. Well, definitely don't waste it on me. You look good, but in my formidable experience, banker types aren't good conversationalists and they're selfish in bed." I threw him a wide, sassy grin. I didn't have Kat's dimples, but I had straight white teeth and some cute eye crinkles myself.

His nostrils flared as he suppressed a surprised laugh. "That is very good to know. Thanks for sharing your assessment, and I'll remember that the next time I run into a banker. Just out of curiosity, what would impress someone of your significant experience?"

I checked my phone briefly to make sure Abigail hadn't texted back, glanced over the room for a twitchy guy in a hoodie, and then considered his excellent question. How would a guy actually impress me in a bar? "A widespread knowledge of bourbon—and generosity in procuring it. An encyclopedic knowledge of movie quotes. Proof that one has read an actual book in the past month." I looked at his mouth. "And being a good kisser. Naturally."

He returned the look at my mouth. "Naturally."

There was a moment of silence, and I expected him to make an excuse to turn away. This wasn't normal flirting behavior for me. Usually, I'd be astounding the targeted male with my wealth of Chicago sports trivia or asking him dozens of questions about his fascinating work. But this conversation was going to end the moment I spotted my potential hacker, so the refreshing honesty was worth the indulgence.

He took a deep breath. "Bourbon is a type of whiskey made in America. It's a barrel-aged distilled spirit made mostly from corn. It can be made anywhere in the United

States, but the best comes from Kentucky. Popular bourbon cocktails include Manhattans and old-fashioneds, but I prefer boulevardiers, myself." He waved his empty glass in the air. "In terms of brand, I like Angel's Envy straight, but Knob Creek, Booker's, and Blanton's will all do. One of these days, I'm going to save up for a bottle of Pappy Van Winkle, which is—"

"I know what it is," I interrupted, laughing. "And consider me impressed on the bourbon thing."

He inclined his head. "Do you want to quiz me on movie quotes, or should I pluck some from my head at random?"

I gestured expansively. "Pluck away. I will know them all."

He did an amazing Michael Douglas impression. "Greed, for lack of a better word, is good."

"I knew you were a banker." I said. "*Wall Street*. Blech."

"If you build it, he will come."

I shook my head. "Why do men always love *Field of Dreams*? So boring."

His eyes gleamed at me from behind his glasses. I couldn't tell if they were brown or very dark blue. "I'm going to pretend you didn't say that. Um, how about: 'A boy's best friend is his mother.'"

I shuddered. "Are you a creepy *Psycho*?"

"You can't handle the truth," he volleyed back, and I had to bite my lips together to keep from laughing.

"Sweetheart, I can always handle *A Few Good Men*," I said, enjoying myself immensely. "Listen, I appreciate the effort, but you're really underwhelming me with all your obvious choices. Not one surprise in the bunch."

But then he absolutely surprised me by taking his hand off the bar and lowering it so it hovered above my arm. The way he hesitated before allowing a finger to trace the inside of my wrist made me wonder if it was unusual for him to make the first move. "Of all the gin joints in all the towns in all the world, she walks into mine."

Heat spread from the spot on my wrist where the tip of his finger rested to all the way up my body. "*Casablanca*," I sighed. "A true classic. Now that one I like."

"Good," he said simply. "I'm Max, by the way."

"Tess."

We looked one another right in the eyes. For a full minute. One of those long minutes that make you realize how rare it is in daily life to have speechless, sustained eye contact. Usually people are too busy with their phones or some spectacle or with the words coming out of someone's mouth. I'd forgotten what it was like to just look at someone and feel the zing. It was one of those time-stands-still looks that happen so rarely you remember them years later because your body and brain are both tingling and your mouth waters and you hold your breath and everything inside you says "Oh my."

He broke our gaze to look down at his phone, and I felt foolish. Clearly, he hadn't felt the same sparkle. Not that it mattered. I should probably get up and walk around anyway, maybe call Abigail and get the hacker's phone number.

"Here." He—Max—handed me his phone. "Proof that I've read a book in the last month."

My mouth dropped open—his Kindle app. I felt my lips turn up as I nosily poked through his large library. "Wow." I bowed my head and handed his phone back. "OK, I concede that you're a reader. Well done, you."

His fingers danced on my wrist one last time and then returned to the bar. He adjusted his glasses with his other hand. "Have I done well? Have I impressed you?"

I pretended to consider. "You didn't knock it out of the park," I lied. "But I give you an A+ for effort."

"And so we've come full circle," he said, a note of triumph in his voice. "Apparently, I brought my 'A' game after all."

"I'd toast you," I said dryly, "but I still don't have a drink."

He chuckled, a low rumble that I could have listened to for hours. "You know, I'm starting to think my colleague is standing me up. I'm going to call him to find out. If that's the case, I'd be honored to buy you the bourbon of your choice."

"I'll be choosing the most expensive one on the menu," I informed him, a stupid grin on my face.

"Save my seat." He stood up for the first time, and I realized he was well over six feet tall. "Tess."

My stomach muscles clenched. When he said my name, it sounded like a promise.

Chapter Six

WHILE MAX STEPPED outside to call his colleague, I sent a final text to Abigail. *Why aren't you answering me? Your friend didn't show. Text me his number so I can contact him tomorrow.*

I opened the bar menu and perused the long list of bourbons. I should have been more upset about the hacker standing me up, but I couldn't deny that this Max guy had put major butterflies in my stomach. Despite my many evenings on the bar scene, it had been quite some time since I'd had clever repartee with a stranger. And I didn't even remember my last "oh my" moment. Chemistry was a tricky beast.

It probably wouldn't last. He'd probably say something off-putting as soon as he got back. He'd probably go on and on about some obnoxious podcast he listened to every day. Or tell me that CrossFit changed his life. Or insist the food truck parked outside his office building had the best tuna poke bowl in the city. Probably he was allergic to gluten. Or, worse, he did the paleo diet and actually *chose* not to eat carbs.

"Want to share some French fries with our bourbon?" he asked, plopping back down next to me.

Oh.

"Yes, I do," I said. It didn't matter to me at all that I'd just finished dinner. "French fries are my green eggs and ham." Ugh, what? Of course. This was going much too well. Perfect time for a little Tess weirdness to pop out.

But Max just laughed and countered, "You would eat them in a boat? You would eat them with a goat?" He put the order of fries in with the bartender.

Oh.

When our bourbons arrived, we silently clinked our glasses together and took a sip. It was so delicious that I closed my eyes as it slid down my throat. "Mmm." When I opened them, he was looking at my lips again.

"Tell me something random about yourself," he said, jerking his gaze up.

I blinked. "Something random?" An unusual request, but certainly more fun than the typical questions about what you did for a living or which city neighborhood you lived in. "Can you narrow it down for me a little?"

He swirled his drink. "The most embarrassing thing you've done lately. Or a favorite high school memory."

Well, shit. Asking a coworker to delete a sex tape I made was the most embarrassing thing I'd done lately, and I wasn't about to bring that up. And for me, the high school memory was a tougher question than it probably seemed. I didn't really like to think about that general time period at all. "You go first," I deflected.

He hesitated, apparently unprepared to have the ball back in his court. "OK. This is probably going to shock you, but I wasn't very 'cool' in high school." I loved that he did actual finger quotes. "In fact, I would say my shining moment would be my winning performance at the state finals of the Illinois Math Competition."

"Incredible." A former champion mathlete was definitely not my typical Saturday night drinking buddy. I couldn't resist poking at him. "Do you keep your medal displayed in a glass case over your fireplace?"

"Bedside table," he deadpanned. "I like to be able to look at it every night before I go to sleep."

I snort-laughed loudly before I could stop myself. "That's not disturbing at all. Wait—was that your embarrassing story or your favorite high school memory?" I teased.

The tips of his ears went the tiniest bit red. He grinned down at me, shoulders shaking with silent laughter. He pointed an admonishing finger in my face. "Clearly, it was my favorite high school memory. I'm not embarrassed by being completely awesome."

My stomach did another slow flip at his wide grin and the twinkle in his eyes behind those dark frames. All those stupid women's magazines said that confidence is the sexiest attribute of all. I hadn't always agreed with that sentiment, maybe because I met so many arrogant guys at work...and in my opinion, arrogant guys are about as sexy as toads. But Max just seemed confident in who he was, comfortable in his own skin. And damn. It *was* incredibly sexy.

"Your turn," he said. "Tell me a Tess story, any story."

I was stymied. Maybe because there were actually so many Tess stories—but none I wanted to share at this moment. Not when I wanted him to keep looking at me like he was right now. Like there was some sort of magnetic current tugging his eyes to my face.

I finally settled on describing the night I met Roz. "I moved into my current apartment three years ago. Shortly after I moved in, I came in late one night and saw a guy, about forty-five or fifty years old, all dressed in black, jiggling the knob and trying to get in the door of my next-door neighbor's apartment. I hadn't been introduced to her yet, but I'd seen her—a tiny, seventy-year-old woman."

Max leaned forward. "Did you call the police?"

"Not exactly." I wrinkled my nose and cocked my head, sheepish. "I'd had a fair bit to drink that night, and I'd also recently completed a self-defense course. Suffice it to say that I was feeling invincible." Max groaned, which I accepted with a nod. "I charged him." Poor guy, he'd dropped like a stone. Which made it super easy for me to keep whacking him with my purse while shouting obscenities about men who preyed on old ladies.

"Then one of your neighbors called the police?" he guessed.

"Noooo," I said, slowly, drawing it out. "Actually the seventy-year-old woman, Roz, opened her door and started screaming at me."

"Why?" he asked. "Did she not understand what was going on?"

A big laugh bubbled out of my chest. "She understood perfectly. I was the one who didn't. The guy wasn't a burglar. He was...ah...her 'date' for the evening."

"No!" Max exclaimed.

"Oh yes." I nodded sagely. "I now know that Roz occasionally prefers the evening company of a younger man."

His eyes twinkled at me. "So the two of you are sworn enemies to this day?"

"Nope!" I grinned and took a sip of my bourbon. "We're actually best friends," I said, hoping Max would laugh. And he did, that low chuckle.

Just as the French fries arrived, my phone rang. It was Abigail. Ugh, could her timing be any worse? Why didn't she just text? I thought people her age were actually allergic to making phone calls.

I jumped off my stool. "I'm so sorry, but I need to take this. It's really important. I'm just going to run back there." I pointed to a back hallway and took off.

The Gage had an enormous back area that held its large bathrooms, long-abandoned little booths where pay phones used to be, and private dining rooms used for corporate events. Luckily, cell reception was good and it was much quieter than the bustling bar with its loud soundtrack.

"Where have you been?" I hissed into my phone.

"Don't get pissy with me," Abigail retorted. "I've been in a movie. I'm sure you're one of those assholes who lights up the theater by texting during a film, but I'm not."

I was definitely one of those assholes. "Why didn't your guy show up? I've been waiting thirty minutes." I skipped the fact that the wait had been pretty darn fun.

"I think you and he are the dumbest people I've ever met," she said. "He's been there, looking for you."

"He has?" Had I been too wrapped up in Max to notice someone looking for me? "What did you tell him I looked like?"

She paused. "I didn't say anything about what you

looked like. I just said that my boss needed help with an area of his technical expertise and asked if he was free for an impromptu meeting tonight."

I rolled my eyes to the ceiling and counted down from ten. For such a smart person, Abigail was occasionally clueless. "Maybe just send me his number? I'll find him."

"Fine," she snapped.

I hung up and waited. Was there any way I could quickly meet with Abigail's friend and still do bourbon and French fries with Max? I absolutely needed to get my awful situation taken care of, but I met guys in bars all the time and none of them ever made me this jittery or interested.

As if I conjured him up by simply thinking his name, Max came strolling down the empty hallway. When he saw I was off the phone, he held out my glass of bourbon. "If it was going to be a long conversation, I thought you might want your drink. Everything OK?"

He peered down at me with concern; my stomach did a slow flip. He was so long and lean in that dark suit, and something about those glasses was just really doing it for me. "Everything's fine," I said, accepting the glass and taking a swallow. "Thank you."

"Welcome," he said. His gaze dipped to my cleavage and then rested briefly on my lips before meeting my eyes again. We were alone in the hallway. How had it gotten so warm back here so fast?

"I just realized something," he said, voice soft. "I regaled you with my bourbon knowledge and bowled you over with my comprehensive movie quotes and absolutely stunned you with my phone full of books. I even bought you a drink. But

I omitted something very important from the 'Impress Tess' list."

I quickly thought back to all the nonsense I spouted about impressing me… Oh. A good kisser. Boy, did I like where this was headed. Impishly, I batted my eyelashes and licked my lips. "I thought maybe it was on purpose. That you intentionally avoided the subject."

"And why would I do that?"

I showed him a lot of teeth. "Maybe you're just a terrible kisser."

He laughed, long and deep. His eyes were appealingly crinkled when he looked down at me. "Could be."

I gave him a sympathetic squeeze on the arm. "Had a few complaints?"

He leaned down so that our noses were almost touching. "Not one," he whispered.

Whoa. My mouth was actually watering. I was more turned on from talking about kissing with Max than actually kissing anyone else in recent memory. He backed away slowly and took a long drink of his bourbon, never breaking eye contact.

"While you were on the phone, I even took the liberty of looking up movie quotes about kissing," he said.

Delighted, I leaned back against the wall. "Did you find a good one?"

Nodding, he lowered his voice and gruffed it up a bit. "You should be kissed. Often. And by someone who knows how."

I let out a half moan, half sigh. "Clark Gable. *Gone with the Wind.* Oh yes, please."

Max's brow crinkled, and he did that fantastic chuckle again. "Is that a 'yes, please' to Rhett Butler or to me?"

"You," I whispered, so happy to be in this back hallway with him that I felt almost dizzy. Abigail's friend was just going to have to wait.

He deposited his bourbon glass in one of the old phone booths and then tipped my chin up with his thumb. Instead of my eyelids fluttering closed, I stared into his eyes. This close, I could finally see their color. They were an unusually dark shade of blue.

Now that he was so close and touching me, I could feel the slight quiver in his hand and see the way his pulse was racing in his throat. He was either nervous or excited or the perfect mixture of both. "I'm not usually the guy who comes on strong in a bar..."

My pulse was racing too. And since I was pretty much always the girl who came on strong in a bar, I decided not to wait one more second. With the hand not holding my whiskey glass, I reached up and cupped the back of his head. The short hairs were soft and warm against my fingers. I tugged his head down, loving the motion. In my boots I was five foot eleven, and his height made me feel small and feminine.

Then his lips were brushing against mine, softly, as if we had all the time in the world to stand here and make out.

I drew in breath through my nose. This was always an important moment in kissing for me, that first whiff of your partner's scent. I love the mystery of it, the human chemistry, how some people smell good and right and some people don't.

Max smelled perfect. I liked it so much I made an urgent whimper of approval in the back of my throat. He liked *that* so much his lips moved faster and harder. I opened my mouth and pulled him closer to me by the back of his head.

Inside his mouth was heat and bourbon, and I wanted more. I moaned again and suddenly our gentle little kiss went insane. Our lips and tongues moved furiously together. He had me pressed so hard against the wall I could feel the wainscoting digging into my thighs. My hand slid from his head to his nape, and I gripped him with my fingernails. When the kiss started, he'd had one hand on my chin and one at his side. But now one was in my hair and the other was clutching my hip and making a slow slide toward my ass.

Bing! Bing! Bing! Bing!

Both of our cell phones erupted with a flurry of sound. Startled, we broke apart. Or at least, our lips released one another. My hand was still holding him by the neck, and he still had me by the hair and hip.

He stared down at me. "Wow."

I nodded emphatically, taking advantage of the angle to look at the shape of his lips up close.

Bing! Bing! Bing! Bing!

OK, OK, Abigail. Reluctantly, I let go of him. He did the same. Before his hand fully left my hair though, he gave it a little tug. He looked at me with the most adorable shy smile on his face. I could feel a goofy mirror on my own face. He was right. WOW.

I squinted at my phone's screen, confused. Instead of just sending me a phone number, Abigail had started a new text thread to me and to a number not stored in my phone. The message included two photographs along with text in all caps.

One of the photographs was my professional headshot from our company's employee directory.

The other photograph was of a familiar-looking man with dark hair and glasses. "What the…?"

Oh God. Oh please no. Gasping, I read the message: *TESS, MEET MAX. MAX, MEET TESS. BOTH OF YOU, LEAVE ME ALONE NOW.*

I dropped the phone to my side and looked up at Max, my mouth hanging open. He wore an identical expression. He may have even been a bit pale. "You're Abby's boss?"

I nodded. "You're her…coding friend?" I wanted to scream. No! I couldn't reconcile it in my head. Abigail said her friend was an unemployed antisocial guy who wore only sweatshirts. (Hadn't she? Or had I made a little leap?) In front of me stood a gorgeous, slightly disheveled—because of my roaming hand—man wearing a nice suit. Who smelled great, tasted great, and made me laugh.

I thought back over everything we'd said earlier. "So you just assumed her boss was a man?"

He lifted one shoulder in a half shrug. "I guess. Shitty assumption," he admitted.

Indeed. "Did you wear that suit to meet me? Why?" I shifted my weight. "I was expecting someone dressed, uh, more informally."

He crossed his arms over his chest. "It was supposed to be kind of like a job interview," he said, his tone defensive.

Damn Abigail's terribly written text. "No," I said slowly. "What I need doesn't have anything to do with our company."

"Oh." Disappointment was clear in his tone and etched all over his face. I wondered how long he'd been out of work. "What do you need then?"

At the moment? An escape route. There was nothing in the world I wanted less than to confess my current predicament to the man who'd just given me the best kiss in memory.

Well, nothing except having my sex tape available to the world. Which, according to the ticking timer in my head, would happen in approximately twenty days.

I didn't see any point in trying to dress it up. Either Max would agree to do it or he wouldn't. Either he'd be completely turned off by the whole situation—and therefore me—or he wouldn't. Whichever it was, I'd have to deal with it.

But I didn't need to look him in the eyes while I was talking.

I chose a spot on the wallpaper behind his head and focused on it. "Abigail told me that you had a particular set of skills—" Oh God, now I sounded like Liam Neeson in *Taken*. I cleared my throat and tried again. "She told me you were a good hacker. Several years ago I met a real jerk." I sped up my words as fast as I could. "I-went-home-with-him-and-made-a-sex-tape-and-he's-going-to-post-it-online-in-twenty-days." *Breathe*. "He calls himself the FSG. The Fucking Sex Ghost. I need someone to hack his overseas server and delete my video."

Dead silence.

I mustered all my courage and looked at his face. He was gaping at me like I was an alien from outer space. The disappointment that had shaded his features minutes before was transforming into something that looked a lot like shock. Even though he hadn't exactly acted like one tonight, Abigail had called him a Boy Scout. Probably Boy Scouts didn't think much of women who went home with Sex Ghosts. I lifted my chin and met his eyes defiantly. He could be Mr. Judgy if he wanted to; I didn't need to explain myself.

Might as well finish. "I'll pay you a thousand dollars." No answer. "Or whatever you think is reasonable," I hastened to add.

He finally closed his mouth. Adjusted his glasses. When he spoke, his tone was glacial. "I've seen on the job boards that Abigail's department has an open position." I cocked my head. It was true. A senior programmer had recently quit to go work at one of our competitors.

It sounded like he was speaking through gritted teeth. "I don't want a thousand dollars. I want that job."

Sheesh, that was ballsy. I narrowed my eyes at him. Way to really pin a desperate woman to the wall. Of course, he'd literally just had me pinned to a wall and I'd loved it.

Swallowing hard, I forced myself to focus. The senior programmer position reported to Paul. He hadn't had time yet to interview applicants, but the process was starting very soon. I was always on the interview team and part of the decision. Maybe this could work. Paul took my opinion pretty seriously. If Max was as brilliant as Abigail said, he should be able to do the job.

"I'm not the hiring manager," I said. "But I can influence the process. If you have the right qualifications—"

"I do." There was anger in his cold tone. Because I'd

questioned his abilities?

I held out a hand. "Then I guess we have a deal." He shook it quickly and then dropped it, practically flinging my hand away like I had cooties. He started to walk away, but I just couldn't let him go without addressing our little interlude in the hallway.

I was not going to apologize for it; it had been very mutual. One could argue that he was the instigator, actually. And I wasn't going to apologize for going home with the asshole five years ago either.

But I didn't want him to think that what happened with him tonight was anything like what had happened with the FSG. For both my brain and body, the two experiences were night and day. "Wait." He didn't even fully turn around. He just looked over his shoulder.

A rare occurrence—words failed me. "Max, tonight. Before the texts. The kiss."

He shook his head and wrinkled his nose. Light glinted off the lenses in his glasses, and I couldn't see his eyes at all. "No big deal," he called. "We were both just out for a good time."

Oomph. I absorbed that phrase like a gut punch as he disappeared into the bar.

Chapter Seven

I GOT AN email from my mom on Monday morning. My mother and I did some of our very best communicating via email. She and Kat chatted on the phone at least every other day and constantly texted one another. But for me, there were only occasional emails. I truly didn't mind. I could read her words, get as annoyed as I wanted, then cool down and respond. It may have been a little formal, but we avoided a lot of family feuds.

Tess, I think we should do a lovely send-off party for Kat. I'm thinking a fancy brunch somewhere downtown. Block your calendar for November 1. I'll be in touch about the venue and invitations.

I leaned back in my office chair and sighed. If Max was able to delete my video, I'd certainly be ready to celebrate. If things didn't go well, my sex tape would be live to the world that day. If I was extremely unlucky, someone could have tagged me on social media with it by then. Once that happened, there'd be no stopping it. Even if people didn't pay to see it, the gossip alone would be brutal. "Did you hear that Tess Greene made a sex tape with some amateur porn star?" That shit spread like wildfire; there could be people at Kat's party who'd already know. I'd be a pariah. I'd humiliate my sister and mother.

Been there, done that.

Think positive. Abigail wouldn't have recommended Max unless she was sure he could do it. As if on cue, an instant message window from Abigail popped up on my laptop screen. *How'd it go on Sat. night?*

I shook my head. She sat literally twenty feet away from my office. Wouldn't it have been easier to ask me in person? But I dutifully responded. *Good. He didn't want money though. He wants the open position on your team. Am gonna work my magic with Paul.*

Now, to respond to my mother. I typed: *Let me know how I can help with the party*—and then deleted it. Between the Sex Ghost ridiculousness and the extra hours I'd need to work to impress Jack Sorenson, the last thing I could handle right now was working closely with my mom on my sister's going-away party. Kat's ninth birthday had taught me a hard lesson. My lip curled.

Kat had been so excited because she was going to have her very first slumber party. She'd handwritten fancy, old-fashioned invitations to her six best friends and handed them to my mom to stamp and mail. "They'll be so surprised! It's so fun to get real letters!"

I was sixteen and not exactly looking forward to having our small apartment invaded by giggling *High School Musical*–obsessed preteens. But Kat's anticipation was contagious. As the day got closer, we spent lots of time discussing the night's movie lineup, the possible snack options, and debating if an ice cream cake was cool or not.

The night before the big party, Kat came home crying. None of her friends were coming. "They told me they didn't know about the party, but I think they're lying. They just don't want to come." Not possible. There was always some "mean girl" stuff brewing at school, but Kat was too pretty and sweet for her own good. She wasn't the kind of girl others turned on. (I was.)

She put her head down on the kitchen table. "I don't get it. Why do they hate me?"

In an instant, I knew what had happened. I made some random excuse and forced Kat to go to our next-door neighbor's. Then I burst through the closed door of my mother's bedroom. She was actually sleeping this time instead of just lying there, but I didn't care. I shook her shoulders until she woke up. "You forgot to mail Kat's invitations, didn't you?"

She just stared at me. I grabbed her purse from the floor and rummaged through it until I found the stack of carefully addressed envelopes. I held them up in triumph, and she said, "Oh God," and dissolved into tears. Six months before, that would have erased some of my anger. But not anymore. Especially since she didn't even climb out of bed.

I called the parents of all of Kat's friends and lied. I said that I was supposed to mail the invitations and I had forgotten. I said, as punishment, my mom made me call and that also I'd be happy to pick each girl up for the party and drive them all home the following day.

Three of them were able to come, thank God. I stole my mom's credit card and got custom T-shirts made with each girl's name displayed in glitter. Kat and I caravanned around to pick them all up, and they were duly impressed to be driven by her older, cool sister. We blasted that stupid *High School Musical* soundtrack. I took them through the Taco

Bell drive-thru and let them order anything they wanted on me. I let them watch R-rated movies and giggle all night long. In the morning, we went to Dunkin' Donuts before I took everyone home.

Kat still has the T-shirt and ranks that as her favorite birthday party of all time. I can't remember it without feeling vaguely nauseous.

Abigail poked her purple head through my office door, a very welcome interruption to my noxious trip down Memory Lane. "Got a minute?" I nodded, and she came in and shut the door.

"Paul is never going to give Max a job," she said without preamble.

For Christ's sake. What fresh hell was this? "Why not? You said he was brilliant," I reminded her.

"He is," she said. "But something went down at his old company, SideDoor. Something bad. Supposedly, he got let go during a planned round of layoffs, but there has to be more to it. Right after it happened, he got plenty of interviews. But every time Max got close to getting an offer, they would rescind. It's like he's blacklisted."

I shook my head. "Blacklisted? What do you mean?"

She shrugged. "He told me that he suspects the CEO of SideDoor personally calls the hiring manager of the company about to offer and talks shit until they change their mind about hiring him."

That made no sense, particularly given the reputation of SideDoor's CEO. Cole Taggert was something of a legend in the Chicago business community. He'd created a next-generation antivirus software and released it as open source to the public instead of selling it for a gazillion dollars. He was like a Robin Hood for code, for God's sake.

Why would a guy who willingly sacrificed a bunch of cash for the greater good be so vindictive? "What in the world could Max have done to make Cole Taggert personally invested in making sure he can't get another job? Why would any CEO be that petty?"

"I asked him that once," she admitted. "He turned bright red and wouldn't answer."

This sucked. If Paul had already retired, the position would report to me and it would be a done deal. But in my current role, I was only able to hire temporary contractors for small projects—nothing like the senior role Max wanted. I knew I could get him on the docket to be interviewed for the position. I was fairly sure I could get Paul to choose him from all the possible applicants. But there was absolutely nothing I could do if Paul got a phone call from one of the most respected CEOs in the city.

"Shit."

"He's been unemployed for almost a year," Abigail said, opening the door to leave. "He must need money. Offer him more."

More? Between the amount I was paying the lawyers and now this…I'd be very lucky not to go into credit card debt this month. No shopping for me this holiday season. Many fewer nights at Fizz. A sudden, visceral urge to see the FSG overtook me. I had some very violent and bloody revenge fantasies to work through.

I GOT OFF the Brown Line at Western and followed the directions on my phone to a nice but older-looking home about six blocks north. I'd found a listing for Max on whitepages.com at this address. Since he'd ignored the various text messages I'd sent him in the afternoon, I didn't see another alternative to following up with him in person. Tick-tock on the sex-tape-release clock.

I rang the doorbell and waited. The house didn't seem right for a single guy in his thirties. It was a family home that looked comfortable and worn, the kind of home where children had beat the crap out of the floors, doors, and walls. As I suspected from my very first conversation about him with Abigail, he was probably living in his parents' basement. A little bratty of me, but it made me feel better to know this. Maybe he thought I was an idiot, but at least I could afford my own apartment.

I heard footsteps jogging inside, and Max flung open the door. His mouth dropped and his eyebrows leapt over his glasses. No suit today. He was wearing dark jeans and—ta da!—a hoodie. I waited for my dancing pheromones to retreat in light of his geeky IT attire, but no. Turns out Max looked pretty good in casualwear. His navy sweatshirt matched the dark blue of his eyes, and it looked incredibly soft.

"What are you doing here?" he asked.

"We need to renegotiate," I announced. "You snubbed all my texts today, so I hunted you down."

He ran a hand through the hair on the right side of his head. I tried hard to block the memory of how silky his hair felt in my fingers. "I wasn't snubbing you," he said. "I've just been busy. I haven't looked at my phone in hours."

He opened the door wider and gestured for me to come inside. I looked around curiously, wondering if his mom might pop out of the kitchen with a plate of chocolate chip cookies. With its two La-Z-Boy recliners, circular crocheted rugs, and multiple throw blankets, the living room had that Toll House kind of vibe.

"No one else is here right now," he mumbled. "My parents are closing on their new condo downtown. I'm helping them get organized." There was definitely evidence of an upcoming move, I saw now. Boxes lined the hallways and stacks of books and folded clothing were all over the floor.

I wondered where he would live after his folks' house had sold, but decided that would be inappropriate to ask. We had business to cover. I perched myself along one arm of the sofa and crossed my legs. "Abigail told me about your issues getting hired. If the position reported to me, I'd hire you no matter what sicko thing you did to piss off your old boss. But the job doesn't report to me, and I can't guarantee it if my boss Paul gets a call about you."

My booted foot started twitching. "But I still really need your help. So name another price."

He didn't say anything so I looked up at him. His shoulders were slumped, his chin lowered, and his eyes were hidden behind a glint of light off the lenses of his glasses. I wondered if he always knew the exact right angle to tilt his head to hide his eyes.

I felt a pang of sympathy. I'd be a basket case without my job. Aside from how great Kat turned out, my professional success was the thing I was absolute proudest of in my whole life.

He still didn't answer, and I grew uncomfortable with the silence. Hopping to my feet, I circled the living room and poked my head into the dining room and kitchen, which were in an even more advanced state of disarray. Winter clothing was strewn out from the mudroom. Cookware had been pulled out of the cabinets and piled in stacks on the counters.

I tried to lighten the mood. "Are your parents hoarders?"

Ha! One side of his mouth turned up, just a smidge. "No. Or at least not major ones. This house has just become the dumping grounds for all the detritus of my siblings and their kids. It's one reason they're trying to downsize."

Good, at least he was talking now. "How many siblings do you have?" I asked.

A faint smile. "Four. Two older brothers, two younger sisters."

"Aw." I winked at him. "Max in the middle?"

He winced. "Don't start with that."

"You should be proud of being a middle," I said. I'd recently read an article about birth order while in my dentist's office. "Middles are known for being skillful manipulators, trailblazers, and justice seekers. Fifty-two percent of US presidents have been middles," I added helpfully. The article had also mentioned that middles were more open-minded and adventurous about sex than other birth orders, but I needed to banish that kind of thinking right now.

He stared at me. "And since you come strolling in here like you own the place, I'll go out on a limb and guess that you are clearly a firstborn."

Naturally. "Yep."

He crossed his arms over his chest. "So you're bossy and Type A and—"

"—a good leader and extremely self-motivated," I finished for him, smiling cheekily. His lips twitched.

I looked around at the chaos in each room. "If you don't mind me asking, what exactly are you trying to, er, organize?"

He flicked his eyes to the ceiling. "My mom asked me to go through all the closets and cabinets and pick items to throw away, items to donate, and items to keep. Sounded straightforward at the time, but now I just keep pulling things out, and I have no idea how to categorize them." He walked around me and gestured at the mudroom. "Mom said there's nothing in there they want to keep, but I have no idea what's right to toss and what's right to donate."

Hmm. I joined him at the threshold of the mudroom and took a good, long look. "Actually, this is pretty easy," I said. I pointed at the floor where there were a dozen pairs of worn-out tennis shoes, flip-flops, and loafers. "Throw all that stuff away. Donation centers don't want items that beat up."

I dug into a cabinet and whooped with excitement at my find. One pair of gently used rain boots and two pairs of barely worn children's snow boots. "These! These are golden to donate! Take these to the Goodwill or Salvation Army or wherever. These are a find!"

He quirked an eyebrow at me, and I nodded emphatically. "Snow boots are expensive and obviously necessary in Chicago. Children's feet grow so fast, and it can be really hard for families on a budget to keep up. When my sister was ten, her feet grew three sizes in one winter. I almost bawled my eyes out when there was a late snowstorm in March and she just couldn't squeeze into her pair—"

Abruptly, I shut my mouth. What was I doing? I never talked about that time.

His eyes were on my face again. I cleared my throat and opened another cabinet. "Looks like you have some winter coats in good condition. Those are a treasure as well."

I went through every cabinet in the mudroom, doing a little monologue. He watched with a neutral expression, but I got the feeling he was listening to everything and making mental notes. "A lot of places don't take used children's toys," I finished. "You can give that stuff to people you know or toss it."

Whew. Maybe I'd gone on a bit too long. But it's hard to shut me up once I'm on a roll and know what I'm talking about. "Do you want me to look at any of your other closets?" I asked.

He actually smiled at me. "No, I think I've got the framework now. Thanks."

To my surprise, he went into the kitchen and opened the fridge. "You want a soda?"

"Yes. Please." *I will not think about the last time we had a beverage together.*

He handed me a root beer. "Have a seat." He pointed to the kitchen table.

"Thanks." I plopped in a chair and he sat across from me. We each took a long swallow. It was a nice peaceful moment...which I had to ruin by having a tactless thought slide right through my ragged brain-to-mouth filter. "So, did you do something really bad at SideDoor? Is that why Cole Taggert hates you?"

He paused, the can halfway to his mouth. He didn't look upset though. He looked amused. "I thought you said you were only candid with strangers."

"We're still strangers." I smiled uncertainly. His curved lips were creating that inconvenient zing that whipped up from my stomach and stole some of my breath. "Tell me what you did."

He took a long chug of root beer. "Nah. Too long of a story. Unlike you, I'm only candid with very close friends." He put the can on the table and leaned forward. Now I could see his eyes clearly through the lenses. "Many people *would* consider what I did to be a bad thing. But I stand by my actions; I did what I did for a good reason." He glanced down. "It was naïve of me though to not realize that all the consequences would come straight from the action and not the motivation."

My hands started to tremble. I wasn't wearing my lucky silver ring, so I put them under my thighs and sat on them. Good God, did I know this scenario. Doing something wrong for the right reason. Dealing with the aftermath. Seven years ago, I'd been screaming this exact tune in my head. And I was positive my indiscretion was much, much worse than Max's. I still sometimes woke up from nightmares of Daniel's crestfallen face.

"What frustrates me," Max said, "is that if I could just get in somewhere, I really think that my work would speak for itself. And I'm a good team player. I get along with everyone. If I could just work somewhere for a month, I don't think anyone would believe what my ex-boss tells them." He sighed. "But I can't get in the door."

I nodded in sympathy. So true. With everything online and so much social media and networking, there was no walking in with a clean slate anymore. Everything was scoped out ahead of time, first impressions formed, and you couldn't escape the pre-judgment. I cyber-stalked all of our job applicants.

Wait a minute. I sat straight up in my chair and bounced a little. "I have an idea. I'm allowed to hire short-term contractors for projects where we need high-volume, unskilled work. Usually, it's for data entry or testing or other mind-numbing stuff."

Max went still, probably following my train of thought to its conclusion. "What if I brought you in as a contractor for something like that? Like you said, to get you in the door. Then Abigail and I could work with you to astound Paul with your tech skills and go-getter-ness."

He was nodding along. "And then I would apply for the senior programmer position."

"Exactly!" I clapped my hands together. "When the SideDoor CEO calls Paul, he'll already know you and maybe he won't believe whatever your ex-boss says."

Max waited a beat and then reached his can across the table at me in an attempted toast. "It's a long shot, but I'll take it."

I didn't clink his can. Not yet. "But you will help me with my...situation?"

He looked annoyed. "Of course. A deal's a deal." Fair enough. I completed our root beer toast. "In fact," he said,

"I've already started researching your Sex Ghost."

"Don't ever call him *my* Sex Ghost again," I warned. "And 'research,' eh? Watching lots of his videos?"

He shuddered. "God, no. That shit is horrible. I watched thirty seconds of one and felt dirty. I've been poking at the offshore site. It uses a variety of different server farms on the dark web for his videos. I'm starting an analysis on their security weaknesses. That way, when your video goes up and I can isolate its home, I'll have a strategy for how to take it down quickly."

Oh.

For the first time since Micki took me into her office at Fizz, the complex knot in my stomach loosened. "Thank you," I whispered.

Max cocked his head. "Why'd you do it?"

"Why did I make a sex tape?" Inwardly, I sighed, preparing to give him the same sort of speech I'd given Joe that night at Fizz. And I was unaccountably disappointed that I needed to.

But then Max said, "No. I can understand wanting to experiment. I was more asking why you'd go home with such a tool."

Caught off guard, I laughed. "Fair question. He didn't behave in person the same way he does on his site though. He said he was an actor. I think he has his obnoxious 'ultimate bro' FSG persona and a completely different picking-up-girls persona that's a bit more charming." I sighed a little. "Honestly, the moment I saw beyond his looks, he became really unappealing. But I didn't find that out until too late in the evening."

Max was quiet, listening to me so intently. I squirmed under his gaze and gave in to the impulse to turn flippant. "Anyway, I was crazy and careless and stupid."

He shook his head. "No. That doesn't seem like you. Well, maybe the crazy part." I tensed—until I noticed the upward curve of his lips and the glint in his eyes. He was teasing me.

Then his face went serious. "But definitely not the stupid part."

Perhaps it was a sign I needed more compliments in my life if one so small made me almost drop my soda. Or maybe the fact that I was so relieved he didn't believe I was normally stupid was a blatant reminder that I was still crushing on him.

Even though my soda was still half full, I stood to leave. Between my flashbacks to Goodwill shopping, my memories of Daniel, and my gratitude for Max's site research, I was feeling uncharacteristically emotional. I needed to go before I did something ridiculous, like launch myself across the table and wrap myself inside that hoodie with him.

"I'm out." I manipulated my voice to be light and carefree. "It's time for my cocktail hour, and you need to keep helping your hoarder parents." I forced my mind back on work. "I need a day to complete the contractor paperwork. Come down to the office first thing on Wednesday, and we'll start Operation Paul Loves Max."

"We need a different name for that," he said dryly, walking me out.

Challenge accepted. "Operation Max Attack! Operation Persuade Paul! Operation Acquire the Hire! Operation

Hobnob for the Job!"

He burst out laughing. It was even better than the chuckle I'd liked so much on Saturday night. His chuckle was low and rumbling, like a cozy fire in a grate. His laugh was loud, raucous, and slightly higher pitched, like an unexpected firecracker. I could get addicted to those.

He got himself under control and opened the front door to me. "See you in two days."

I wasn't going to count down the hours. Not at all.

Chapter Eight

ON WEDNESDAY MORNING I got to the office super early. If I'd spent a little extra time blowing out my hair, so what? I was also wearing my absolute favorite green turtleneck sweater and pencil skirt combo with fishnets and my sassiest, highest heeled boots. On my way out of the building this morning, Roz had declared my outfit "a little bit boardroom, a little bit bedroom." I adored her assessment.

While pretending I wasn't waiting for Max to show up, I tore through my email backlog, sent out instructions to my various teams, and updated Abigail via IM on Operation Paul Loves Max.

It was still shy of 9:00, so I began my weekly review of my mother's and Kat's bank accounts. One of these weeks I'd get over the compulsion to do this, but old habits died extremely hard, and making sure my family was financially solvent was just one more hang-up from my teenage years.

Kat kept her password, *GreeneGirlzRock123!*, on a small yellow Post-it Note near her laptop in her apartment. Not that I'd needed to see it. She hadn't changed it since I took her to set up her bank accounts eight years before. I scanned through her recent transactions from both her checking and savings. Nothing abnormal. Her credit card, however, had been hit with an unusual charge. Frowning, I drilled in deeper, only to realize it was for the U-Haul rental that would take her to San Francisco.

I sighed and logged out of her accounts, redirected my browser to my mother's bank. Years ago I'd had to guess her password, but it had been simple. I'd gotten it right on my third try: *Katharine1208*. Kat's name and birthday. My mother's checking account looked lower than normal, and I scrolled down to confirm that she hadn't been paid last Friday. My mother worked as an office manager for a CPA, a lovely older gentleman who'd become a family friend. But to my continual frustration, Mr. Gupta didn't believe in automating his payroll. She was supposed to be paid every other Friday, but I'd often seen the funds appear as late as the following Tuesday. He was even later than usual this time, but I wasn't worried. I'd check again in a couple of days.

"Knock, knock." Max stood in my doorway. Today he wore khakis and a blue button-down shirt, the eternal answer to the question: What is the safest thing to wear in a business-casual environment?

"Good morning," I said cheerily. "Ready for a long day of tasks well beneath your intellect and education?"

He grinned. "Strangely enough, yes, I am." Oh, that grin. A bespectacled, on-the-skinny-side guy had never been my type before, but I was suddenly worried that my type had changed for good.

"Great." I called Abigail and asked her to come over. When she appeared, she and Max gave each other an awkward one-armed hug. "Abigail, take him to get a temporary ID badge and give him the rundown on where everything is. He can sit in the empty cube next to you. You and the rest of the programmers can use him for testing or debugging or brainstorming or whatever."

"Nice! You can do all my bitch work," she told him. He grinned down at her now, and I analyzed every microinch of his face. He didn't smile at Abigail the same way he smiled at me. I couldn't pinpoint the difference, but I was fairly sure I'd spend several hours this evening trying.

Paul walked by my open door, his face in his phone. There was no time like the present to jumpstart Operation PLM. "Paul!" Max and Abigail both looked at me with wide eyes.

"Morning, everyone." Paul's eyes were puffy and bloodshot. I knew why.

"The game last night was a real barn burner, wasn't it? I'm still holding my breath." I laughed. The Cubs playoff game on Tuesday night had gone into extra innings before they won with a walk-off home run in the eleventh. I hadn't actually watched the game, but I always listened to sports radio on my way to work in the morning so I'd be ready for him with a verbal highlight reel. Hopefully, Max was taking notes on my skillful approach.

Paul's whole face lit up. "Yes! It took me hours to calm down enough to sleep. What did you think of Rizzo's error in the eighth?"

Well, shit. There was no error mentioned in the summary I'd listened to. Before I could fall back on one of my usual generic answers, Max said, "Totally uncharacteristic, right? Normally, he's as solid as they come. I couldn't believe it when he bobbled that ball."

"Me either!" Paul exclaimed. Then he focused on Max's face and threw me a panicked glance.

"Paul, meet Max Hampshire," I said smoothly. "He'll be contracting for us over the next several weeks. The programmers have a ton of tight deadlines coming up, so Max is going to take some testing and debugging work off their plates. Today is his first day."

Relieved, Paul shook Max's hand. "Aha. I knew I didn't recognize you. Welcome!"

I pointed down the hall and gave Abigail a tiny push. "Go get Max settled, and I'll check in with you both later."

As they walked down the hall, I leaned toward Paul and did a stage whisper. "We're getting a bargain with that one."

"What do you mean?" he asked.

"Max is like, a genius programmer with a ton of experience," I said. "He's trying to decide which company he goes to next. He could go anywhere, but he's really dedicated to finding a good corporate culture. So he's temping around before he decides where to apply." I looked around and lowered my whisper. "Fingers crossed that he'll apply for our open position."

"Interesting," Paul whispered back. He loved being "in" on any sort of office gossip even though he never was. It was one of the things I'd always liked about him. "And a Cubs fan to boot!"

Paul ambled off to his office, and I smiled to myself. Operation PLM was getting off to a great start.

I MEANT TO get with Max and Abigail to discuss strategy right after lunch, but something rare happened. One of our clients encountered an actual disaster. Most of my job involved creating disaster recovery plans, documenting them, and testing them. Actually enacting them in real-life situations happened only once in a blue moon.

But Northern California was having a terrible year of wildfires, and on Wednesday afternoon, one of our clients lost their data center to a blaze. Panicked, my client contact called to alert me of the situation. I consoled her and reassured her the recovery solution was one hundred percent automated—but then put out a Code Red to one of my teams so they could verify everything was working exactly as planned.

After slipping my lucky silver ring on my finger, I stalked around the floor all afternoon, barking orders and demanding status updates. Luckily, I continually received a thumbs-up from the team monitoring the account. The client's recovery databases, located on servers in Alabama, came up right on schedule with no hiccup, and their customers experienced no system outages. I was on the phone with the client every thirty minutes, providing statistics and assurances.

When I finally hung up with her, I walked back to the project team who'd worked with me to design the solution and gave them each a high five. I was always confident in our work, but it was a huge win when a client went through an actual disaster and everything went seamlessly. When the dust settled, our marketing team would have a great new opportunity for a glowing testimonial.

After giving Paul the good news, I sat down at my desk to catch my breath. Whew. A glance at the clock told me it was getting close to 5:00 p.m. I was going to Fizz tonight for sure. A day like this deserved a stiff cocktail.

But then I noticed a new email from my mom.

Tess—

I found a great venue for Kat's party. It's a restaurant called Pop's for Champagne and it's only a few blocks from your office. Can you swing by? See if they have a private room available on November 1st? Get the pricing for catered events? I'm just so swamped at work. If you could do it today, that would be best. Send the info to me in email when you have it. Thanks!

This was just so typical. My mother volunteered to throw Kat a party, but I would end up doing all the work. Take my engagement, for example. When Daniel had proposed, my mother had been over the moon at the idea of a large, fancy wedding. But when it came to the invitations, seating arrangements, or any of the other thousands of details where I could have used some help, she always had something better to do.

Gritting my teeth, I forced myself to inhale and exhale ten times. My therapist had a strict rule for me about this: whenever I got pissed at my mother for something that happened in the past, I had to counteract by actively thinking of a good memory involving her. Fine. I exhaled through my nose and closed my eyes.

Before my father died, he traveled constantly on business. There was one winter in particular when he was gone for weeks at a time. Kat was going through her terrible twos and cried constantly. I was in fourth grade and in a daily battle with myself over whether to let myself be bullied by the reigning Mean Girls or let my bad self loose and become the biggest Regina George of them all.

One afternoon I fought back tears on the school bus only to explode with them as soon as I'd let myself through the front door of our house. My mom looked up in surprise. She was bouncing a wailing Kat around the kitchen and now she had two bawling daughters to deal with.

I blubbered to her about how Sarah Liberty, my archnemesis, had gathered a bunch of the other "cool girls" in a corner of the playground and how they'd whispered and pointed at me. This was not my first Sarah Liberty story, and normally my mother would listen with a sympathetic ear and then say fair, mom-ish things about trying to be kind to everyone and ignoring girls who behaved badly, blah blah blah.

But that afternoon, she said none of those typical things. Probably she was completely exhausted from having to work and single-handedly parent two difficult children. I'll never forget it. After I broke down sobbing about Sarah's nasty whispers, she just shook her head, moved Kat to her other hip, and said, "That girl sounds like a little bitch. Maybe you should just punch her in the nose."

I was shocked into silence. I'd never heard my mom swear or advocate violence. My eyes flew to her face where red blotches covered her cheeks. Her long, dark hair was loose on her shoulders, and her eyes were blazing. In that moment, she looked like Wonder Woman to me. An extremely tired, pissed-off, on-the-edge-of-a-nervous-breakdown kind of Wonder Woman, but still.

I burst out laughing. After a second, her nostrils flared and she did too. We laughed and laughed until Kat even stopped crying and gurgled, trying to join in on the fun. That night we ate Cheetos and peanut butter toast for dinner. I slept in my parents' bed with my mom, and we listened to Kat howl herself to sleep while we created elaborate verbal traps for old Sarah.

Now, I opened my eyes. My therapist was right again; my anger fire had been downgraded to a spark of irritation. Sighing loudly, I reread my mother's email.

Honestly, had she even called this place? She only worked twenty-four hours a week. How swamped could she be? I'd walked by Pop's many times, and it looked pricey. She probably hadn't even looked at the website to see if it was affordable.

Damn it. I logged off my computer and put on my coat. I'd walk over there now and get it figured out. The party was in less than three weeks. They probably didn't even have an open room on such short notice.

"Oh, you're leaving?" Abigail and Max hovered in the doorway. "Thought you might want to discuss things," Abigail said. "Nice job on the wildfire recovery, by the way."

"Thanks." Shit. I really needed to get a plan together with them. Time was a-ticking. "Any chance you guys want to swing over to Pop's for a quick drink? We can talk about it there."

Abigail and Max looked surprised but agreed. They

walked behind me, gibbering about code, as I tried to get my mind away from wildfires, away from my mother, and back on task.

Chapter Nine

"TABLE FOR THREE?" The gorgeous Pop's hostess offered a perfect smile.

"Yes," I answered. "And can I please see your catering menu?" I'd check the prices first. No need to inquire about availability if it was beyond reach.

She seated us at a window table that overlooked Clark Street. Grudgingly, I admitted that Pop's was a very pretty place. The décor was all chandeliers and champagne bottles. Light jazz played in the background, and the crowd of patrons was pretty darn pretty too.

Abigail glanced around the softly lit room and shifted uneasily on her stool. I bet she was more accustomed to hipster pubs with dartboards and sticky floors than the understated elegance surrounding us.

Max had fit in well at the Gage, and he looked right at home here as well. I suspected he was a chameleon, like me. I was actually more of a pub girl myself, but I enjoyed a trendy scene every now and then.

"Drinks on me," I said, passing them a leather-bound cocktail menu.

Abigail quickly read through the long list of champagnes by the glass and then just shrugged. "I'll have whatever you have," she said. "Be back in a sec."

As she headed to the restroom, I examined the catering menu. Jesus. What had my mother been thinking? There was no way she could afford to throw a party for twenty people here. I closed my eyes and rubbed my temple, already dreading the phone call I'd have to make to her. I'd tell her it was too expensive, and she'd get quiet and disappointed, as though somehow it was my fault.

"Tough day?" Max asked.

I dropped my hands back to my lap. "Not really."

"How often do you manage actual disaster situations?"

I had to remind myself that he was talking about the wildfire and not my mother. I closed the menu. "I think the last one was almost three months ago. Something similar happened to a Florida client with a hurricane." I rolled my neck from side to side. The tension must have gotten to me more than I realized, because I was stiff and sore. "But it's definitely not a daily occurrence."

"You handled it like it was." Max leaned back, closing his own menu. If I weren't mistaken, there was a strong note of respect in his voice.

I looked up, a little surprised. His eyes were scanning my face, and I guessed that he was...reevaluating me? Trying to recategorize however he'd filed me away before, maybe. That kind of adjustment happened sometimes when you saw someone out of context. Kind of the way the Fizz crowd was always taken aback when I showed up for happy hour in my work clothes as opposed to my Saturday night clothes.

Now that I thought about it, Max had seen several different iterations of me in the short time I'd known him.

Which was strange and discomfiting. I was usually pretty vigilant about keeping my life more segmented.

Abigail returned, and I ordered us both glasses of sparkling. I wondered if Max would order some sort of bourbon cocktail, but he played it safe with a beer. When the drinks arrived, I said, "Cheers," and took a long sip of the bubbles.

"Let's talk about ways to ingratiate yourself to Paul."

Max frowned at me. "Do I really need to? If I do a great job with the programmers, won't that be enough?"

Abigail looked up at him from under her lashes. "You're already doing a great job. We made insane progress today!" Oh no. Was Abigail making googly eyes at him?

"Thanks, Abs." On the table, Max's phone began to vibrate. He looked at the display. "I better take this. One sec." He left the table and walked away, the phone to his ear.

It was always best to be as direct as possible with Abigail. "Do you have a thing for Max?"

She blinked at me, confused. Then her expression cleared. "Ew! No! Gross. He's even older than you."

"Then why are you looking at him like this?" I looked sideways as if a tall man were sitting next to me, and fluttered my eyelashes.

"Not funny." She crossed her arms over her chest. "He's so smart," she said finally. "Working with him today, I learned so much. He's just impressive. Get your mind out of the gutter." She sniffed. "Besides, Max is totally hung up on his ex."

I took a careful sip of my champagne and turned the pages of the catering menu nonchalantly. "Oh?" He hadn't seemed very hung up on anyone Saturday night, but what did I know? Maybe I was just a distraction. Or an experiment. Maybe I was his Sex Ghost. Wasn't that a sobering thought!

"Yeah." She glanced backward to make sure he was still across the room. "That's her on the phone. I saw her name on the screen before he answered."

Max reappeared and sat down before I could figure out a surreptitious way to pump Abigail for more details. "Sorry for the interruption. Like I was saying, why do we need any sneaky strategy for Paul?"

"Because we don't have time for good word of mouth to get to Paul's ears," I said. "He's not involved with the programming team on a day-to-day basis. He leaves that to me. You need to connect with him and impress him quickly if we want the timing to work."

"She's right," Abigail said. "I worked here for three months before Paul stopped calling me Allison."

I brought up the notes app on my phone. "Some ideas. You're from a big family, right? Find a way to chat with him about that. Paul has five children and twelve grandchildren."

Which was utterly insane. Hadn't they heard the world was going through an overpopulation crisis? Of course, Paul's dopey devotion to his family was sort of endearing. His office was wallpapered with photos of children, and he called his wife every day at lunch. If some gigantic-ass family was going to gobble up all of Earth's natural resources for themselves, at least they were the kind of family who got together for Sunday dinners.

"More sports stuff like this morning," Abigail contributed. "Years ago, Tess figured out the way to Paul's heart was through Chicago sports babble."

I nodded. "I'm usually up on the Cubs and the Bears. But sometimes I struggle with the Bulls and Blackhawks. And don't even get me started on the Fire."

Max took a long pull of his Stella Artois. "OK, family and sports. Got it." He was definitely patronizing us, but I would power on.

"Those kinds of conversations will make him like you on a personal level, which is key. But he also needs to quickly think of you as invaluable." I picked up my phone and shook it. "Paul is really good at his job. The big decisions, the high-level technology discussions. But he's terrible at small technology."

"Oh God, yes." Abigail drained her glass. "His phone. His laptop. Microsoft Word. The printer. The scanner. When he comes out of his office with that frown between his eyebrows, everyone tries to run away."

"Max won't," I said, smiling in spite of my challenging day. "Max is going to run to Paul's aid whenever he jams the printer or downloads the latest virus on his laptop."

He grimaced into his beer. "I will be a one-man help desk." He gave a philosophical shrug. "How bad can it be?" Abigail and I traded smirks. He had no idea. Max's proactive intervention was going to save the rest of the department a ton of time. Honestly, I should have hired a contractor for this sole purpose years ago.

There was one item left on my list. It was a long shot. "Is there any chance you've rescued a dog?"

Paul had not one, not two, but three bumper stickers of dogs on his Subaru Outback that read "Who rescued who?"

In the past, I had considered keying cars spouting that sanctimonious bullshit.

Max's mouth dropped open. "Uh, no."

I gave him a hopeful smile full of teeth. "Any chance you're in the market for one?"

Abigail burst out laughing. After a moment, Max joined in. My stomach muscles clenched in response to his chuckle. I acknowledged defeat. "We'll save that one for an emergency."

Our waitress, a platinum blonde with Cleopatra-style hair and six-inch pink stilettos, paused at our table. "Another round?"

Since we were done with our Paul prep, I was about to decline. But Max said, "Sure." I looked at Abigail, and we both did that sort of shrug-nod.

I was a little worried we'd have nothing to talk about, but before I knew it, we were having a loud debate about the best '80s movie of all time (Abigail: *The Breakfast Club*. Max: *Back to the Future*. Both were solid choices, but I had to go with *Goonies*) and we'd actually had *two* more rounds.

I'd switched to red wine on the third drink because two glasses of bubbles on an empty stomach had gone straight to my head. Abigail was downright tipsy by the time her third glass arrived. Not surprising considering she probably weighed eighty-seven pounds soaking wet. "Let's get French fries!" she demanded.

My eyes jumped straight to Max's before I could stop them. His nostrils twitched, and he looked down at the table. But I could have sworn he muttered "green eggs and ham" under his breath.

Before Abigail could flag down blonde Cleopatra, Max's phone began to vibrate on the table. "Is that Aria again? She sure calls you a lot for an *ex*-fiancée," Abigail slurred.

Ex-*fiancée*? Whoa. Aria. What a lovely and exotic name. Only four letters but three beautiful syllables. My name was also four letters and it rhymed with "mess." Fucking unfair.

Max quickly ended the call and avoided both of our gazes. "Let's get you those fries," he said.

"Sorry, Max," she said quickly, sounding a touch more sober. "Didn't mean to be bratty. I know it was a hard breakup." She gave him a sloppy pat on the shoulder. "Good riddance though. She was always too nice anyway."

Max did one of his patented head angles where the glare off of his glasses prevented a clear look at his eyes. When he spoke, his tone was patient but a little irritated. He plainly did not like her last comment. "I like nice girls," he said firmly. "Nice girls are my type."

I flinched. Thank God we hadn't gone further on Saturday night. I was—unapologetically—about the furthest thing there was from a traditionally defined "nice girl." Which would have been abundantly clear to Max even before the big sex tape revelation. I'd worn a boob shirt, I drank brown liquor straight, I kissed men I just met in back hallways at bars. If Max was in the nice girl camp, he must have just been looking for a distraction that night. Thank God we'd been interrupted before things had gone further.

Max took Abigail's hand off his shoulder and gently placed it on the bar. "Should we get food?" he asked me, widening his eyes, clearly looking for help with our blasted little friend.

Nope. I was ready to go home now. Not only that, I felt a perverse desire to make it clear that I was not and never would be a nice girl. Kat was always exasperated with this contrarian aspect of my nature. If someone didn't like something about me, I'd flaunt that one aspect to death instead of toning it down. My mother had once remarked that she disliked my beloved knee-high black boots. Instead of just throwing on a pair of pumps to make her happy, I now wore the boots every single time I saw her.

"Actually, I've got to run," I said. I signaled the waitress for our check. "I'll cash us out here and you guys can go grab dinner or whatever."

But before I left…I cocked my head in Max's direction. "You were engaged?"

He slumped back in his seat. "Yeah. It ended a year and a half ago." His entire face tensed as though waiting for a barrage of follow-up questions.

I surprised him instead. "I was engaged once too. Seven years ago."

Abigail pulled her face out of her champagne glass and stared at me, incredulous. "*You* were engaged when you were young? To a boy?" I rolled my eyes at her astonishment and nodded. "That's hard to imagine." She waved her hand at me. "I think of you as a sort of boozy Amazon."

I hooted. Now that was funny. And not a terrible depiction.

"What happened?" she asked.

The waitress appeared with the check, and I handed over a bunch of cash before the others could move. "We called it off the morning of the wedding."

I waited until their faces softened with sympathy before I added, "It was completely my fault, of course. He found out, just in the nick of time, that I wasn't the nice girl he wanted to marry."

I considered dropping the full bomb, explaining my transgression in lurid detail. But no, let their imaginations run wild instead of releasing another of my dirty secrets out in the wild. Of course, this one wasn't exactly a secret. Daniel's mother had been with him when he found me, and so most of our wedding guests knew what had happened before lunchtime.

As their eyes grew as large as the fancy coasters on the table, I stood and slid on my leather coat. "Anyway, I'll see you guys tomorrow." I winked at Max. "Can't wait for you to blow Paul away."

I lifted my chin and walked out.

Chapter Ten

THE REST OF the workweek passed very quickly, in spite of the fact that I was barely sleeping. With only two weeks remaining until the sex tape release, I'd started waking up from nightmares that featured a giant red countdown clock, much like the one that used to appear before every commercial break of the TV show *24*.

Paul and I helped sales land two new clients, so forming project teams and high-level solutions took up most of my time. Jack Sorenson dropped by my office for a status update, which he'd never done before. I took it to be a good sign that he was taking me seriously as a VP candidate. Zack Morris, the Away-Ho CEO, canceled two meeting appointments, driving both the sales team and me a little nuts.

From Abigail I learned that the entire programming team was now in awe of Max, already treating him as the senior team lead he wanted to be. I mentioned this to Paul as casually I could, carefully planting the seed.

But our first big Operation PLM win came on Friday, when Paul plodded out of his office with that telltale frown between his eyebrows. Unfortunately, he saw me before I could escape. "Tess! My phone is saying that it can no longer back itself up! Something about no space in my cloud. But I purchased an enormous amount of space the last time I was at the Apple store. It's also not recognizing my Apple ID password. This is horrible!"

"I bet I can help." Smooth as can be, Max appeared out of nowhere and gracefully took Paul's phone. "I've recently had similar issues with my iPhone. Should I come into your office and see what's going on?"

Paul's face relaxed. "That would be great. Thank you."

As they walked away, I heard Max say, "Is this a picture of your children and their kids? Aren't big families the best? I have four siblings and three nieces and nephews myself."

Nice. Excellent progress. I plopped back down at my desk and finished composing an email to my mother. Because Pop's was too expensive, I'd done some research on more affordable options with availability on November 1, and now I was sending the list over to my mom for her decision. I'd made sure to get Kat's stamp of approval on each option so my mom couldn't use that as a rejection point.

Kat's time in Chicago was evaporating so quickly. I was going to go into major withdrawal when she left.

"How did that date go?" she'd asked me on the phone last night.

I pictured Max kissing me and saying "wow"...and then looking at me with shock after my Sex Ghost explanation. "It had its ups and downs."

"Will you see him again?"

Sure. Every day at work for the next several weeks. "Maybe. I think he's hung up on his ex though."

Kat paused, and when she spoke again, there was an odd

note in her voice. "Speaking of exes, Tess, there's something I've been wanting to tell you." Whoa. She was finally going to tell me about the picture I'd seen on Facebook. "I had brunch with Daniel a few weeks ago."

"Oh?" I swallowed and kept speaking calmly. "How was it?"

"Really nice! We've kept in touch via email for years, but this was only the third time we've actually met in person." Her usually sweet tone turned bitter. "He wouldn't even talk to me right after it happened, you know. Said it was too painful."

The lump in my throat started to burn. I'd started dating Daniel when I was twenty-one and Kat was fourteen. We'd dated for four years, which meant that he was around the house all the time during her teenage years. He was fantastic with her. She was a girl who'd desperately needed a strong, kind male role model, and Daniel fit that perfectly. Their strong attachment was one of the main reasons I almost went through with it. *Almost.*

"Anyway, I just wanted to tell you I'd seen him so you heard it from me and not Mom or someone else. Are you mad?" The hardness of her voice said plainly that she didn't care if I was.

"Of course I'm not mad. You have the right to be friends with anyone you want. Especially Daniel. He was like..." I had to clear my throat.

"A big brother," she said flatly.

Of all my mistakes, the thing I regretted the most was that my actions took away someone so adored from her life. About six months after the non-wedding, Kat started speaking to me again, but she'd never quite forgiven me. She'd never understood how I could do something so awful to someone we all loved.

The picture on Facebook had shown the two of them smiling big, his arm around her shoulders. Daniel was several years older than me, which meant he was twelve years older than Kat. He had gray in his hair now, but the same easy smile and open affection warmed his face. He even still wore a familiar-looking navy fleece. He'd captioned the photo: "My honorary little sis."

Her response had been what upset me so that night. She'd written: "I'll ALWAYS wish things had gone differently. Biggest disaster EVER."

Now, Max knocked on my open office door. His hair had grown out a little bit this week, giving him a slightly less-tidy look. "You weren't kidding about Paul," he said bluntly. "I have no idea what he did to obliterate his entire phone, but we needed to restore from a backup and make two separate calls to Apple."

I laughed, pulling a bag of potato chips out of my office drawer. "You got off easy, my friend. At least there was no physical labor. Or ink stains. Wait until he jams the copier. He can get that thing FUBAR'd in less than five minutes, and no one else can use it until multiple elusive sheets of paper are pried out of every nook and cranny."

His lip twitched. "Something to look forward to for next week." He shut my door. "Would you like a quick update on your personal situation?"

My pulse sped up. Had he made progress eradicating my sex tape? Was there a chance I'd sleep nightmare-free tonight? "Of course."

He sat in my visitor chair and folded his hands on his knee, as though we were having a very normal business discussion. "I have an exhaustive list of every server the Ghost has ever used since the site went live. I'm confident I can breach the firewalls to each one and delete or corrupt files."

I inhaled sharply, almost choking on the chip in my mouth. "That's great! So you think you'll be able to take it down super quick once the video is live?"

He nodded. "I do," he said simply.

Relief washed over me, almost making me giddy. "That's such good news!" Maybe the knot of impending doom that had been twisting in my stomach for weeks would finally disappear.

He leaned forward in the seat and pushed his glasses higher on his nose. "There is something else though."

His face was very serious and his tone grave. The knot in my stomach transformed itself into a noose and settled around my neck. I groaned and set the chips aside. "I'm going to hate it, aren't I?"

He nodded and took a deep breath. "I searched through all the newsletters he's sent out prior to new city releases. Occasionally, before a city's release, the FSG has sent out a link to his mailing list for a free 'major teaser.' The teaser is a very graphic, sixty-second montage from his videos from the upcoming city."

I went rigid in my seat. For fuck's sake. A video of my whole encounter with the Sex Ghost was unbelievably horrible, but any snippet of a graphic video that showed my face could ruin me almost as fast.

Max gave an apologetic wince. "He hasn't done one for every city." A hesitation. "From researching the pattern of the teaser releases, I'm guessing he does it when traffic to his site is slower than desired in a given month."

I spoke through gritted teeth. "And how's traffic this month?"

He looked me straight in the eye. "It's the second slowest since he's been live. He gets a ton of hits on his release days when he has brand-new content, but there are big lulls mid-month."

The potato chips in my stomach threatened to make an abrupt reappearance on my desk. Max held up a placating hand and said, "It's OK though. We can plan for this."

A plan. Yes. I was a project manager. I loved plans. "How?"

"The Ghost always sends out a warning blast to the email list thirty minutes before the major teaser itself is sent. He does this as a way to warn his bros not to open the teaser email if they're at work or with their girlfriends or whatever."

"How thoughtful," I bit out.

"And useful." Max grinned. "I added myself to his mailing list, obviously. You should do the same if you haven't already. If he plans to send out a major teaser this month, we'll have thirty minutes to react."

"Is thirty minutes enough time to do anything?" I asked doubtfully.

Max made a big show of looking offended. "Of course. I already found the file location where he stored the previous teaser videos."

He went on, describing in detail what he'd do. It all made perfect sense technically—well, except for some geeky coding gobbledygook that I nodded and pretended to understand—but the detailed plan still didn't get rid of the sick feeling in my stomach. "Hmph," I grunted.

"Tess, I won't let him send it out." His voice was quiet and rock-solid. "I promise."

For some reason, his self-confident promise did what his explanation of the plan couldn't—it made me feel better. "Thanks," I whispered.

"You're very welcome." He stood to leave.

"Any weekend plans?" I asked quickly as he opened the door. Just idle office chatter. A vague curiosity about how he spent his leisure time, nothing more.

He paused in the doorway. "Some. A nephew's soccer match. A niece's birthday party." He shifted his weight. "Tonight I'm helping a friend build some IKEA furniture."

I made a rude gagging noise. "That part sounds terrible." I gave him a knowing glance. "You're an awfully nice ex-fiancé."

He managed to smirk and look sheepish at the same time. "How'd you know it was for Aria?"

"Please." This was not hard-hitting investigative journalism. "Guys don't build IKEA for other guys, and Abigail told me you were hung up on your ex. Building IKEA furniture is exactly what a guy who is still hung up on his ex would do for her." I thought through possible exceptions. "Unless she's paying you."

He looked offended. "Of course she's not paying me! Look, it doesn't have anything to do with being hung up on her or not being hung up on her," he protested. "She asked and so I'm helping. She's not very good at that kind of thing."

"Neither am I," I said. "But I am very good at using my credit card for the additional IKEA assembly fee." It was completely not my business, but that never stopped my big mouth with anyone else. Why should Max get an exemption? "She dumped you, right?"

He flushed and narrowed his eyes. That was a yes.

"In doing so, she forfeited the right to your free labor," I declared. "Friday nights are for fun: friends, cocktails, movies, board games, a good book, extra sleep—whatever you're into. Furniture building? Only if wine and sex follow in rapid progression."

Max's eyes were wide behind his glasses. He'd probably gotten a little too used to office-appropriate Tess this week. But it was after 5:00 on Friday, and I was off the clock.

"You talk a lot," he said finally. "You have a lot of opinions."

Master of the obvious. I just laughed. "Always."

He took a step closer to my desk. "Last Saturday night," he started. The smile dropped right off my face. I swallowed, hard. One of these days we were going to give each other whiplash with the subject changes during our little chats. "I wondered something. Tess is an unusual name for someone in our age bracket. It makes me think of Tess Trueheart in *Dick Tracy*. Is that who you're named after?"

Oh. Ha. I wished. "No. Actually my mom was obsessed with the movie *Working Girl*. She's seen it a million times. There are two women characters in it, Tess and Katharine. I was the oldest, and when I was born, I already had some of this." I picked up a piece of my strawberry-blond hair and shook it. "In the movie, Tess has reddish hair, so I had to be Tess. My younger sister got to be the elegant Katharine."

He looked amused. "So you're named after a movie character."

Indeed. "A scrappy bridge-and-tunnel gal trying to break into the business world in the big city," I agreed. "And sleep with Harrison Ford."

He chuckled. "You know, you do remind me of a movie character sometimes, but not that one."

Oh really? "This I have to hear." So what if my eyes were wide and I was leaning forward with my lips slightly parted? I was not flirting. I was in my own office and chatting with a temporary coworker who was in love with his ex. That's what was happening.

He leaned against the door frame. "The character that you remind me of is feisty, manipulative, good at getting in and out of scrapes, and enjoys a bit of witty banter."

I couldn't help it. I totally batted my eyelash extensions at him. "That does sound like me. Tell me more. Is the character...attractive?" OK, fine. Maybe I was flirting a little bit.

He didn't react, except the smile lines around his mouth deepened. "Yes. This character is very attractive. Like you, the character has tawny hair and huge eyes. Most importantly, the character likes to tromp around in boots, just like you."

I figured out where he was going with this and felt unaccountably disappointed. I'd give him credit for humor, but this wasn't a sexy comparison.

Oh hell, it *was* kind of funny.

I narrowed my eyes and pursed my lips. "Are you comparing me to Puss in Boots?"

He burst out laughing. God. That laugh. "Yes. Isn't it perfect? You're Tess in Boots."

I shook my head. Good or bad, I would admit that any conversation with Max left me feeling unusually invigorated. "You know what? I'll take that. Have a good weekend, Max."

He left my office, looking over his shoulder. "Tess."

Chapter Eleven

"HOW'D YOU AND Abigail get to be friends?" Max asked me on Monday morning. I was in his cube pretending to show him how to do his timesheet, but really we were lying in wait for Paul. Over the weekend, the Cubs had advanced in the playoffs, the Bears had lost to the Vikings, the Blackhawks scored four goals against the Wild, and the Chicago Fire did…something. I couldn't remember; hopefully, Max did.

"We're not really friends," I said. "Not outside of work anyway."

"Still," he answered. "I've never seen her comfortable with another woman the way she is with you. She thinks you're funny. She trusts you."

"She should," I retorted. "She did something dumb once, and I prevented her from getting fired."

He leaned closer, glanced around to make sure no one else was nearby. "What did she do?"

I hesitated, but I was pretty sure Abigail wouldn't mind Max knowing what happened. "She found a vulnerability in our HR system and accessed payroll data she's not authorized to see."

He whistled. "That's a pretty serious offense."

"Yeah. A guy on one of my teams noticed it when he was reviewing security logs late one afternoon. Luckily, he came to me instead of going to Paul or straight to HR." I hadn't slept a wink that night. I'd been positive I'd have to fire her. I had no problem firing people when they deserved it, but something told me that Abigail didn't. I didn't know her as well then, but I knew she was bright and worked really hard.

"First thing the next morning, I called her into my office and asked her why she did it." Abigail's face had gone sheet white, and she'd started trembling. I felt like a high school principal chastising a freshman who cheated on a test.

"Why did she?" Max asked.

"She suspected that she was paid less than all of the men on the programming team, even the ones who were hired at the same time she was." I grimaced. "She was right too. I do have authorized access to that information, and I checked as soon as she left my office. She went about things in a totally inappropriate way, but she uncovered something really unfair."

Max abandoned our pretending-to-look-at-the-timesheet game. "What'd you do?"

"If I'd discovered the breach, I would have just ignored it. I don't condone what she did, but in this case—as in a lot of cases—the *why* was really important. But it was Nick who found it, and I knew he was expecting some sort of action to be taken." Max nodded quickly, fascinated.

Another glance around to make sure we were still alone. "Luckily, I had a scintillating little tidbit of information about Nick as well. A month before all this happened, I found his phone in the conference room. It was blowing up with texts, and I looked at a few to see if I could figure out whose phone it was." I snorted. "It was a conversation about how a particular brand of pot makes meetings with your boss tolerable. Apparently, Nick is an avid user of weed during workdays."

Max teased me, winking. "And did you reflect on the *why* in Nick's case?"

Straight-faced, I nodded. "Absolutely. I came to the conclusion that Nick smokes pot because getting high is awesome."

Max closed his eyes, suppressing one of those big laughs. I finished the story. "Anyway, I mentioned to Nick that we all made poor decisions at times and let him know I knew about his not-sanctioned-by-the-workplace habit, and I said that Abigail had done it by accident, blah blah blah. He knew it was bullshit, but he also knows it's a fireable offense to be high at work."

"So is this how you came into your position of power?" Max grinned. "By becoming a keeper of secrets?"

"It never hurts to know where the bodies are buried," I said matter-of-factly. A familiar gray head was bopping along the hallway. "Showtime."

Paul ambled by, only too happy to be stopped with an exhilarated spazz-out from me concerning the Cubs game five victory over the Nationals. After a sentence or two, I pretended to answer a call on my phone, letting Max take over. From a short distance, I watched Paul and Max commiserate together about the Bears' miserable offense.

Max didn't even really need Abigail's or my help, I knew now. He was surprisingly social for a techie, and he would have been able to charm Paul all on his own without our hints. For the thousandth time, I wondered what he'd done at his previous job to get fired and blacklisted. Genius programmers with strong social skills were unicorns. He must have done something really unforgivable. Which did not jive with his true-blue Boy Scout persona. Of course, he said it was for a good reason.

Ah well, I'd learn his secret sooner or later. I always did.

A FEW DAYS later, Paul came to my office with a short stack of résumés. "I've been looking through all of our applicants for the open senior programmer position."

I pushed my reading glasses up on my head. "And?" *Please say Max is the most qualified by far. Please say Max is the most qualified by far.*

"It looks like that young man who's been contracting for us, Matt, is the most qualified applicant by a long shot."

"Max," I corrected gently. My least favorite of Paul's quirks; I'd been Jess for longer than I'd care to admit. "I agree. He blows the other candidates out of the water."

"We still need to interview three different people, per our HR regulations," Paul said. He handed over two other résumés, and I scanned them quickly. "I'll set up the interviews for next week."

"Great!"

I gave him my most professional smile and turned back to my computer, pretending not to feel the accelerated thumping of my heart. I wished that my stupid heart wasn't excited at all. I was ecstatic that the "hire Max as payment" part of the plan was working so well, of course. But my asinine heart was pounding not at that, but at the thought of Max being around past the end of the month.

Which was beyond stupid. There was absolutely no romantic future possible between Max and myself, and I needed to resolve this disconnect between my brain and my body ASAP. I wasn't his type. He liked nice girls, and his ex in particular. *He's not your type either.* I hadn't dated a guy like Max in seven years. Max was a rare breed, the kind of guy I thought of as a "long-term" guy. Long-term guys were smart and funny. Long-term guys usually had their shit together in terms of career and savings. Long-term guys weren't afraid of emotional attachment or commitment. Long-term guys put other people's happiness before their own.

After I'd smashed Daniel's life and pride into a trillion pieces, I'd decided I'd never date a long-term guy again. I liked and respected them. In some cases, I lusted after them. But I'd never get involved with one again.

To put it simply, I wasn't a long-term girl.

ON FRIDAY AFTERNOON, I watched Paul sneak out of the office around 3:00 and did a little cheer. Perhaps I'd head to an early weekend myself. I stood and did a little shimmy to the door. *Fizz, here I come!* But then my desk phone rang, damn it. Resigned, I plopped back down in my chair and answered it.

"Tess, thank God. We have a serious problem!" It was Ron, our VP of sales. His voice was panicked.

"What's up?"

"You know our meeting with Zack Morris from Away-Ho?"

"Of course." After the infamously difficult CEO had canceled on us twice, we had him pinned down for a meeting on Monday morning. Paul and I had worked on a strategy and prepared for the meeting all week. Sales was supposed to do a high-level discussion on pricing, but the meeting was mainly designed for our IT solutions to shine. The plan was for me to do the presentation and field all their questions, but Paul would sit in as backup.

Ron lowered his voice to a whisper. "There was some sort of mix-up with the scheduling. They're here right now!"

"What?" I stood and craned my neck so I could see down the hall to our nicest conference room. Sure enough, four or five dudes in trendy-looking shirts and sneakers were standing there looking at their phones. "That's crazy. I have a long string of emails confirming our 9:00 a.m. meeting on Monday. Can't you just explain and tell them to come back then?"

Ron's laugh was desperate. "Yeah, I tried that, and they got super pissed. They're not available on Monday, and they're blaming the whole thing on us. Said if we were really as good as advertised, we'd be able to do the meeting now." He paused. "So we're going to try."

"That's absurd," I said firmly. "Paul's gone for the day—"

"Yeah," he interrupted. "My counterpart is out as well. But their little punk of a CEO said it's today or no day. I'm going to do it on my own. Can you fly solo too?"

Jack Sorenson had told me that I had to land Away-Ho or forget about the VP promotion. There was no doubt in my mind that he'd order me to handle this meeting ASAP. I sighed, all thoughts of an early day vanishing. "As long as you explain the situation to Paul and Jack in an email immediately after we're finished."

"Done," he said, relief evident in his whoosh of an exhalation. "Come on down."

Fighting against nerves, I glanced at my reflection in the small mirror on the back of my door and smoothed some wild hairs back against my braid. I threw on a black cardigan over my sleeveless black sheath and belted it. I pulled my lucky silver ring out of my purse and slid it on the third finger of my right hand. A coat of lipstick went on like armor, and I was ready.

No need to freak out. Paul and I had prepared more for this meeting than any other I could remember. I'd memorized all the relevant data and run through it so many times I'd been having very boring dreams about it. No worries.

But twenty minutes later, I was very worried. Ron and I were going to lose the account, and it wouldn't even be close to our fault. Sorenson had described Zack Morris as a hyperaggressive little shit—and wow, was that an accurate description.

He wouldn't let me finish a goddamn sentence.

My gorgeous presentation—one that I'd created after weeks of research about Away-Ho and actual input from their own IT team—was stalled on slide three. The meeting agenda had clearly stated our intention to deliver a presentation that would outline high-level possible solutions. Zack Morris had approved the agenda via email just yesterday, but he clearly had no interest in it.

From what I could see, the only thing he did have an interest in was interrupting. I tried again to move on to the next slide. "We've partnered with dozens of companies that have similar infrastructures to yours, so we—"

He held up his hand while shaking his head violently back and forth. "Let me stop you right there. Don't presume for one second you know anything about our business, Miss Greene." He'd called me Miss Greene no fewer than three times, even though I'd asked him to call me Tess.

He leaned back in his chair, glowering at me. With his beefy build, ruddy skin, and generically good-looking features, he looked like a grown-up frat boy—one with a cocaine habit. He didn't sit still, and he liked to make jabbing motions at me when he spoke. It made me feel like I was being physically stabbed with his obnoxiousness.

"We're a technology company," he said, his tone of voice implying that he was speaking to a three-year-old. He jabbed at me again. "We probably understand what you do better than you do."

I bit down hard on my lip and fought the urge to turn to Ron and roll my eyes. Really?

Zack Morris didn't have any issues with giving me a disgusted eye roll. *Jab!* "We're only outsourcing this project at all because our IT staff needs to focus on revenue opportunities and can't waste their time on this donkey work."

I wished that I could run him out the building. And then I wished for Mother Nature's most horrible disaster to wipe out their entire company. I mean, donkey work? Was he kidding me?

Satisfied that he'd slammed me into silence, Zack Morris made a fake-bewildered expression and gestured up at the large screen at the front of the conference room. "Is there something wrong with the presentation?"

Swallowing, I took a deep breath and clicked forward. "Not at all. If you look at these sample architecture diagrams, you'll see that we recommend one of these approaches—"

He cut me off again without even looking at the screen. A double air jab, aimed at my throat. "Uh, Miss Greene. What is your role here? If we were to work with you—" he snorted, looking around at his cronies until they snorted too, as if the idea of working with us was a huge joke "—what is it you'd be doing?"

I paused here, which was a bad idea. Blood in the water for sharks and all that. But I wasn't sure how to answer, because if I got the VP promotion, my role with Away-Ho would be different from my current position. No, it was best not to presume. Hands under the table, I twisted my silver ring, willing it to help me turn this meeting around.

"I'd be your project manager," I said calmly. "I'd be the liaison between your team and our technical people. Internally, I'd work with our developers to design your solution and lead all testing efforts. I'd also—"

He held up that imperious hand again. "Right there, that's going to be a problem for me."

"How do you mean?" I asked politely.

He crossed his arms over his chest and looked down his nose. "I don't speak to project managers on technical issues.

You guys always speak in bullshit acronyms and nonsense rather than giving concrete information." He laughed a little to himself, flicking his eyes briefly in my direction. "I've always thought that project manager is kind of a fluffy, bullshit role. Not real work. No offense."

Don't let him provoke you, I lectured myself over the dull roar in my ears. *Just figure out what he wants and give it to him.* If I couldn't handle little shits like this, I wasn't cut out for the VP role. "I work with many technology clients, but I apologize if I'm not providing you with the level of technical detail you were expecting." Not that he'd looked at any of the slides anyway. "Perhaps I could document a list of your questions and work with our programmers to get you some answers?"

"Waste of my time." He sniffed. He made a big show of looking at his Tag Hauer watch before air-jabbing at the door. "Why don't you run and get one of them in here now? Then I can decide if it's worth moving forward."

Shit. No. That would be highly unusual and a terrible idea. The programmers didn't come to potential client introductory meetings; that wasn't their role, and no one would be prepped for this kind of conversation. It was my responsibility to bridge the gap between the tech team and clients—and I was really damn good at it.

I tried again, sweetly. "Why don't you ask me your questions?" I was positive that I could answer anything this douchebag would throw at me.

He pulled out his phone and started tapping away. "No, not interested." Of course not. He probably didn't even have questions. He just wanted me to jump through hoops to prove he was a big, important man.

I looked at Ron with wide eyes, willing him to shut down this situation like the VP he was. "Could you grab one of your team, Tess?" he said instead, selling me down the river. For Christ's sake. I narrowed my eyes at him, sending a clear message that I was going to fucking flay him later.

"Let me go check." I stood and left the conference room. As soon as they couldn't see me from the glass doors anymore, I sprinted to Developer's Corner. Who could I get? This was not a job for Abigail. She'd mumble and stammer under Morris's brand of questioning. Possibly Bryant, our longest-standing developer, would work. He wasn't witty or clever, but he was good under pressure.

But when I ran up to the developers' cubes, practically panting, the only person sitting there was Max. "Where is everyone?" I demanded.

"Quiet Friday," he agreed. "Abigail and Anand are off today, Steve and Nick are down in the server room, and Jose left early."

"Bryant. Where's Bryant?"

Max frowned in concentration. "Oh! He had a doctor's appointment."

"Shit!" I kicked the side of a cubicle with my boot.

He half stood from his chair. "What's wrong?"

I quickly summarized the Away-Ho situation, concluding with, "He's just an asshole throwing his weight around."

Max stood fully and tucked in the back of his shirt. "I can do it."

I put my hands up in a full stop position. "No way. You've been here less than two weeks, buddy."

He winked at me behind his glasses. "We're not going to tell them that, Boots. I know enough about the technology here to answer the appropriate level of questions—and I know just the type of asshole you're describing too. Just pretend I'm already a senior programmer and together we'll send Zack Morris happily back to Bayside High."

That surprised a laugh out of me. And the fact that he included the word *together*...well. I'd have to dissect the warm feeling in my chest later. I hesitated, but what choice did I really have? If I couldn't produce a developer, who knew what kind of story Morris would spin up? If he complained to Jack Sorenson, the situation could reflect horribly on our whole team.

"OK, OK, let's do it."

Ron's eyes widened when Max and I came into the conference room, and I gave him a small shrug. He knew Max was a temp, but I dared him to say anything after putting me in this situation.

"Mr. Morris?" Max shook hands with the little prick. "I understand you have questions of a more technical nature you'd like us to address."

"I do," Morris said, a glint in his eye. He put his phone back in his pocket, then put his hands flat on the conference table and leaned forward. His lips twisted in an evil little grin, as though he was about to battle an enemy in which his opponent had a pen knife and he had an Uzi. In his patented rapid-fire approach, he began to pepper Max with questions about our code, platforms, frameworks, and APIs.

I could have answered all of the questions. But I had to admit, Max did better than I would have. He used an absolute shit-ton of technical jargon and spoke even quicker than Morris. When Morris attempted to sneer or put down a response, Max would immediately state three or four reasons for the decision, often citing well-respected coding resources. The harder Morris interrogated him—with those nasty air jabs—the more relaxed he became.

After ten minutes of back and forth, a light sheen of sweat formed on Morris's forehead. I bet he spent his days trying to humiliate people wherever he went—and it probably worked a lot of the time, since most people don't expect to be attacked for no reason. But here was Max, as comfortable as could be, conceding nothing—and Morris was literally perspiring. It was... It was... It was *beautiful.*

It was also a real wake-up call. Morris was speaking angrily at Max—but he was engaging with him and treating him as an equal. I'd gone wrong with Morris from the first instant, I saw now. Everyone had prepped me for how difficult Morris was, so I'd incorrectly assumed that the best approach to take was to be endlessly accommodating. Which, in his brutish little mind, immediately made me seem weak and worthy of contempt. I'd been so focused on the fact that winning the Away-Ho business would propel me to my promotion that I'd left my usual swagger in my office.

Well, that ended now.

Morris took a deep breath and fired another shot at Max. "What about your own disaster recovery plan? If this is what your company does for other companies, I'd sure like to know what your plan is."

Max opened his mouth, but I shook my head, and he

snapped it closed. Under the table, I twisted my lucky ring so hard it popped right off my finger and landed somewhere on the carpet. Shit. I'd have to pick it up later.

"No," I said loudly. So loudly that Morris's eyes widened, and he made eye contact with me for the first time all afternoon. "That's proprietary information. It's not something we share with external clients. Just as your disaster recovery plan will be completely private to your company."

Mimicking his aggressive posture, I put my hands on the table and leaned forward. I considered doing an air jab back in his face, but decided that was a little too on the nose. "To be honest, I think we've gone above and beyond on honoring your data requests today, particularly as none of this was on the agenda that you agreed upon in writing earlier this week. Not to mention the fact that this meeting wasn't even scheduled for today."

Morris glared at me, and Ron visibly flinched, no doubt fearing Morris was about to storm out. But I just held his gaze and raised my eyebrows. "Unless you want to cover the topics on the original agenda, we're done here."

He couldn't quite let it go. Without responding to me, he looked back at Max. "One more question—"

"Nope," Max said, standing to leave. "*She's* the boss." He gave a cursory glance around the table. "Nice meeting you all." He left the conference room with a respectful nod to me and without a backward glance at them, and I could practically feel my pupils dilating with pleasure.

I threw some business cards on the table. "You're welcome to follow up with us next week. But even if you don't, I have plenty of 'real work' to do for the forty-six other companies I personally handle." I laughed, long and loud, as though I'd found Morris's earlier comments on my role to be amusing and clever instead of insulting. "You know, in my fluffy bullshit role."

The Away-Ho bros filed out quickly, no doubt to harass some poor cocktail waitress at the newest happy hour hot spot. But Zack Morris paused in front of me and Ron, eyes on his phone. "My assistant will set up some time next week," he muttered.

Jackpot. I wasn't exactly sure what had improved his opinion of us. Maybe it was the fact that I'd finally stood up to him, or maybe it was that Max, a person who'd obviously known his shit, had deferred to me so respectfully. I didn't really care. There was no reason to meet again except to get closer to a signed contract—and that's what Jack Sorenson wanted.

"Wonderful. Have a great weekend!" I chirped.

Ron looked like he might faint with relief. A look that quickly turned to fear once we were alone in the conference room again. "Sorry, Tess," he piped, no doubt dreading my legendary temper. "I should have handled that much better. You and Max were terrific."

The tantrum I'd been about to throw at him disappeared.

You and Max were terrific.

Chapter Twelve

I FOUND MAX sitting in his cube with his coat already on and his cell phone to his ear. I didn't mean to eavesdrop, but I did. "What a jerk. They're still not speaking to each other? Oh wow."

He looked up and saw me hovering. "I gotta go, Mom. Still at work. I'll think of something."

I could have pretended that I hadn't overheard anything, but it sounded too darned interesting. "Is everything OK?"

He closed his eyes briefly. "Family drama."

I leaned on his cubicle wall. "Tell me everything. I'm a master of family drama."

He glanced at his phone again, checking the time. "I have plans in an hour, and I need to meet a ticket scalper on the Riverwalk before then. Walk with me for a bit?"

A butterfly fluttered in my stomach, and I paused for a moment to set its imaginary wings on fire. The man just said he had plans, which probably meant he had a date. Going for a quick walk meant nothing.

"Sure." I'd been planning to return to the conference room and get down on my hands and knees to search for my lucky ring. But I really wanted to walk with him. I'd just have to come back to the office afterward and find it then.

I hadn't been outside all day and was relieved to feel the temperature still hovering around fifty degrees. It wouldn't be that cold, even on the waterfront.

"So, family drama?" I prompted as we navigated the large stone stairs down to the pedestrian walkway on the south bank of Chicago River. It was getting late in the year for boat rentals, but the restaurants and bars on the Riverwalk were a popular happy hour destination and the steps were crowded.

He groaned and gripped my elbow to steady me on the stairs. "I swear, Tess, it's like the plot of an old Lindsay Lohan movie."

I bounced up and down, clapped my hands together. With that description, I was clearly going to love it.

"Apparently, my two younger sisters were dating the same guy and didn't know it." He winced. "Everything was somehow revealed this week, and now it's Armageddon. They're furious at each other."

I almost tripped on the last step. "That's insane! But wait—did the guy realize he was seeing sisters?"

Max squinted, and for a minute he looked so angry I shivered. "Yeah."

"Asshole!" I declared.

Max nodded hard and gestured to an empty bench. "This is where I'm supposed to meet the scalper."

We sat on the cold wood, and I angled my body to face him. "Why are your sisters mad at each other though?" I was always curious about sister dynamics because I was well aware that my relationship with Kat was unlike that of other siblings. She was my best friend. But I also felt unusually maternal toward her, no doubt because of the big age gap and what our household had been like when I was a teenager.

He shrugged. "According to my mom, they both liked him and they're just hurt. So they're taking it out on each other." He gave a look that was a mixture of adoration and exasperation. "They're both enormous drama queens."

"Did they not think it was odd that they were both dating a guy with the same name?" I asked.

"I asked that too!" Max exclaimed, and then his face got even darker. "The dickhead's name is Andrew. He told Beth to call him Andy and he told Sarah to call him Drew. That's one reason they didn't put it together sooner."

Diabolical! "The dickhead must pay," I said, my mind racing.

"Way ahead of you," he muttered. "When I get his last name, I'm going to find him and beat the shit out of him."

I couldn't help it. I started laughing. Max was tall and fit-looking, but absolutely nothing about him said: "I routinely beat the shit out of people." He'd probably come home with a broken nose.

When he glared at me, I smothered my laughter. "Good instinct," I assured him. "But have you ever punched anyone in your life?" He pinched his lips together. Before he could answer (in the negative), I went on. "What needs to happen is that your sisters bond over the revenge. The plotting and execution of a truly excellent 'fuck you' will unite them."

"I'm listening," he said stiffly, probably still annoyed I found the idea of him as an avenger kind of funny.

"Some ideas," I said briskly, counting off some favorites on my fingers. "1. Remove the license plate from his car and then call the cops from an anonymous phone and suggest there's a sketchy person in the neighborhood with a potentially stolen car. 2. Post on Craigslist on behalf of dear Andrew. The posting should express the desire for intimate contact with ex-convicts with massive tattoos. Make sure you post his work email address for the contact and with the request to send pictures; his employer *will* notice. 3. If your sisters can get into his apartment somehow, they should buy some shrimp or oysters and put them in unfindable places. Like, remove a light switch cap and plant one in the wall. Put them in the ventilation fans in the bathroom and kitchen. It'll smell godawful. 4. The old laxative in a hot chocolate is a classic—"

I broke off because Max was staring with his mouth open. "I am honestly terrified of you right now," he finally said. "Did you actually do any of those things to an ex?"

"Not to any of *my* exes," I said quickly. "But to some of my sister's exes. If they were jerks to Kat, then absolutely yes." I'd done them all. The smelly fish was my personal favorite. The others were over too quickly.

"Mention some of these ideas to your sisters," I continued. "It'll make them laugh, it'll intrigue them, and before you know it, they'll be concocting a plan. Together." I shook my finger at him for emphasis. "Nothing brings people together like a common enemy."

I thought he'd refocus on his sisters, but he surprised me with his next question. "Why did you never do any of that stuff to one of *your* exes?"

The words popped out before I could think about it. "I never really cared about any of them enough to—" I bit the sentence off. That sounded downright pathetic. "Tell them to go with the shellfish," I advised. "It's the best one. They get the excitement of a B and E and the ongoing satisfaction of knowing he'll be miserable in his own home."

He started to chuckle. "It's a pretty good idea," he admitted. He pulled out his phone and started a long text. I tried not to watch him but failed. His glasses had slid partially down on his nose, and I could see the navy color of his eyes. His lips were turned up at the sides and twitching slightly, his brow furrowed as he crafted his message. He wasn't Clark Kent and he wasn't some Calvin Klein eyewear model. But I would have stared at him for hours if that wouldn't have been super creepy. I just really liked his face, particularly in unguarded moments like this.

He looked up and caught me staring. "Thanks," he said. "My sisters will love this." He grinned down at me, his eyes crinkling. "And I might be a little relieved not to have to pummel someone."

I'd never felt physically warm under someone's gaze before. "Well, I owed you for earlier. You really saved our meeting this afternoon. So, thank *you*."

"My pleasure."

Sometimes when out at a restaurant or the park, I'd see a couple smiling at one another. Not speaking or laughing, but just solely connected to one another from the eyes and lips. They didn't feel you watching because they were seeing only each other. These smiles were private moments happening in public, and you almost felt like a voyeur watching it. On the few occasions I'd witnessed that kind of smile, I'd felt odd, physically. A pain my chest, a shortness of breath, a sting in the eye. At this moment, smiling at Max, I knew what those physical symptoms represented: jealousy. Because I'd never experienced one of those shared smiles that spoke of pure enjoyment and appreciation and connection and all that sappy bullshit.

Until now.

Max blinked and cleared his throat. "I almost forgot." He dug around in his pocket, pulled out my lucky ring, and held it up. "You dropped this earlier."

I inhaled sharply. He'd noticed me dropping it during the meeting and then took it upon himself to go back to the conference room and find it?

"Thank you! I was going to go back to the office and search for this. Wow!" And now I needed that damn ring because my hands were starting to tremble. I snatched it from his palm, almost dropped it again, and finally fumbled it onto my index finger. Close enough.

Max cocked his head. "Isn't that the wrong one?" He reached over and tapped the longest finger on my right hand. "You don't wear the ring often, but when you do, you wear it on this one."

My breath caught in my throat. What did it mean, exactly, that he was watching me so closely he would notice something like that? And what did it mean that I liked it?

I looked away, just in case little red hearts were actually appearing in my eyes. The wind blew wisps of hair out of my braid, and I busied myself with tucking them neatly behind my ears. A guy wearing a baseball cap came strolling down the sidewalk, his eyes trained on our bench. "There's your scalper."

Max turned, stood, and waved. I watched as he handed

over a wad of cash and looked carefully at whatever was in the envelope the scalper offered. Finally they shook hands and the scalper took off.

"Cubs playoff seats?" I guessed.

He grinned down at me. "Actually, they're *Hamilton* tickets. My parents' anniversary is next week. My dad will be skeptical, but my mom's been dying to see it. She'll be thrilled." He sighed. "As long as my sisters are speaking."

I thought he might say good-bye then, but he just sat back down next to me on the bench.

"Are you always the family peacekeeper?" I asked. "It's another classic middle child trait."

His lips turned up as he considered my question. Most people, myself included, didn't bother. They deflected, answered with the same answer they'd provided dozens of times before, or said the first thing that came to mind. But Max always appeared to genuinely think about your words and give a thoughtful answer. It made people feel valued to be taken so seriously. I'd made a note of it earlier in the week to try this approach with my team. Past staff evaluations had told me many of them considered me to be too blunt and mouthy.

"I guess I am," he finally answered. "And yeah, I think it has to do with being the one in the middle. My two older brothers are twins, and my sisters are only sixteen months apart. I'm separated from each of those pairs by three years." He showed me a picture of his large family on his phone, tapped his finger on the image of an older brunette woman. "Or it could be I'm so much like my mom that she knows how to guilt me into helping whenever there's a crisis."

He put his phone back in his pocket. "What about you? Are you more like your mom or your dad?"

"Oh. Well." I shifted on the bench. "My dad died when I was eleven, but I think he was more like Kat. She's very sweet. Not in an annoying way," I assured him. "She's smart and funny too, but she's never harsh or makes a joke at anyone's expense. That's how I remember my dad."

"I'm sorry," Max said, serious. "That's really young to lose a parent."

I nodded. It fucking was. "Yeah. But it was a long time ago."

I was about to change the subject to something lighter when he asked, "So are you more like your mom then?"

I almost made a gagging sound and said, "God, I hope not." But I'd just been admiring the way he actually responded to questions, and I wanted to give him the same respect, even if I generally avoiding thinking about this particular topic.

"Probably," I grudgingly admitted. "She can be very feisty and fun, but she can be a little cruel and weak too."

Max did a sort of gasp-laugh. "I see you're still being candid." Was I ever. Sheesh. I looked across the river, desperate for a funny subject change before I started blurting out more family demons.

Max's phone buzzed in his pocket, thank God, and he pulled it out and looked down. "One of your sisters?" I asked eagerly, already thinking of new, undetectable hiding places for the shellfish.

He blanched, reading the message. "Uh. No. Crap. I'm really late." He stood quickly and looked up the stairs at the street signs as if trying to orient himself. "I totally lost track of time."

The nasty taste of disappointment filled my mouth. Why did I keep forgetting all the important stuff? The way I lit up around him wasn't a sign of something growing between us. It was a sign I had a serious problem. If he was this unnerved at the prospect of being a few minutes late, he wasn't looking at me the way I was looking at him.

"Aria?" I assumed.

He glanced back at me. "Yeah. We're having dinner, and then I'm taking her to the airport. She's on a red-eye tonight."

I snorted. Even though I knew better, I just couldn't shut up. "So last Friday, you built Aria furniture, and tonight you're taking her to the airport?" I fisted my hands so that I wouldn't put them on his shoulders and shake him. "Most people don't take their ex to the airport, you know."

His nostrils flared and his voice was cold. "Most people don't have a list of elaborate revenge plans for their exes either." That stung. It was also true, but I'd only mentioned it to help his sisters.

"You're right. None of my business." I stood too and started to march up the stairs without bothering to wait for him. We weren't going the same direction anyway. "None whatsoever."

IT TOOK ME only forty minutes to go home, change from my work clothes into proper Friday night attire, and get myself to Fizz.

In front of the mirror as I adjusted my cleavage, on the edge of my bed as I exchanged my work boots for spiked heel boots, in the Uber (because I couldn't walk the three blocks in said boots), I beat myself up for getting stupid over Max. It was just a crush and one I needed to get over ASAP. He was going to work at my company. I couldn't exist with permanently hurt feelings.

What I needed was a palate-cleanser guy. I hadn't been out on the town at all since Max had come along and messed me up with his words and his kiss. Maybe if I found a nice, ordinary guy to spend some naked time with tonight, I'd get over my Max problem.

My determination must have been etched on my face because when I passed Roz in the hall she'd burst into the classic song "Maneater" by Hall & Oates. Normally I would have found this hilarious, particularly because Roz sang it in a baritone voice, the word *maneater* coming out as loud as a foghorn. But tonight I only managed a weak laugh.

At Fizz, Micki slid me a bourbon and raised an eyebrow. "I haven't talked to you all week." She looked around and lowered her voice. "What's the latest with the Ghost?"

"I'll tell you later." Talking about the FSG would inevitably lead to talking about Max, and I was *not* doing that tonight. Breezily, I changed the subject. "Nice crowd."

Fizz was extra busy tonight. Lots of happy Cubs fans and lots of folks just drunk with Friday night freedom. I nursed my drink and surveyed the room. Plenty of possibilities for male company. After chatting with Micki for a while, I set my sights on a muscular, sandy-haired guy drinking beer with a couple of buddies across the room. He was the physical opposite of Max, which was perfect. Nothing about him set my heart a-thumping, which was...normal.

I threw my shoulders back, tossed my hair, and walked slowly toward him until he noticed me coming. He paused, his beer bottle halfway between the table and his mouth, to give me an appreciative look up and down. "Hey there," I said, flashing my teeth. "I'm Tess. Want to play pool?"

I let him win the first game while wowing him with my sports trivia knowledge. Kat would have called him a total Jerry: an affable guy with a sales job, Blackhawks season tickets, and a strict gym habit. He offered to buy me a drink and complimented me on my hair and earrings.

I was so bored I wanted to scream.

My phone buzzed with a text message just as Rich? Rick? started to rack the balls for another game. It was from Max, and my foolish heart cannonballed into my throat. He must have just finished up dinner. It was a simple message and surprisingly personal.

I feel bad about earlier. I'm sorry. I shouldn't have snapped at you.

True. But I didn't really need to give him shit either. My crush was my problem, and he was entitled to spend his Friday night mooning over his ex on the Kennedy Expressway if he wanted. I thought about texting back "I'm sorry too," but...no. I needed to get further away from emotional exchanges with Max, not prolong them.

So instead I flipped my phone to the camera app and called Rich/Rick over. Then I took a selfie of us. In the photo, my eyes were half-closed, I was smiling hugely, and Rich/Rich's gaze was stuck to my propped-up boobs. Perfect.

I texted that back to Max with the comment: *No worries! Happy Friday!*

We played another round of pool. This time I lost because I couldn't concentrate. Not that Rich/Rick could tell. I still smiled, nodded, and cooed appreciatively over his shots. When the game was over, he offered to get another round, but I didn't need one. "Be right back," he said.

"Great!" I peeped—but I didn't want to go home with Rich/Rick. I just wanted to go home.

Because my eyes were on the front door eyeing my escape, I saw Max the moment he walked in.

I froze. What in the world was Max doing here? The city was too big for a coincidence like this; he was here for me. He must have felt my flat-out gaping, because we locked eyes in an instant. His jaw tightened and he tore across the room, grabbing my wrist and pulling me to a dark, back corner.

"What the hell are you doing here?" I yelled.

"Trying to keep you from making a drunken mistake." His tone was so self-righteous I wanted to punch him in the face.

Instead I took a deliberate step back, causing him to drop my arm. I spoke clearly and directly and made perfect eye contact. "I'm not drunk," I said truthfully. My tolerance was high, and I was holding my second drink of the evening. It was full.

He examined my face. "Oh." He let out a frustrated huff. "In the picture you sent, you looked hammered."

"Is that how you found me?" I demanded. "The picture?"

A dark flush crawled up his neck. "Yeah," he mumbled.

"Most smartphones embed GPS coordinates in the photo files. All you have to do is enter the coordinates in Google Maps to see where they were taken."

Jesus. Modern-day technology was going to be the death of me. "Well, the first thing I'll be Googling when I get home is how to change that privacy setting on my phone," I informed him.

We stood in silence for a moment. I did the timing math in my head. He couldn't have had dinner and driven to the airport and back since I'd seen him last. My silly picture must have absolutely panicked him into savior mode. Tess the Disaster Girl about to strike again! I couldn't believe he came dashing across the city to save me from myself. How pathetic I must have seemed to him.

He looked down at the floor. "Sorry about the photo-stalking. I didn't want..." He paused. "I, uh, I was worried about you."

I suddenly felt weary. "You don't have to worry about me, Max." Not sure what it was about this guy, but the blunt truth just seemed to burst from my lips whenever he was around. "I'm thirty-two. I've lived in the city for a long time. I know self-defense, and I'm very careful. Despite the fact that I should have made sure the video with the damn Sex Ghost was deleted, I've managed to live my life—including having a sex life—and I've survived just fine."

He nodded and swallowed. "You're right. About everything. I'm sorry I intruded on your evening. I—"

"I hate that the first thing you learned about me was that I made a sex tape with a stranger!" I interrupted with a vengeance. I still wasn't ashamed of the video, but it should have been my choice to share something I'd done in the past—not an act of desperation that forced me to talk about it. And I hated that Max was probably judging me for it. "I'm forever branded in your head as an idiot, aren't I?"

He shook his head vigorously. "No, Tess. That is *not* how I think of you."

"You should have seen your face in the Gage the night we met," I retorted. "When you heard why I needed to hire you, you ran away like you were completely disgusted."

Max's mouth dropped open. "I ran away because I was mortified! Here I'd been having the most surreal encounter with a girl, and then all of a sudden she knows that I'm unemployed and I've made a completely false assumption about the job." He paused. "To be perfectly honest, I didn't love the story about the sex tape. For God's sake, you blurted out two sentences about being a victim of a sexual predator who's about to infringe on your privacy in the worst way. I didn't know the right way to respond!" He pushed his glasses up higher on his nose. "I did think it was pretty awesome that you'd concocted a plan and were hell-bent on executing it. But, Tess, I swear, when I think of you, that video is not what first comes to mind."

"You came running across town tonight because you think I'm a weak woman who makes bad decisions," I reminded him.

"I came running across town because I didn't want you to have sex with the guy in the photo," he muttered.

Was there a difference? I rubbed my eyes and left them closed. "I'm not perfect, Max, but I've been taking care of myself for decades. I'm not the kind of woman you have to protect."

"I know. I think that's the reason I'm so attracted to you."

My eyes flew open. He was speaking so softly. I couldn't have heard him right. I looked up, searching for his eyes, hoping he hadn't guarded them by angling his chin to cause a glare on his glasses.

He hadn't. He was ready to meet my gaze, even though the flush had moved up from his neck to his jaw. "You charge around the office in those goddamn boots, and I can't take my eyes off you. I sit in meetings and watch everyone get nervous when you zero in on them with your smart-ass mouth."

He took a step closer to me. "You are the most independent woman I've ever met, and it turns me on like I've never been turned on in my entire fucking life."

Where did all the air in the building go? There certainly wasn't any left in my lungs. I had to be having some sort of auditory hallucination based on wish fulfillment.

"The sex tape was not the first thing I learned about you." He took the bourbon glass from my hand and held it up. "I learned you love this stuff. I learned that you're a quick wit." He let his eyes leave my face and linger for a long, long moment on my breasts. "I learned that you're sexy and confident." His gaze traveled up to my lips. "I learned how you kiss."

My heart pounded so hard I was sure he could see my pulse in my throat. I was so warm that steam would rise off me if I stepped outside into the cool night air. "We're circling back to my problem." I sighed. "The problem that's been consuming me all week and especially tonight."

He raised an eyebrow above his glasses, stepping even closer.

"I don't want to have sex with the guy from the photo," I whispered. "I want to have sex with you."

He leaned down so that his lips brushed against my ear. "I don't see why that's a problem at all."

Chapter Thirteen

I WAS SHAKING as we left Fizz. Max's large, warm hand was on my back, propelling me forward until we were outside. A light rain had just started, but we were lucky and caught a taxi right away. "Damon and Grace," he said to the driver before I could give my address.

What? That was nowhere near the house where I'd ambushed him a few weeks back. I gave him a puzzled look. "That's where I live," he said in response.

"I thought you lived with your parents," I spouted before I could remind myself that not every dumb preconception I had about him needed to be spoken aloud in his presence.

Instead of getting offended, he chuckled, that low, rich, toasty vibration that made my thighs reflexively tense. "I need to talk to Abigail about the way she describes me," he said.

The intersection of Damon and Grace was a quick six-minute cab ride from Fizz. Actually, his apartment wasn't even a mile from my own. At some point I wanted to pepper him with questions about his living situation. How long had he lived here? Did he, like me, enjoy the neighborhood-in-the-city feel? Which were his favorite restaurants in the area?

But right now, I was strangely anxious and tongue-tied.

My body was already warm, wet, open, and so ready for what we both knew was coming next...but my brain was more unsure. While I'd had my share of casual boyfriends and one-night stands, it'd been a long time since I'd slept with someone who zinged for me like Max did.

"Second thoughts?" Max asked, watching my face as we climbed out of the cab.

I shook my head and pressed my lips together before something weird popped out of my mouth.

He took my hand and guided me to the front door of his building, a four-story walk-up. When we were under the awning and safe from the rain, he gave me another out. "Seriously, Tess. In the entire time I've known you, you haven't been quiet for more than thirty seconds. If you've changed your mind about this, I'll just grab you an Uber."

"I want you." Yikes. My husky words came out sort of forceful and caveman-ish, but at least it was true and simple and there was no way he could misunderstand.

He shuddered and pulled me to him. In my spiked boots, I was almost his height, and our hips pressed together. "Thank God," he whispered. Something hot and bright bloomed in my chest. I'd never made a man shudder before. It seemed a strange little miracle, that he could want me as much as I wanted him.

His apartment was on the second floor. We held hands, climbing the stairs in charged silence. He pulled a set of keys from his coat pocket and then we were inside. His apartment was dark and cool. The only light was from the streetlamps outside. A steady thrumming of rain beat against the windows. Max must have been feeling nervous too. Once the door shut behind us, he took a deep, quivering breath and just looked down at me, his eyes unusually large behind his glasses. There were a few drops of rain on the lenses.

Swallowing, I unzipped my jacket, shrugged it off, and tossed it on the floor. As I knew they would, his eyes went straight to my breasts, which were lifted high and pushed together by my best bra and displayed thoroughly by my favorite plum-colored halter top.

As nervous as I was, I still couldn't help making a joke. "So you're a boob guy?"

Max laughed, one of those unexpected firecracker bursts. "Honestly, I never have been before." He walked straight into me until my back was pressed against the wall of the hallway. "But then you sit down next to me in a bar, I look over, and now these…" He ran his fingertip lightly over the swell of skin. "These take up an inordinate amount of space in my head."

His fingertip trailed gently in the other direction, and I licked my lips. "You're always completely covered in the office," he mused. "But I know what's under all those sweaters and button-downs and long-sleeved dresses, and it makes me crazy."

His words were making me crazy. Light-headed. I took a deep breath before I passed out. It had the additional benefit of lifting my breasts even higher. Max groaned—and then he lowered his mouth to them.

"Oh. Ohhhh." My exhalations were loud in the silent apartment but quiet compared to the kind of noises I really wanted to make. My breasts were sensitive, and his lips were warm and firm and left no inch unexplored. After he kissed all the available skin, his shaking hands gently pulled the shirt over my head.

I laughed aloud at the way he stared at my almost-naked breasts, bolstered high. His intense focus and delight made me wonder if Aria was extremely flat-chested—but I immediately pushed her right out my mind, right out of this apartment. I wasn't a girl who liked to share. Tonight, Max was all mine. The way he kept staring told me he felt the same way about me.

I was wet just from the way his eyes were worshipping me, but it was time for...

"More," I said firmly. "Touch, lick, suck, bite."

A satisfied grin transformed his face. "I should have known you'd be bossy."

I grabbed both of his hands and put them on my damn boobs myself. "Yep." His thumbs rolled over my nipples and pinched gently. "Harder," I breathed.

"Say please," he said with that sexy chuckle. I whimpered; the man just undid me.

"Please." He pinched again, absolutely perfectly this time. I bit my lip because it felt so good.

"You're so ridiculously sexy," he whispered. With his hands still on my breasts, he kissed me. It was everything I remembered from the Gage. The perfect smell and taste of him, the way his lips moved furiously over mine, the way our tongues slid together until we moaned in unison.

Everything dissolved into madness. His teeth pulled at my earlobe and scraped my neck. I shoved his jacket off his shoulders. Our hands collided as I tried to unbutton his shirt and he tried to unfasten my bra. When we were both completely naked from the waist up, he pressed himself against me and I wrapped my arms around him.

My God. Maybe it was the sensation of warm skin pressed together or that amazing kiss, but I was on the verge of coming and all we'd done was get to second base. Not that either of us was going to settle for that. "More," I said again.

"Bedroom," he answered. He half pulled, half shoved me into a room a few feet away. His bedroom was brighter than the hallway because it was on the corner of the building and windows were on two walls. The rain was pelting hard against the glass.

I was too self-conscious to let Max tug off my boots and skin-tight jeans, so I perched on the end of the bed and did it myself, as quickly as I could and with as few wiggles and wriggles as possible. Not that he seemed to notice any awkwardness. Standing a few feet back, he just watched me take them off. When I was finally free and only in my panties, I stood again, planning to pull him closer.

Instead, he took a step back and looked up and down, a small smile on his lips. "You're always wearing boots. I don't think I've ever actually seen your calves before." He unbuckled his belt. "They're beautiful, just like the rest of you."

Sheesh, a woman could get used to this kind of bedroom talk. Lots of guys said stuff during sex, but it was usually just bursts of enthusiasm ("Yes!") or cheesy general stuff ("You're so hot, baby!"). Max, though, was looking at me, seeing me, and telling me that he liked what he saw—specifically. Just one more thing about him that could quickly become addictive.

He fumbled with his pants, and I finally got an opportunity to look at him. I'd thought of him as skinny, but that actually wasn't the case. He wasn't skinny; he was wiry. Thin but strong and taut. His muscles were lightly defined, and he had a smattering of light brown hair on his chest. I'd loved the way it had felt against my breasts in the hallway.

His jeans finally fell to the floor, revealing plain blue boxers—and a very nicely muscled set of thighs. Soccer player thighs. "Wow," I said, pointing. "You have great legs."

He snort-laughed. "That's a strange compliment to give a man."

I shrugged and kept looking. "I like."

Still laughing, he walked toward me until we were an inch apart. "I like *you*."

And my heart went BOOM.

I was saved from having to respond because the instant my lips parted, his pressed against them. Oh, the kissing. I didn't remember other kissing like this.

Maybe because I'd developed a bit of a pattern with the guys I'd recently hooked up with: 1. a few drinks, a few laughs, 2. cab to whoever's apartment was closer, 3. kissing, sometimes good, sometimes sloppy, 4. clumsy removal of clothing, 5. the good ones attempted oral on their own, the others were given firm instruction, 6. intercourse, some who took about three pumps and some who took so long, I constructed work emails in my head.

In most of the couplings, even the subpar ones, I enjoyed myself. I reveled in the anonymous physicality of it all and the way the encounters allowed me to escape my own head for a precious period of time.

But this...this was different. It was an escape, but it

wasn't anonymous. This was *Max* kissing me. And no one had ever kissed me like him. Like the kissing was the end goal instead of a maneuver to get elsewhere. He pushed me back until we were both lying on the bed, entwined in each other's arms. Then we kissed more. I lost track of the minutes in his sighs, in the warmth of his lips, in the dance of his tongue. I wanted to kiss him for days.

Perhaps it was because the man could multitask. His mouth was busy with mine, but his hands cupped my breasts, slid down my arms, gripped my hips, paid a visit to the inside of my thighs. I had to touch too. I squeezed his broad shoulders, ran my palms along his sides, dug my nails into his ass. So hard he yelped—and then bit my bottom lip.

"Tess," he whispered, coming up for air.

"What?" I continued to nibble at the soft skin on his neck.

"Nothing. I just like saying your name." Now I shuddered. He was Trouble. I was going to be a complete Max junkie by the time this was over.

He chuckled. "I have to take off my glasses. They're completely steamed up." He propped himself on an elbow and took off the black frames.

As soon as he put them safely on the bedside table, I grabbed his face with both hands and stared. "I've never seen you without them." I looked hard, wanting to memorize his face. The strong jaw, dark eyebrows, high-angled cheekbones. I wanted to trace the shape of his nose with my fingers, but that might be a bit odd.

"And?" His voice sounded strangled. I supposed my review had been rather thorough.

I rolled my eyes and made a disgusted sound in the back of my throat. "Uck. You're even better looking without them."

We dove at one another again, our teeth clicking together in our urge to rejoin our lips and tongues. He rolled on top of me, then pulled me to his other side.

His hand, finally, slid inside my panties. *Yes!* I wanted to cry. Oh please, God, yes. Instead, I pushed his hand deeper and lower with my own so that there'd be no confusion over where I wanted it.

"You're so wet." His voice was shocked.

"I've been wet since you walked through the door at Fizz," I admitted.

With a groan, he kissed me harder and stroked me gently until, to my utter surprise, I came on his hand.

I cried out, clenching around his fingers while the world fluttered and disappeared except for the sweet waves I rode to mini-oblivion.

When I opened my eyes, he was grinning down at me, looking very smug. "Don't be so proud of yourself," I said airily. "That always happens."

"Shut up," he said, the smirk not disappearing at all. He kissed my cheek and carefully removed his hand from my underwear. "You were beautiful to watch."

He started to pull away, presumably to give me some recovery time. Which I did not need. "Where do you think you're going?"

I climbed to my knees and pushed him on his back. He looked up at me with a corner of his mouth quirked and his eyes crinkled. I held up three fingers. "How bad is your vision? How many fingers am I holding up?"

He snickered. "Three. You're a foot and a half in front of my face, goofball. I'm not legally blind."

I took the superior look right off his face by slowly pulling off his boxers and taking the length of him in my hand. Oh. My. Just like the rest of Max, this part was perfect for me. I stroked him until he was trembling.

"Three," I informed him. "Three is the number of orgasms I plan to have tonight." Even though his face was contorted with lust, he did his firecracker laugh, and I felt a burst of pleasure in my chest.

"You got the first one out of the way. Well done. Now, if you have a condom, I'd like to move on to my second," I said primly. Max scooted backward and twisted until he could access the drawer on his nightstand table. He had that condom unwrapped and on in no time flat.

We looked at one another, wondering. I hesitated. Would he like it better if I took charge and climbed on top? Or would he prefer me on my back? Or on my stomach?

In the end, he just said, "Come here," and we lay on our sides, facing one another and kissing feverishly until we couldn't take it anymore. I lifted my top leg over his hip and guided him inside me. The moment he slid in deep we both gasped.

"Wow," he said, reminding me of our first kiss. I nodded and flexed my core, bringing him as deep as I could.

We went wild—rocking, rolling, slamming our hips into one another. I scratched his shoulder blades with my fingernails, trying to get even closer. His fingers dug into my ass so hard I knew I'd have Max-fingertip bruises there tomorrow. I tasted sweat on his lips during frantic kisses.

I didn't last long. I started to quake, to break down around him again, to flood in joy and bliss. "I'm coming." I screamed it this time. Hello, neighbors.

"Mmmm." Max made the best sound I'd ever heard. A sort of growl and purr and sob. "Tess. Fuck. *Yes.*" His hips jerked, and I clung to him for dear life before practically blacking out in the throes of *yes, yes, YES.*

Chapter Fourteen

LIKE A LOT of other people who often have sex without an emotional connection to one's partner, I usually dislike all the stuff that comes after orgasm. The awkward cuddling and excusing myself to pee so I don't get a UTI and the finding a nice way (or a blunt way) to explain that a sleepover isn't happening. I don't like sharing a bed, and I don't like waking up with a stranger.

I should have known that everything with Max would be different.

The orgasm left me almost catatonic for a few minutes. I was vaguely aware of Max leaving the room to get rid of the condom, and I felt the mattress dip when he got back in bed. My body felt deliciously banged around, and my brain was mushy enough that I was almost dozing. I didn't even squeak in protest when I felt Max's fingers caress my face.

I did, however, shriek in pain when he yanked out one of my eyelash extensions. "Ow!" I smacked his arm as hard as I could. "What is wrong with you?"

He ignored my outburst, examining the eyelash between his fingers with fascination. "Look at this beast. It's enormous. Stop your whining—they're not real, right? How much could it hurt?"

In another bed, with another man, I probably would lie and say they were my natural lashes. But with Max, the filter between brain and mouth was just never where it was supposed to be. "It hurts a ton, you ass," I snapped. "They're stuck on with medical-grade glue. It hurts ten times more for you to pull out one of those than if you pull out a normal lash."

Finally, he looked sheepish. "Sorry. I didn't mean to hurt you." A telltale flush on his neck. "I've just looked at your eyes so much lately. I've been curious. Why do you get fake eyelashes?"

What a dumb question. "Because I'm vain, you imbecile." I was also a strawberry blonde, which meant my own lashes needed a heavy coat of mascara to be visible. With the extensions, I woke up already looking like my eyes were done for the day and without any smudging. A solid investment, in my book.

He rolled the lash between his fingers. "It feels like a pine needle."

I started laughing. This was the oddest post-coital conversation. "You might be the strangest person I've ever had sex with."

He looked between the lash and my face, laughing along with me. "Ditto."

He blew the lash away very deliberately. Had he made a wish? Did wishes made on false lashes count? "Lie on your stomach," he said.

Curious, I obeyed, curling my toes over the end of the mattress. Max pulled the sheet down, exposing my bare back. "You have a tramp stamp." I could hear the smile in his voice.

"You already knew that from the countdown picture on the Sex Ghost website." I tried to yank the sheet back up to cover the tattoo at the base of my spine, but he wouldn't let me.

"When did you get it?" he asked, dancing his fingers over the decorated skin.

I snorted. "When every girl gets a tramp stamp. I was eighteen."

"Why did you choose an anchor?"

Normally, I deflected when someone asked this question. I'd say, "I just liked the design" or "I have a pirate fetish" or "I dream of sailing around the world someday." I always found it kind of funny-sad that no one ever looked at me skeptically and commented that none of my explanations sounded like me.

Maybe that was why I didn't lie to Max. If he hadn't been skeptical, I would have been so disappointed. Which would have been idiotic since I'd known him for a matter of weeks.

Daniel and Kat were the only two people to whom I'd tried to explain why I'd chosen that particular image. Daniel had immediately co-opted the meaning, which I didn't appreciate. Kat didn't really understand, but that was my fault because my explanation to her was incomplete.

So I didn't lie to Max. I didn't tell the truth either though. Instead, I deftly changed the subject. I gave a dramatic sigh. "I'd like you to know that the phrase 'tramp stamp' was not in the common vernacular when I was eighteen. If it had been, I would not have chosen to get a tattoo on my lower back."

I was rewarded with his laugh. His hand rubbed harder, from the base of my spine all the way up to my neck. I arched my back like a cat. I hadn't had an unprofessional back rub in years. I meant to make a flirtatious comment, something along the lines of "You're good with your hands." But what actually popped out was "I like the way you touch me."

I immediately stiffened. That sounded both goofy and way too serious. I should probably get up and go now. It was definitely time to make a graceful exit. But Max just chuckled again and lay next to me, so close that we brushed against one another from shoulder to toe.

"Good."

IN THE MIDDLE of the night, cozy in a nest of blankets and comforter, I was shaken awake by large hands and an irritated, sleepy voice in my ear. "Stop stealing all the warmth, woman."

I snuggled in deeper. Poor Max had fallen victim to my patented covers-hogging move in which I somehow cocooned all the top layers of the bed around myself and secured them to me with my body weight. Kat has told me many times that this technique is not only stealthy but impossible to unravel without my cooperation. The cocoon move was why she brought a sleeping bag when she and I had to travel and sleep in the same bed.

Max wasn't having any of it. He pushed my shoulders,

turned me around, and yanked at the blankets until they were somehow flat on top of us again. It took at least ten minutes. Then I felt his lips on my cheek. "Greedy pain in the ass," he whispered.

"Mmph," I mumbled, mostly asleep but still not thrilled about losing my covers cave. "Sorry. I shoulda gone home. I never do sleepovers."

"Never?"

I was too sleepy to answer.

MAX'S ROOM WAS bright in the morning. Way, way too bright. Melt your eyes bright. Ugh. I raised my head to see the clock on the bedside table. It was only 8:00 a.m. I was never awake at 8:00 a.m. on a Saturday morning. "It's like the sun is in your ceiling," I wailed.

Max lifted his head from his pillow. From the grumpy slant to his eyes and mouth, I guessed he was also not a morning person. "Go shut the drapes then, bratface."

I got out of bed, crossing the room completely naked. Was Max watching? It was one thing to be wanton and bare in the middle of the night with only lightning flashes illuminating a dark room. Quite another for the horrible sun to shine a spotlight on every patch of cellulite and random hair and wrinkle. In case Max was watching, I threw back my shoulders and strutted to the window with a swing in my hips. Brazen self-confidence can mask just about anything.

To my relief, the drapes actually made the room quite dark. I'd probably be able to sleep for another couple of hours. As I sat back down on the edge of the bed, Max popped his head up again and smirked. "Since you're up, why don't you go cook me some breakfast?"

"Fuck all the way off," I said with feeling, and pulled the covers over my head.

I woke again a few hours later. I'd slept hard, which wasn't unusual because I tended to sleep hardest during the morning hours. But it was very unusual for me to sleep so hard with someone else in the room. Max must have slept very still. Carefully I rolled over, but the bed was empty.

I used the attached bathroom and forced myself not to go through the medicine cabinets or drawers. Looking in the mirror wasn't terribly pleasant, but I did the best I could to freshen up by splashing water on my face, downing some mouthwash, and brushing my hair with Max's brush. I put my jeans and boots on before realizing that my halter top was still out in the hallway somewhere. I opened one of Max's drawers and pawed through his T-shirts, trying to figure out which one he wouldn't mind me borrowing.

I was stalling, I suddenly realized. I was actually sort of afraid to leave the bedroom and face him in the light of day. It made me a little angry—this wasn't who I was. I didn't wake up in a man's apartment half giddy, half fearful about the night before and wondering what it all meant.

It always meant nothing.

Out in the hallway, the buzzer from the front door rang. Did Max have a visitor? I heard his voice say, "Come on up" and then, a few minutes later, "Thanks, man."

Curious, I stuck my head out into the hall just in time to see Max take ownership of a familiar, large, pink bakery box.

"Oh my God," I screeched, shyness forgotten. "Did you get Stan's Donuts delivered?"

The Stan's glazed donut was a holy creation, an absolute marvel of sugar and butter and pure magic. I gave thanks daily that there was no location between my apartment and the office or I would weigh four hundred pounds.

"Are there any glazed?" I asked, breath held.

Max snorted. "Are you kidding? They're all glazed."

My mouth dropped open. "You. You are a god."

He laughed, shifted the box so he could hold it with one hand, and used the other to tug me down the hall. "I would have preferred you to say that in bed last night, but I guess now is OK too."

He already had coffee brewing in his small kitchen. I perched on a stool at his breakfast bar, torn between snooping around the rest of his apartment and tearing right into my first donut. He took a glazed from the box, zapped it in the microwave for ten seconds, and placed it ceremoniously on a plate in front of me with a steaming mug of coffee. I felt like a queen.

A crazy-hungry queen with overactive salivary glands and an unhinged jaw. That donut was gone in approximately eight seconds. I ate the whole thing with my eyes closed, practically quivering with delight.

"Impressive," Max said, when I was down to crumbs and licking my sticky fingers. He cleared his throat. "And arousing."

I choked on my coffee. "You're aroused by watching me eat a donut?"

"You make the same face eating a glazed donut as you do

when you're orgasming," he informed me.

I giggled, holding up helpless hands. "They're similar experiences."

I eyed the pink square of temptation. Too soon to dive in for donut number two? Unable to stop myself, I said, "I will eat them in a box. And I will eat them with a fox."

Max burst out laughing. "Does that make me a fox? Well, thanks. Stan's Donuts are another of your *Green Eggs and Ham*, eh? Can't say I blame you."

Max plopped next to me and wolfed down his own first donut. He waggled his phone. "So, you're a new hero in my family. My sisters have reunited and are hell-bent on joint revenge. As we speak, they're at the grocery buying a load of shellfish."

I grinned. "Do they need any help breaking into his place? I have lots of ideas about how they can get ahold of his keys."

Max closed his eyes and groaned. "Maybe we'll let them try to figure that out without your generous help."

"Suit yourself." I grabbed a second donut and gave in to the urge to wander around his place. It was small but nice, with dark hardwood floors and lots of windows. The main living area didn't have much furniture, just a large comfy-looking sofa, a scarred coffee table, and a bookshelf. Several black-and-white photographs of Chicago decorated the walls.

Most of all, I was struck by how tidy it was. Thank goodness we'd come here instead of my place last night. My apartment wasn't dirty, but it was messy. There was old mail, magazines, and books on every available surface. My clothes were never contained to my bedroom. They lived on the backs of chairs and sofas and hung from every doorknob. Whenever Kat was coming over, she gave me a twenty-minute warning so that I could stuff all nonessential debris into the bedroom. Otherwise, she said she felt attacked by clutter. Judging from the austerity of Max's space, I'd better implement a similar twenty-minute rule if he came over.

Not that he'd be coming over or anything. Would he?

Max refilled his mug and gestured out the window, where a heavy rain had replaced the early morning sunshine. "I have an idea."

I walked back to the kitchen and helped myself to more coffee. "Don't keep me in suspense."

"It's October, a week from Halloween, and it's nasty outside. Let's watch a scary movie."

I blinked. In the back of my mind, I'd been calculating how long was too long to linger over coffee and donuts. I definitely didn't want to overstay my welcome. I'd figured I'd be hitting the Uber button on my phone in another ten minutes.

"You want me to stay and watch a movie?" I asked like a dumbass. But I was just so surprised. So flummoxed, in fact, that my next comment was entirely inappropriate. "Is this how you normally do mornings-after?"

Max's eyebrows jumped over the rims of his glasses. "You mean, do I ask all the girls to hang out and watch movies after I bring them home the night before for sexual intercourse?"

I brought the hot coffee mug closer to my nose so that my pinkening face could be blamed on the steam. "Sorry. Not sure why I said that."

Max watched me carefully for a minute while I examined my mug, his kitchen, his extremely clean countertop…everywhere but his face. "After my engagement broke off, I did go through an ill-advised sort of rampage of taking women home." I looked up at him. He shook his head. "But that's not really me, never has been, and it actually just made me feel worse about everything."

"I wasn't asking—I'm sorry—it's *so* none of my business—" Stumbling, muttering, humiliated, I put my mug on the counter. What the hell was wrong with me?

Max didn't seem upset though. He actually had the sweetest smile on his face as he continued to talk. "In answer to your morning-after question, Boots, no. I would not say this is normal for me."

He reached over and took ahold of my chin with his thumb and finger. I allowed him to push my face up until I was looking straight at him. "Would hanging around to watch a movie be part of your normal morning-after routine?" His lips were still curved in that sweet smile, but his eyes were serious behind those glasses.

I wasn't sure why it made something in my chest twang to say, "No."

Max leaned in and gave me a quick, soft kiss on my lips. Then, as if our bizarre little aside never happened, he leaned back and gave a considering look. "Maybe an older scary movie? I don't feel like any of the crap horror stuff that's come out in the past few years."

"Nothing with evil children," I declared. "They freak me out too much."

"What about *Poltergeist*?" he suggested. "Carol Anne isn't

evil."

"Absolutely not," I said. "She's still super creepy. What about something with vampires? *Fright Night*, maybe?"

I followed him over to the couch. "Vampires," he said. "I've got it. What about *The Lost Boys*?"

I fluttered my eyelashes (sans the one he'd yanked out the night before) at him. "Oooh, a classic. Now tell me, are you a Corey Haim or a Corey Feldman fan?" He threw a pillow at me, which I luckily was able to catch with my left hand before it hit my coffee mug and sloshed coffee all over his nice gray sofa.

Bickering and laughing, we somehow got settled with my feet in his lap and the remotes in his hand. We spent way too long negotiating in Netflix before making our choice. He was just about to push play when we heard a knock on his apartment door. That was odd. No one had buzzed from the street.

Then his front door opened and a woman called, "Knock, knock! Max? You decent? It's me. My flight got canceled last night, so I thought I'd see if you wanted to go to the farmer's market. It's a little wet out there, but that just means shorter lines, right?"

I launched off that couch and sped across the room as though I'd been shot from a cannon. Holy shit. This had to be Aria. My pulse raced, and for a crazy moment, I wondered if I should try to climb out a window.

But no. No. We weren't doing anything wrong. Max had asked me to stay. He and Aria weren't together anymore. A small, mean part of my brain wondered what it meant that she still had keys to his apartment and felt comfortable walking right in.

As her heeled footsteps came down the hall, clicking on the hardwood floors, my eyes cut to his face. He looked like he was holding his breath and trying not to vomit.

"Hello? Max?" A brunette head popped into the kitchen.

"In here, Ari," Max finally called.

Into the living room walked my complete physical opposite. I would have guessed that I wouldn't resemble Aria in the slightest, but it was still somewhat jarring to behold Max's ex-fiancée in the flesh and get a good eyeful of the anti-me. I'm five-nine in socks; Aria was wearing heeled boots and couldn't have been more than five-three. I'm fair-skinned with long, bright hair and my share of freckles. Aria had a sleek cap of black hair and olive skin. My boobs aren't the only curves on my body. My love of booze and French fries and donuts ensures I'll never be what you'd call skinny. Aria was wearing tight jeans and a fitted T-shirt that displayed just how tiny and petite she was. I could scoop her up under my arm and carry her around like a perky football.

Aria stopped short as she entered the room to two people frozen and gaping at her. I recovered first. "Hi!" I walked over to shake hands, suddenly very aware I was wearing Max's shirt. It fit me just fine, but I wondered if she'd recognize it. "I'm Tess."

Max twitched and shook off his trance. "Yes, sorry! Ah, Aria Jameson, this is Tess Greene."

Aria shook my hand firmly and looked up at me with a stiff smile. "So nice to meet you!" She looked over at Max with big eyes. "I am *so sorry* to burst in on you like this! At dinner last night you said you weren't doing anything today, so I thought I'd see if you were up for one of our errand days."

She looked at me now. "I should have texted first," she said firmly. "I'm so sorry to interrupt."

I don't know if it was the reminder that they'd eaten together the night before or the new, fun knowledge that they did "errand days" together, but all of a sudden, I had to get out of there.

"No interruption at all!" I yelped. "I was just leaving so…perfect timing! You guys can totally go to the farmer's market." I jogged down the hall to grab my jacket before Max could argue.

He didn't argue.

In fact, he didn't say anything at all to me as I gathered my bag and surreptitiously picked up my halter top from the hallway floor. He just chatted with Aria about the rain and her rescheduled flight. Even when I paused at the front door and we made eye contact across the long hallway, he didn't leave the living room.

"Bye!" I shouted and slammed the door.

Chapter Fifteen

I CALLED MICKI and convinced her to join me for a double feature at a movie theater on Saturday afternoon. I didn't want to be alone, but I didn't want to talk either. Which is why I love Micki; she knows when to pry and she knows when to just buy a mega-sized popcorn and chill. We saw some space adventure that got a lot of laughs from the crowd and some action movie with race cars. After it ended, the only thing I remembered about it was that a ton of stuff blew up, and I appreciated how the roaring soundtrack made it impossible to think about anything else.

When we left the theater, the rain had finally stopped and the early night was crisp and cool. Micki checked her watch and whistled. "I have just enough time to go home and change before work. You coming in tonight?"

I shook my head. "I'm probably going to hang with Kat." Not true. I'd gotten a text from Kat earlier saying she was going to spend the night packing. We'd have our normal brunch date in the morning.

Very uncharacteristically, I just didn't want to go out. I was already picturing my favorite pair of pajamas. Micki eyed me sympathetically. "Come to Fizz if you change your mind. I'm experimenting with a new bourbon cocktail. You can help me name it."

It was a solid enticement. Every year she held a contest to name a new concoction and, much to my chagrin, I had *never* won. Winning was on my current bucket list. "Tempting." I smiled weakly. "But have a good night if I don't see you."

She gave me a shoulder squeeze as her Lyft pulled up. "Cheer up, Tess. We still have lots of time to stop the FSG." I waved at her, bemused, as she climbed into the car and it pulled away. I hadn't thought about the FSG all day. I'd been moping about a very different man.

In my apartment building, Roz strolled out of her unit just as I cleared the stairs, wearing a killer red suit and matching heels. She caught sight of me and did a slow twirl. "On a scale of one to ten, how gorgeous do I look?"

Easy answer. "An eleven, at the very least." Once a month Roz enjoyed dressing up on a Saturday night and treating herself to an outing at a gay martini bar up in Andersonville. I went with her sometimes, and it was always a hoot. But even that didn't sound fun tonight.

She took a long look at my sourpuss face. "Bad bikini wax? Yeast infection?"

From Roz, this was a fairly pedestrian conversation-starter. Still, "Jesus, Roz. No!"

When I didn't immediately counter with a question about menopause or senility, her expression went from expectant to mildly sympathetic. "Lawyer hasn't gotten the video off the site yet?"

Roz had been on a business trip in New York this week and I hadn't updated her. "Ah, no. And she doesn't think she will." I summarized my meeting with Natasha Long. Roz's mouth turned down at the corners and she squared her shoulders like a general about to go into battle. Terrified that she was about to change her evening plans, I said, "But I've found a plan B. I hired another kind of help."

Her eyes brightened. "Oooh. A hit man? The mob?"

"Solid Chicago thinking." I laughed. "But no. A hacker. A really smart guy."

"Oh wow. Don't see too many of those with you." Her lips trembled as she suppressed a smart-ass grin.

"Yeah, yeah. You're hilarious. Don't call me for help up the stairs if you have too many Manhattans tonight," I threatened.

She sniffed and headed for the stairs. "There's no such thing as 'too many' Manhattans."

"Night, Roz."

After pulling on my coziest pajamas, I poured a glass of red wine and fidgeted on the computer for a few minutes with some vague idea of getting a head start on the workweek. But I was just clicking around blindly. I couldn't focus on anything.

Closing my laptop, I took a deep breath. Years ago, my therapist had suggested a surprisingly effective technique for me when I was spinning on an emotional issue and feeling numb. Spinning on emotional issues and feeling numb had directly contributed to the horrible explosion of my engagement. I needed to be more in tune with what was going on in my brain or else I'd cause mass destruction.

The therapist had instructed me to speak aloud and explain what I was feeling as though I was talking to a ten-year-old. Apparently, ten years old was what she considered the actual age of my psyche. The concept sounded asinine, but for some reason, hearing myself explain my emotions in my own voice using simple language always did help.

Clearing my throat, I started. "I am very attracted to Max physically. He was attracted to me too. We had *really* good sex." That was the easy part. "But we also have fun talking and being together, and I like him a lot." I almost laughed, my voice was so robotic. "I like him a lot," I said again, forcing myself to hear it. "I'm feeling like shit right now because my feelings were hurt this morning when he didn't ask me to stay after Aria got there." Deep breath. "I am sad because I think he likes me but he's still in love with her."

More wine, please. I'd forgotten that while it was good to have clarity kick aside some of the numbness, it could also hurt like a bitch once I melted. Which was actually very stupid. Even if Max wasn't still pining for Aria, there was no way I should be mooning like this. Max was clearly a "long-term" guy, and I shouldn't be messing with him anyway.

Ugh, I really hated the occasions where the smart part of my brain couldn't override the "but this is what I want" part.

After a glass and a half of the Cabernet, my phone became magnetic. I wanted to reach out to Max so badly my fingers itched and twitched. But to say what? He could still be doing errands with Aria for all I knew. Maybe the farmer's market turned into lunch, which turned into a museum visit, which turned into laundry together, which turned into dinner...blah blah blah. I gulped down the rest of my second glass. Hell, aside from no diamond ring, maybe their relationship hadn't changed at all since ending the engagement. Maybe they even still slept together sometimes.

The allure of the phone became so strong I put it under a pillow and went to take a shower. A long, hot shower to wash away every trace of him. I'd worn his shirt all day, and now I was afraid I had a new scent addiction to his fabric softener. When I finally emerged from the steam, I crawled back into my pj's and collapsed on my bed with a stack of books. Might as well take advantage of my antisocial feelings to catch up on some reading.

My phone buzzed and my heart skipped a beat. It was just about the same time as last night when Max had texted he was sorry. Maybe the man always felt a little apologetic around 9:00.

I didn't want you to leave this morning.

Oh really? *Then you should have asked me to stay.*

He didn't like that. He responded immediately. *I'm the one who asked you to hang out and watch a movie! You're the one who ran out like the house was on fire.*

The nerve of him! I glared at my screen as my thumbs went crazy. *I think you're forgetting something rather important that happened between you asking me to stay and me deciding to go.*

There was a longer pause this time. *OK. I didn't handle it well when Aria showed up. But you were gone before I knew what to do!*

Not good enough. Frankly, it seemed obvious that he didn't know how to handle it because he was more concerned with Aria's feelings than mine. Which hurt, but I understood. He'd been engaged to her, for God's sake. He'd known me for a couple of weeks. We'd slept together once.

It's not like we were seriously involved.

No worries! Hope the farmer's market was fun! I was always good at defaulting right back to Tough Girl.

Damn it, Tess. I didn't go to the farmer's market. I hate the farmer's market.

That made me smile a little. I hated the farmer's market too. Who wanted to spend all morning picking out fruits and vegetables from a bunch of stalls that all sold the exact same fruits and vegetables? God invented supermarkets for a reason.

He kept typing. *Aria left four minutes after you did, and I watched the movie we picked out and ate more donuts and felt sorry for myself. Does that make you feel better??*

Actually, it did. *Yes.*

Are you out somewhere?

I leaned back against my pillows, considering. *If I am, are you going to lecture me about drunken mistakes?*

No! he answered quickly. *I was just making conversation.*

I couldn't help poking at him a little. *Sure, sure. Is this a booty-text?*

I wished I could see the expression on his face. Had I made him laugh? Texting was awesome, but it left a lot to be desired when you were as strung out on someone else's facial expressions as I currently was on Max's.

His response: *Booty-texting? That's a thing?*

Oh please. *Everyone under the age of seventy-five knows that booty-texting is a thing. Actually, people in nursing homes probably booty-text too. Saves them the effort of going to the TV room down the hall to see if anyone's interested in a hookup after the Blue Bloods reruns are over.*

A longer pause this time. Then: *You're an odd woman, Boots. And no, this is NOT a booty-text.*

Good. Truly. I absolutely did not want Max booty-texting me. (Sometimes I'm even good at lying to myself.)

He shot another one over. *I do feel sort of bad though. You were such a snoring, covers-hogging sleepyhead last night that I wasn't able to deliver on your demand. You didn't get your third.*

I bit my lips together to keep my face from cracking in a wide smile. He was right. I hadn't gotten my third orgasm. But I could be generous. *We can count the Stan's glazed donut as my third.*

No, no. My masculinity can't take the concession. Next time there will be three. Good night, Tess.

I corked the bottle of wine and got back in bed, unable to straighten the goofy smile on my face. It was amazing how two simple words had saved the evening. The entire day, in fact.

Next time.

"YOU'RE IN A good mood this morning." Kat raised her coffee cup to her lips.

I snapped my menu closed, unsure why I even bothered to look at it after all these years. Kat and I had been going to this diner every Sunday since she started college. Kat was a dedicated runner, and liked to do a long run on Sundays. The diner was a perfect six-mile run from Evanston. When she moved into the city after college, I'd insisted she take self-defense classes. She'd agreed on the condition that I join her, and so that became our new Sunday morning tradition: "punch and brunch." It was so much fun we'd repeated the course three times until the instructor told us we were more than qualified to defend ourselves against a variety of attackers. Now we just met to eat. And without fail, I ordered the number three: two eggs over easy with bacon, hash browns, and white toast.

She gave me a knowing expression. "Did you meet a new friend last night?"

"No." I sniffed, then grinned. "Not last night." Truth be told, I was a little giddy this morning because I'd woken up to a text from Max. He'd sent over a picture of Puss in Boots with the simple message: *Thinking of you.*

"It's the guy I met at the Gage a few weeks ago," I said unnecessarily. Yep, this was a bad crush, complete with mentionitis. If Kat hadn't given me such an easy in with her question, I would have found a way to bring the conversation to Max somehow.

The waitress took our order and refilled our coffee cups. "So, what's he like?" Kat asked. "Is he a Jerry?"

"No." Definitely not.

Kat pursed her lips, looking a lot like my mother. "Is he one of your dating disaster guys?"

I rolled my eyes and spoke primly. "It's been ages since my last bout of silliness."

"Oh really?" Kat scoffed. "How long ago was it that you and some guy fell asleep on the Red Line all night and called me in the morning to come meet you in Chinatown?"

I put my napkin in my lap and waggled my coffee cup at her. "You choose to remember it that way. I choose to remember it as the morning we discovered the best dim sum in the city."

She did my favorite husky-trill laugh. "Fair enough. But

now I'm at a loss. If he isn't a Jerry and he isn't some rando you picked up for a night of fun, what is he like?"

I imagined Max grinning down at me, his eyes crinkled behind his glasses. The way he rolled up his sleeves at the office and hunched over his keyboard. "He's super smart and kind of nerdy. Really good at his job."

Kat's jaw dropped. "That's not how you usually describe guys," she said slowly. "Usually you just describe how they look." Sad but true. Since I didn't date seriously, the guys I hung out with didn't always have a lot going on that interested me beyond their looks.

"He's tall," I offered. "Wiry. He wears black-rimmed glasses." I smiled to myself, remembering how he'd had to remove them on Friday night when they'd gotten all steamed up.

"You like him!" Kat exclaimed. "Holy cow." She leaned forward, putting her elbows on the table. "I have to meet him before I leave."

Oh boy. I needed to knock it off. "I doubt it'll go anywhere," I said quickly, hoping to dampen her enthusiasm. Unfortunately, it also dampened my own.

"What do you mean?" she asked, pushing her dark hair behind her ears. "If he's so smart and he puts that silly look on your face..."

Aria's pixie face flashed in front of my mind's eye. Might as well be blunt. "Worst case, he's still in love with his ex-fiancée. Best case, he has serious boundary issues with her."

Kat frowned. "Oh."

The waitress put our steaming plates on the table. As usual, Kat had gone healthy with a bowl of oatmeal and a side of fruit. I took advantage of the distraction to change the subject. "Are you getting excited for Mom's big Farewell to Kat party?"

She dumped some raisins and maple syrup into her oatmeal and gave it a swirl. "It's so nice of Mom to put it together, but I feel bad she has this on her plate along with being so busy at work. We were supposed to have dinner together on Wednesday night, but she needed to stay late to help Mr. Gupta with some last-minute project."

Alarm bells began to ding inside my brain, causing my stomach to churn. Suddenly the bacon didn't smell good anymore. I put my fork on the table. Mr. Gupta, the CPA and family friend my mother worked for, was a tennis fanatic. His league played on Wednesday nights, and he'd often boasted to me of never missing a single match.

"What's wrong with your food?" Kat cocked her head. Usually my plate was clean approximately two minutes after it was set in front of me.

"Nothing." I picked up a piece of toast and smeared butter on it. "Did Mom say how many people had RSVP'd to the party?" I forced myself to laugh. "Has she decided what she's wearing yet?"

Kat speared a strawberry and shook her head. "She's been so nuts I haven't even spoken to her this week except for a few texts."

And…the toast went back on the plate. "So you haven't seen her or talked to her at all?" That was highly unusual. A flutter of panic crawled up the back of my neck. Although I hadn't needed to in years, I was so used to hiding this particular kind of fear from Kat that she didn't notice anything different about my voice or face. Under the table, I shredded my napkin into tiny pieces.

"I have this theory that she's trying to wean us off one another before my move," Kat admitted. "Also, she knows how busy I've been with trying to get everything wrapped up at work and get myself packed. I think she's just trying to give me some space."

"Makes sense." I nodded several times. "Totally makes sense."

After brunch I drove Kat to the UPS store to grab boxes and packing tape. I chattered on about the movies I'd seen the day before and made her laugh with stories about awful Zack Morris from Away-Ho. I commiserated with her on the rent prices in the Bay Area and debated whether it would be better to visit her the first time in January or March.

All the while, I was counting down the minutes until I could drop her off.

As soon as I did, I drove home like a maniac and sat down at my laptop. Then I logged into my mother's bank account. She still hadn't been paid. I looked at her credit card and debit card purchases for the last month. Again, I found a horrible omission. This month, there was no debit at the Walgreens pharmacy.

Hands shaking, I called Mr. Gupta.

WHEN I ARRIVED at my mother's suburban apartment complex around 2:00, it was raining again. I turned off the engine and sat in my car for several minutes, letting the rain pound on the windshield and hide me from the rest of the world.

Maybe I was wrong. Maybe I'd walk into her apartment and find her reading the newspaper at her kitchen table. She'd look up at me with annoyance and say, "Tess? What are you doing here?" Then she would dazzle me with logical reasons for avoiding Kat, for not showing up to her job, and for not paying for her meds.

Fuck. I laid my head against the steering wheel. I supposed I'd done enough crappy things in my life to deserve a month like this, but Jesus. First the Sex Ghost, then Kat moving, and now this.

My phone rang, and the display showed Max's name. It was like a cosmic reminder from the universe that not everything about this month had been awful. If I hadn't been so utterly destroyed at the moment, the very sight of his name would have lit me up like a Christmas tree. I was already lecturing myself about letting it go to voice mail when my traitorous body went ahead and answered.

"Hey."

"It's raining again," he said without preamble. His voice was warm and flirtatious and it brought unexpected tears to my eyes. "Want to try for round two on the scary movie?"

"I can't," I whispered.

His tone changed abruptly. "What's wrong?"

I swallowed the tears and forced myself to speak as normally as I could. "I have to deal with a family issue today."

"Are you OK? What can I do to help?" he demanded. Sheesh, he really was a long-term guy. I'd known him a couple of weeks and he was ready to give up his Sunday to dive into some unknown shit show. What in the world had Aria been thinking to let him get away?

"Nothing," I said. "I can handle it. I gotta go." I hung up before he could ask any more questions.

Chapter Sixteen

As I LET myself into my mother's apartment building with a stolen set of her keys, I forced myself to follow my therapist's rule again and remember good moments with my mother.

There were actually quite a lot of them before the Bad Time.

When my father traveled, my mom and I were a good team. I helped her with Kat in the evenings so she could catch up on work. She would come to every one of my middle school basketball games, even though I was an abysmal point guard and more likely to start a snarky chant against the opposing team than score any points. On Sunday afternoons, she often got a babysitter to watch Kat and we'd go see movies together. Even now, every time I smell movie theater popcorn, I think of her.

Around the house, music and books were her passion. The house was rarely silent. There was always something playing. She loved artists from every decade: girl groups from the sixties, Jim Croce and Air Supply from the seventies, Bruce Springsteen and Madonna from the eighties, Sarah McLachlan and the Indigo Girls from the nineties. She'd lie on the sofa, reading a book while her propped-up feet bounced along with the music.

My dad was twelve years older than my mother, but it was still a shock when he passed away from a heart attack at the age of fifty. But things were mostly OK for a while. While Kat and I had loved him very much, his constant absence probably made adjusting to his death easier for us than it would have been for other children.

Life didn't slow down much. Kat and I had to go to school, after all, and my mom had to work. The major change was that we sold our house and moved into an apartment. I didn't mind the smaller space, because I still got my own room and I could walk to school instead of taking the bus. It didn't occur to my eleven-year-old brain that maybe there were financial reasons for selling the house.

My mom still read a lot of books in the apartment, but she stopped taking me to movies. And she stopped playing music.

Now, I ducked into the small mailroom off the lobby of my mother's apartment building. As I expected, her mail was overflowing and several brown boxes with her name on the label were stacked on the floor. I picked up as much as I could carry and headed for the stairs.

Like most teenagers, I had been pretty self-involved, and so it took me a while to notice how much my mom changed over the fall I turned fifteen. I'd noticed that she didn't bug me about my grades or ask about my teachers, but I was actually grateful for that because I was struggling with biology and didn't want her to know I was about to lose my lifelong 4.0 GPA. If I thought it was odd that she didn't set a curfew when all of my friends had to be home at 11:00 p.m.,

I was probably too excited to be the last sophomore at a senior party to question it.

But one day in mid-November, I got the stomach flu. It hit me hard just after third period. I'd run out of geometry class with saliva flooding my mouth and barely made it to the girls' room before vomiting. The school nurse took my temperature and sent me home right away. She couldn't reach my mom on her office phone, but I assured her I could make the short walk home.

It was before noon, and the apartment should have been empty. I had to throw up again as soon as I stepped inside, so it was a few minutes before I realized that my mother's bedroom door was closed. I heard a sniffling sound within.

"Mom?" I knocked and opened it before I got a response.

She was in bed wearing her favorite maroon flannel pajamas. Tears streamed down her cheeks and her eyes were scarlet, as though she'd been crying for hours. When I burst in, she looked up quickly and hiccupped. "What are you doing home?" Her voice was hoarse and angry. It scared me to death.

"The nurse s-sent me home," I stammered. "I have the flu."

She cleared her throat. "I do too," she said quickly. "Can you shut the door?"

I backed out of her room and did as she asked. As I lay down in my bed, I told myself that the sweat down my back and fear in my gut were caused by the stomach bug.

That evening, it was like nothing had happened. She changed into jeans and picked Kat up from grade school. She brought me crackers and soup and put a cool hand on my hot forehead. I was so relieved I decided not to ask her why she'd been crying. Everyone was entitled to a bad day now and then, right?

But her bad days started happening more often. I grew to hate the sight of those maroon flannel pajamas because they meant it was a day she'd decided not to go to work, a day she'd spend in her room with the door closed. I fantasized about lighting those horrible pajamas on fire in the dumpster behind our building. Or dumping a bottle of bleach on them so they looked as twisted and wrong as I felt whenever I saw her wearing them.

I didn't know how to explain to eight-year-old Kat that Mommy was "sad" all the time, so I lied and told her that Mom had migraines. Kat's favorite book at the time was *Anne of Green Gables* and Anne's Marilla had "sick headaches" that put her to bed; migraines were something Kat could understand. When Kat fussed over her and said she was so sorry Mommy had bad headaches, my mom accepted her fawning and looked at me with such gratitude I wanted to cry.

She must have lost ten pounds that winter, along with the interest in making us dinner or breakfast. I gained ten pounds because I kept ordering us pizza when she wouldn't emerge from her bedroom in the evenings after stepping in to "take a quick rest." The pizza nights ended, though, when Domino's informed me the credit card had been rejected.

I stomped into my mom's room the night of the Mastercard humiliation and threw a box of Cheerios—our dinner—on the floor. "Do you want me to get a job to pay for food?" I shouted at her. "Or keep helping Kat with her homework like I've been doing every night for months?"

As an adult, I hated remembering those confrontations and how I yelled at her. The way I spoke to her like it was her decision to lie there and feel that way. In my defense, I didn't yet know about fighting against a chemical imbalance. I didn't know that when you're depressed you're engulfed with exhaustion. I didn't know how the brain can be sick and lie to you about being worthy of the time and energy to get help.

When she was able to snap out of it for a while, the relief was overwhelming. We had a solid couple of months in the spring, and I thought she'd kicked it for good. During this good spell, she went to work every day, she ate dinner and laughed with us at night, and she helped me to study for my biology quizzes.

It didn't last. She just got better at hiding her episodes. She'd get dressed in work clothes and drop Kat at school...and then come home and get back in bed for the day. Eventually, she lost her job, which she couldn't hide when spring turned to summer and we didn't have school all day.

Another thing she couldn't hide was the mounting debt. She lost interest in checking the mail, and eventually I started opening it. We were behind on rent, on credit cards, utility bills...everything. The day-to-day needs were piling up too. Like any other family, we had weekly groceries and school fees. Kat had a growth spurt and all of her clothes and shoes were suddenly too small.

Looking back now, it's easy to see that I should have reached out for help at this point if not before. I had finally done enough fumbling internet research to guess that she was suffering from severe depression. But we had no other family. Both my parents had been only children, and we had no living grandparents. My mom had lost touch with most of her friends when she and Dad had moved to Chicago shortly after their marriage. The remaining few drifted away after Dad died.

With no other trusted adult, I would have had to reach out to a counselor at school or something. But I was absolutely terrified at what would happen next. Would they take us away from her? She was still my mother and I loved her. Even worse, would they separate Kat and me? I refused to consider the possibility. I would just have to handle things myself.

As my therapist coached me to say aloud in my mid-twenties: "I was so scared. I was so scared all the time."

I felt remnants of that fear now as I climbed the stairs to my mother's second-floor apartment, my arms full of her mail and deliveries. I set it all down on the floor next to her welcome mat and pressed my ear to the door. Nothing.

The summer my mother spent almost wholly in bed, I changed, practically overnight, from a teenager into an adult. Pretending to be my mother, I called our bank and learned all about consolidating debt. I spent days pawing through a storage unit she'd rented when we'd moved from the house to the apartment. There was enough random furniture, toys, and clothing to hold a rummage sale, which gave us three weeks of grocery money. Best of all, digging through a box of my dad's old files, I found the paperwork for a small life insurance policy. It was enough to pay our rent and utilities for two years. When I found it, I whooped and cried like a showcase-winning contestant on *The Price Is Right*.

I enrolled Kat in summer camp at the YMCA so I could take a full-time job for three months. The weekly trip to the grocery store was my most daunting challenge. Walking through the aisles, I became an absolute expert at addition and subtraction. When meat was too expensive for our budget, I informed Kat that we were going to experiment with vegetarianism. "Like Natalie Portman and Miley Cyrus," I said when she protested. To this day, she won't eat beans because we had them at every single meal for months.

We barely scraped by—but we did.

"Shouldn't Mommy see a doctor for those terrible migraines?" Kat would ask, looking mournfully at the closed bedroom door.

Oh, but Mommy wouldn't. As summer turned to fall and we headed back to school, I'd slide all sorts of mental health pamphlets under her door. I'd clip newspaper articles about depression and put them on her pillow. After Kat went to sleep, I'd sit on the edge of my mother's bed and plead with her to see a doctor. She'd just purse her lips and say, "All I need is more rest to get well." Or "You don't understand this back pain, these headaches."

To make things more confusing, she sometimes had long streaks of good weeks. I'd grab Kat after school and get home ready to microwave dinner...only to find her up at the stove, freshly showered and dressed. She'd have the pantry and fridge stocked with groceries. The next day, I'd find her at the computer, industriously poring over job listings. She'd get her hair cut and her nails done, maybe visit a bit with our neighbors. She'd pore over our most recent schoolwork and ask about boys.

I so wanted to believe she was better I'd convince myself that *this time* she wouldn't relapse again. Of course, now I know a lot more about depression and the fact that it's cyclical and usually recurring and often caused by triggers…but back then I was desperate to believe it could be fixed, once and for all, and that Happy, Healthy Mom would stick around for good.

PULLING KAT'S KEYS out of my pocket, I unlocked the door of my mother's apartment and stepped inside. It was dark and silent, a little smelly as though the trash hadn't been taken out in a week or there were leftovers rotting in the fridge.

No one was in the kitchen or living room or bathroom. The door to the master bedroom was closed. Old habits die hard, I supposed. I took a deep breath and rapped on the door with my knuckles. "It's Tess, and I'm coming in," I announced.

I shoved the door open. My mother stared at me from the bed, the covers pulled up to her chin. She didn't look surprised to see me, exactly. In fact, she looked half irritated and half resigned. I crossed my arms over my chest. "So, we're doing this again, huh?"

Shit. I was *angry*. Definitely not the emotion I should be taking in with me to an intervention. I took a deep breath, but I couldn't turn it off. This whole thing was just too similar to when I was young and wildly confused about the mother who didn't seem to care enough to love me anymore. I should have called my therapist before coming over.

My mother sighed, the little disappointed wheeze of air that never failed to drive me bananas. "You better not be wearing those fucking maroon pajamas," I warned.

"Jesus, Tess," she snapped. "Watch your language. How'd you get in here anyway?"

"I stole Kat's set of your keys while she was in the bathroom during brunch this morning." I stalked around the room, looking for empty vodka bottles, which had come into play at the tail end of her worst episode. Luckily, I didn't see any now.

"There was no need for you to break in." She sniffed. "I just have a cold. I'm allowed to be sick every now and then, you know."

I laughed, an awful cackle with absolutely no humor or warmth. "You're actually allowed to be sick forever. But you're absolutely not allowed to go off your meds. Or blow off your other daughter, the one who adores you. Or get fired from your job."

She blanched. "I didn't—"

"Save it." I opened the blinds to let some of the gray afternoon light in the room. Then I cracked the window. That stale bedroom needed fresh air. "I talked to Mr. Gupta. He said you stopped showing up for work two weeks ago. Even though he doesn't want to, he'll need to let you go if you can't be reliable. Especially with tax season approaching."

That shut her up. She put a hand over her eyes, whether to shield herself from the new light in the room or me, I didn't know. "Also," I reminded her, "Kat's party is coming up, and it'll break her heart if you make an excuse not to show."

Her lips trembled and a tear dropped from the hand covering her eyes. "What do you want me to do?"

I sat on the edge of the bed and pulled out my cell phone. "We call Dr. Gelhorn. We explain everything that's happened since you started feeling lousy again." I was willing to bet it was Kat's announcement of her move that triggered this episode. I almost couldn't blame my mom for falling apart about it. Almost.

Scrolling through my contacts, I found the right number for her psychiatrist. "Dr. Gelhorn will help us figure out the recovery plan—what medication we need to do, how often you need to see her in the coming weeks. She may even want you to go to the hospital for a day or two. OK?"

She didn't put her hand down, and she didn't answer. I counted down from thirty in my head so I wouldn't start screaming. But finally, she nodded.

Chapter Seventeen

DR. GELHORN RECOMMENDED admitting my mother to the hospital. My mom put up a bit of a fight, but Dr. G, thank God, was too sensible for her nonsense. "This is the quickest way I can help you, Helen."

I packed her bag and drove her to the hospital. Dr. G met us, and we got my silent mother settled in a room. She was cooperative, but she refused to make eye contact with me. At last, Dr. G put a hand on the small of my back and told me to go home.

"I'll be back tomorrow." I was going to need to take a personal day. At a minimum, I'd consult with Dr. G, fill my mom's prescriptions, and take the trash out of her apartment.

My mother didn't say good-bye. She did, however, whisper: "Don't tell Kat."

My boots slapped hard against the hallway tile. "I never have."

IT WAS AFTER ten when I got home. I placed an order for Chinese delivery before realizing I wasn't hungry in the slightest. I dashed off an email to Paul about being out the following day. As an afterthought, I also asked him to replace me on the interview team for the senior programmer position. Max didn't need my help to dazzle anyone, and if anyone ever found out that we'd slept together, I didn't want there to be any conflict of interest when he ended up getting the job.

Finally, finally, I let myself fall apart a little. Lowering myself onto the sofa, I put my head in my hands. I'd handled it, right? I'd caught it before things got out of control. "It wasn't so bad," I whispered. Nothing like how it was when I was a teenager. Kat wasn't a child anymore. No one could take her away from me. My mom had a doctor now. I wasn't worried about money. *It's OK.*

I needed to hear it aloud.

"It's OK. Everything's OK." It would have been more comforting if my voice weren't so strained and scratchy.

My phone rang. It was Max. This time, I let it go to voice mail. I was much too vulnerable and broken right now. I'd face him on Tuesday at work, once today was safely in the past and I had my armor back on.

Someone rang my intercom from the street. Right—the food. I buzzed the delivery up and dug some cash out of my purse. But when I swung open my apartment door, I came face-to-face with Max instead of the food delivery man. "Sorry," he said. "I thought I'd talk to you through the intercom, but you just buzzed me up."

"Oh." Flustered, I patted my hands over my unkempt hair and makeup-free face. I didn't want him to see me like this. Ever. And I couldn't be the sassy, flirty, fun girl right now. I was somewhere between hysterical and comatose, and that was not a look I wanted him to witness. "How did you know where I lived?"

He gave a rueful grimace. "You have a large internet footprint."

"Cyber-stalker," I declared half-heartedly.

"I know. Sorry to be creepy. But you sounded so upset on the phone this afternoon, and I just wanted to see if you were OK," he said.

He outstretched his arms as though coming in for a hug. I ducked and evaded, stepping back into my apartment. With one hundred percent certainty, I knew that if someone hugged me right now I'd dissolve into tears. Maybe I'd never stop.

Still walking backward, I caught a glimpse of myself in the hallway mirror. God, no wonder he was worried. My face was white, except for dark purple circles under my eyes. My hair was kinked and weird. I looked like a crazy Irish banshee. If I started wailing, the picture would be complete.

"Now is not a great time," I said. "It's been a bad day and I just got home—"

"Have you eaten?" he interrupted.

"I just ordered food!" I exclaimed, frustrated. "Look, I told you on Friday night. I can take care of myself."

A frown line appeared on his forehead. "That doesn't mean you always have to though."

Yes, it did. It absolutely did. I'd purposefully chosen to live my life in a way where I didn't need anyone to take care of me. In tough times, what worked for me was to be left alone to lick my wounds until I recovered enough to stand up again. This wasn't ridiculous bravado or false confidence on my part; it was actual life experience.

The one other time I let someone take care of me had ended very badly.

"Where's your bathroom?" he asked before I could make him leave. I pointed down the short hallway, and he disappeared into it and shut the door. I cringed, thinking of all the products that clogged the counter. I was fairly sure there was underwear and discarded pajama bottoms on the floor. Hair in the sink too.

My phone buzzed with a text from Kat. *Sorry to bug you so late, but I can't reach Mom. She's not answering my calls or texts, so I'm worried. Thinking about driving out to Glenview.*

Oh no. My mother would not be focused on her phone in the next few days as her body readjusted to her medication and she tried to pull herself out of the abyss. How could I keep Kat away? *Oh, so sorry!* I texted quickly. *Mom and I spoke this afternoon. Wendy's husband is in the hospital, so Mom went to Bloomington to help her out for a few days.* Wendy was an old coworker Mom had been friendly with. Last year, she'd retired and moved a few hours south.

I held my breath and waited for Kat's response. *Well, that's a relief. Weird she didn't let me know though.*

I resisted the urge to throw myself lengthwise on the couch and indulge in a kicking tantrum of frustration. I hated lying to her. And she was right. My mother would never leave town without telling Kat. *I think Wendy was pretty upset, and she was in a big hurry.*

Another pause and then, finally, a merciful response. *Ah. Thanks. Good night!*

Shaking my head, I tapped out a text to my mom. *Kat*

thinks you're with Wendy while her husband is in hospital. I threw my phone on the coffee table. She'd have to take the lie from there.

Five minutes later, the Chinese food arrived and Max was still in the bathroom. Maybe just the sight of me in dishabille had made him sick? Maybe he was in there gearing up the courage to say "Can we just be friends?" to a distraught woman?

I opened the bag and eyed the beef and broccoli with disinterest. Guess I had dinner for tomorrow night taken care of already. I was just about to shove it in the fridge when Max emerged. I raised my eyebrows and waited for him to drop the hammer.

"I drew you a bath," he announced. "Where's your liquor?"

Huh? But I gestured to a cabinet over the microwave. He strode over, opened it, and pulled out my bottle of Knob Creek. Without asking, he rifled through my cabinets until he found my glasses. Ice went into a tumbler, and he poured two fingers of bourbon over it. Then he picked it up and grabbed my hand. "Into the bath with your booze," he ordered.

Wide-eyed, I let him lead me down the hall. It really was beyond time to put my foot down and order him out, but suddenly, nothing in the world sounded better than a hot bath and cold bourbon.

There were bubbles in the tub. It was so surprising that I smiled. "I didn't even know I had bubble bath."

"You didn't." Max winked at me. "I'm a magician." Pointedly, he turned around. "I'm being a gentleman. Get in."

Caught completely off guard, I did what he said. I pulled off my yoga pants and sweatshirt and dipped a toe in the tub. It was on the verge of being too hot, which is exactly how I liked it. I settled into the steamy water and frothy bubbles and fought back a groan as the muscles in my back wept for joy.

In exactly two minutes, my face would be bright red and shiny. "I'm about to become a steamed lobster," I warned him.

He turned around and smiled when he saw me ensconced in bubbles. "Good. You need some color back in your cheeks." He handed me the bourbon. "Instead of a rubber ducky," he said.

"Thanks." For a moment I wondered if he was going to perch on the toilet seat and talk to me. I would have let him, but what I really wanted to do was just close my eyes and sip my drink and think about nothing except how warm I was and how good it tasted.

As if he could read my mind, he left the bathroom, calling over his shoulder, "You, relax. I'm going to snoop around your apartment."

"Enjoy the chaos," I muttered. But I was smiling.

I STAYED IN the bath long enough to get super pruny. My limbs were limp, and my brain a little foggy from the bourbon on a completely empty stomach. Wrapping myself in a robe, I glanced into my living room. Max had made himself comfortable. He was lying on the sofa reading a Lee Child thriller I'd finished a few nights ago. "That was a good one," I said, feeling awkward.

He closed it and sat up. "Got to love Reacher," he agreed. "How do you feel?"

It was embarrassing to admit, but: "About a thousand times better than I did before you got here. Thank you."

"I put your dinner in the fridge," he said. "Want me to reheat it?"

I shook my head. "No."

Max stood. "Then I'll tuck you into bed and head home."

My mouth fell open. No one had tucked me into bed in about two decades. His lips twitched as I stared at him. "Lead the way," he said.

Shrugging, I shuffled down the hall into my messy bedroom and climbed under my comforter. Max followed and made such a big show of tucking it all around my body that I actually giggled.

He sat on the edge of the mattress and put a warm hand on my warmer cheek. "Sleep well."

This was all just…too much. His face was so kind, so affectionate, so focused on me that it caused some sort of nuclear reaction in my chest and brain. All of a sudden, words were frothing out of my lips before I could stop them. "My mom. She suffers from clinical depression. Pretty severe. The kind where she can't get out of bed. It was at its worst when I was in high school, but she had a relapse in the past few weeks."

I could feel the tears building in my throat. I closed my

eyes and swallowed to force them back down. Ugh, this month was going to be the death of me.

Three disparate memories collided in my brain. Max, in Pop's, saying "I like nice girls." My mother, this afternoon, refusing to look at me in the hospital room. My mother, fourteen years ago, looking at me with hatred from her first hospital room.

Max's hand was still on my cheek. I pushed it away and met his concerned gaze. "Don't get involved with me, OK? I'm not a nice girl. I'm the kind of girl who has her own mother committed."

Undeterred, he put his hand on my scalp and started to stroke my hair. I closed my eyes against his azure sympathy. "Sweetheart," he murmured, "I don't think you've been 'a girl' for a really long time."

Gulp. No one had ever called me sweetheart before. I kept my eyes closed hard. "It's not polite to comment on a lady's age," I deflected primly.

He chuckled. "You know very well that's not what I meant, Boots."

He kept stroking my hair, and it felt so good and I was so warm and I didn't open my eyes because I was afraid to see what was in his and...I dozed.

When I woke a few hours later, Max was gone.

Chapter Eighteen

MONDAY PASSED IN a blur. I broke into my mom's apartment again and cleaned out her fridge. I did a small grocery shop and restocked her kitchen for when she'd be home later in the week.

I called Mr. Gupta, explained that my mother was dealing with a medical situation and begged for her to be allowed to come back to work next week. Of course the poor man agreed. I suspected he knew more than he let on about our little family struggle. She'd been working for him for almost fourteen years now. She started at his firm about the same time I started college.

As I did a load of laundry and put fresh sheets on her bed, I took a lot of deep, calming breaths. If only I'd done more of that at the end of the Bad Time.

For much of high school I was too afraid to leave Kat alone with my mother at night. What if Kat got sick or scared while I was gone? My mother was usually in no condition to provide help or comfort. What if there were a fire in the apartment building while they were both asleep? What if one of the neighbors dropped by unexpectedly and discovered our family's dirty little secret?

My anxiety meant that I was always home and desperate

for a distraction. I haunted the local branch of the Chicago Public Library, stocking up on books and tearing through their outdated inventory of rental DVDs. Except for the one blessed month where I figured out how to steal our neighbor's HBO, we couldn't afford cable. So, studying became my default evening activity. Everything else in my life felt so out of control—but my grades weren't. They were the one thing I could control completely. I'd always been competitive. And with no opportunity to play sports, beating my classmates' test scores became the one way I could shine.

My high GPA and SAT scores got me into several name-brand universities across the country, but there was no way in hell I was leaving my twelve-year-old sister alone with my mother to go to school in some other state.

It was actually the arrival of college that forced the confrontation between my mother and myself, the one that finally changed things.

I'd gotten a scholarship to DePaul University in the city, and though it was far from ideal, I knew I could manage the trains to take classes on campus and live at home in our apartment in Glenview. But no matter how I squeezed my schedule, I couldn't make it mesh with Kat's. I couldn't be there to drop her off and pick her up. I couldn't make her volleyball games. I certainly couldn't make both breakfast and dinner.

I knew in my ancient-feeling eighteen-year-old bones that I'd hit an end. I wasn't going to give up college, but there was no way to keep going on as I was. I was so tired.

On an unusually warm day in June, two weeks after my high school graduation, I took Kat out of the city to a week-long sleepaway camp. As soon as I left her in good hands with the camp counselors, I drove to a tattoo parlor and handed over the picture of the anchor. It was agony to get that thing carved into my back, but I already knew it would hurt less than what was coming.

When I returned to the apartment in the evening, I entered my mom's bedroom without knocking. She'd recently added drinking to her repertoire, and that night she looked up at me with a glass of vodka in her hand. "What?"

No niceties, no preamble. "If you do not seek medical treatment immediately, I am taking Kat and moving out."

A sneer formed on her lips, but it quickly disappeared when I said, "You are an unfit parent, and I will not leave her in this house with you when I start college. I will begin proceedings to become her legal guardian." Then I fibbed a little. "I've consulted a family lawyer, who assures me I have a solid case."

"How could you do that?" She stared at me. Her eyes were so dark I couldn't separate her pupils from the irises. Her voice was like a croak, and it seemed to take great effort for her to speak at all. "Tess, you have no idea what I'm going through. If you did, you'd never threaten me by taking my one joy, my baby, away from me."

I wondered when it was exactly that I stopped being a joy, when I stopped being her baby too.

I ignored everything: her words, her tears, her obvious wall of pain. "Tonight. You commit yourself to the hospital tonight. Otherwise, I'll pick Kat up from camp next week and we'll take a nice summer road trip before I move us into an apartment in the city near my school."

"Kat would never agree to that," my mother said, taking a shaking sip of her drink. "She loves me. She'd hate living away from me."

She was right. Kat loved her beyond reason, more than anyone or anything in the world. She thought my mother was the kindest, funniest, most beautiful person in existence. She would have forgiven her absolutely anything.

But I knew my mother's illness wouldn't let her believe that. If I'd learned anything from the dozens of articles I'd read on depression by then, I'd learned that it was a big fat liar. So I used that to my advantage and twisted the knife.

I laughed loudly. "Really? Even after I tell her the truth about your 'migraines'? You think she's going to forgive you for these years? Where you've chosen—you've made the choice—to lock yourself in here? You've never even gone to one of her volleyball games. Did you know she's had her first kiss and that the guy was a total dipshit after? She got her period six months ago, by the way. She has terrible cramps every month, but she didn't want to worry you. For Christ's sake, Mother, you slept through her last birthday!"

I'd meant to be calm, but suddenly I was screaming. "Do you think she will forgive you?"

My mother was sobbing so hard she'd dropped the drink on the bed and it was seeping through the sheets.

I got control of myself and cleared my burning throat. "She doesn't need to know," I whispered. "If you come with me tonight and let me check you in for psychiatric inpatient treatment, if you do whatever the doctors say for as long as they say…I'll never tell her. We'll stay here. I won't take her away."

Faced with losing Kat, she caved. She went to the hospital with me.

We've never talked about that night. I know part of her, a large part, is grateful I forced her to get the help she needed. But another part of her will always be angry about how I did it, at how I used what she loved most against her. What she doesn't know is how angry I was—and will always be—with myself for doing it that way too.

Talking about this night with my therapist was the most painful session in my treatment. "Caregiver burnout is a real thing, Tess," she'd explained softly. "In fact, it's its own trauma."

I wasn't sure about that, but I did know that getting my mother and me to the point where we walked through the hospital doors that night took the temper out of me for a long time. Tess, the bossy, cheeky fighter, disappeared for years.

Now, after I carried my mother's trash to the garbage cans behind the apartment building, I pulled out my phone and called her doctor.

Dr. Gelhorn reassured me that my mother was doing very well at the hospital. She'd be doing two group therapy sessions and one private session with Dr. G every day she was there. Dr. G planned to see her three times a week after she was released as well. "I've also temporarily increased the dosage on her medication," she informed me. "That's worked well in the past when she's had less severe episodes."

That piqued my interest a little; when had she relapsed before? But I knew Dr. G wouldn't be able to tell me. And God knew my mother had never seen fit to confide in me when she needed help. "Should I come to the hospital to see her?" I crossed my fingers, hoping Dr. G would say no.

She hesitated. "That's your choice, Tess."

Aha. "She doesn't want to see me," I stated flatly. I didn't want to see her either—at all—but it stung anyway.

"You know she's intensely private about her illness," she conceded.

Fine. I'd just check on her via phone in a day or two. It wasn't like I didn't have things to do.

ON TUESDAY, I was at the office by 7:00 a.m. I absolutely hated unplanned days out, and I wanted a few quiet hours to catch up on emails and get settled. After an hour or so, my cell rang. When I answered, it was to my lawyer's no-nonsense voice. "Tess? It's Natasha Long. Thought you might want a brief update on your case."

"Oh. Yes, please," I said, surprised. I'd been so focused on Max and our plan to hack the Sex Ghost's site this upcoming Friday night that I'd almost forgotten I was also pursuing legal options.

"No luck on identifying him from the hotel," she said briskly. "We've also tried to communicate with the hosting sites overseas, but no one has responded."

I inhaled deeply through my nose. "No progress then. Kind of what we anticipated."

"Pretty much," she admitted. "However, we did find one other piece of interesting information. One of his video subjects, the one he called his San Francisco Treat? She was using a fake ID the night she met him at a bar. She was only sixteen. Like the other case I mentioned, someone linked to her video from Facebook. When she found out about the sex tape being posted and went to the cops, a John Doe warrant was issued. In that situation, it was not only NCP, it was statutory rape."

I didn't understand the legal terminology. "What's a John Doe warrant?"

"It's an arrest warrant for an individual whose name is not known. The warrant can be issued by a judge when a person is known by sight but not by name."

OK, that made sense. And I was happy to hear there was a warrant out for his ass, but I couldn't see how this related to my case. "Is that helpful?"

"Only if we found him in person," she admitted. "If we did, he could be arrested ASAP without any other immediate steps from us. And if he were arrested, I'm sure his lawyer would advise him to immediately take his site down. It's a long shot though, since we have no way of anticipating where he'll be."

At that moment, Max paused in the entrance to my office. He was wearing the navy suit he wore the first night we met, which meant that his interview must be today. When he saw I was on the phone, he grinned and waved. Flustered, I broke eye contact and swiveled my chair so my back was turned until I heard his footsteps move down the hall.

I'd managed to push our Sunday night interlude out of my mind for a whole day, but the memories were coming back now with a vengeance. I couldn't believe I'd been so open and broken in front of him. No one had seen me like that in my entire adult life. I felt like an insect that had been kicked on its back to flail around, unable to right myself, and with my weak and squishy parts exposed to the world.

I forced my concentration back to Natasha's last words. "Is there any sort of, um, alert that we should do? Some sort of heads-up we could send out to police departments in major cities?" Even as the words left my lips, I cringed. He was a criminal, a complete raving asshole, but he wasn't Ted Bundy. I doubted a national team of crack cops would assemble because a good-looking jerk was able to convince girls to sleep with him.

"I'll think about that, but I doubt it," she said, a wisp of apology in her voice. "I wish there was more we could do for you, Tess."

I appreciated her words, but there was a note of resignation in them I didn't like. I sure hadn't given up yet. Max better be as good a hacker as advertised.

LATER THAT MORNING, I was finishing up a quick status meeting with Abigail in her cube when Max and our HR director exited a nearby conference room. That would have been the first leg of his interview. This afternoon he'd meet with another senior project manager and then with Paul and Jack Sorenson for the tougher questions.

"Max is smiling," Abigail whispered. "It must have gone well. He's the last one to interview, you know. I saw two other people wearing suits in that room with Paul and the others yesterday."

Paul popped out of his office and called my name. "Can we meet in five minutes?" We had a lot to catch up on, including the Away-Ho meeting from Friday afternoon. I'd been both amused and annoyed to find an email from sales this morning, letting me know that Zack Morris would be onsite this afternoon to begin contract discussions. In terms of my possible promotion, it would look good to Jack that Morris wasn't wasting any time signing with us, but I was definitely not looking forward to spending more time with him.

I gave Paul a thumbs-up, and he wandered into the break room for his daily 10:00 a.m. cup of coffee. Max sat down in the next cube, his temp office space. I felt a sudden need to look down at my phone and scroll through Twitter instead of making eye contact.

"Well?" Abigail demanded.

"One down, two to go," he said easily. Oh man, I could *feel* his eyes on my face. Or maybe that was the sensory memory of how he'd stroked my cheek on Sunday night. "How are you, Tess? We missed you yesterday."

I stood quickly, my face growing hot. "Fine, thanks, see you later. Got to meet with Paul." Without looking at him at all, I fled down the hall.

Paul and I met for more than an hour. When I left his office, I avoided walking by the programmers' area even though that meant I had to loop around the entire floor to get back to my office another way. My phone buzzed as soon as I sat down. A text from Max read: *Are you being weird because I've seen you naked or because I've seen you upset?*

I had to laugh. And, frankly, I would prefer to have this

conversation while not looking at his face. *Because you've seen me upset, obviously. Half the office has seen me naked.* Completely false. Until Max, I'd never hooked up with someone at work. At the holiday party last year, I'd slapped a drunk guy from the help desk who'd tried to kiss me while holding up his personal, portable mistletoe. This company, this job, was the most stable thing I had. Long ago, I'd decided to never risk my comfort here for a quick bang with a coworker.

I refused to think about what it meant that I'd known Max would be a possible coworker when I slept with him.

How long will your freak-out last, do you think? Can you get over it by lunch time? Potbelly's? Meet you there at 12:30?

Oh, fine. Might as well. I was going to need to get used to him again by Friday night anyway.

Chapter Nineteen

POTBELLY'S WAS A six-block walk from the office, and even though I shivered during the trek, I was relieved at Max's choice. At that distance, I wouldn't need to worry about people from work seeing us eating together.

Max had beaten me there and grabbed a window table in spite of the massive lunchtime crowd. Two sandwiches and two bags of chips rested on the table in front of him. "Your choice," he said. "You want turkey or ham?"

"Turkey." I plopped across from him and started to unwrap it. "Tell me how the first interview went."

He smiled. "I nailed it." He pulled open a bag of salt and vinegar chips. "I'm ready for this afternoon too. That was smart, by the way, to pull yourself off the interview committee. Thanks."

I nodded, happy he'd understood my intention. I opened my own bag of chips, frowning when I saw that they were barbeque-flavored. Without a word, he pulled the bag away from me and handed over the salt and vinegar.

We ate in silence for a minute that stretched into two or three. I couldn't think of anything funny or clever to say. Ugh, how could I take us back to where we were before Sunday night? I needed to figure out a way to put my armor back on.

But Max didn't give me a chance. "Why are you uncomfortable around me now?" The light reflected off his glasses as he took a bite of the ham sandwich.

I fidgeted against the chair—and against the impulse to lie or deflect. "You know too much about me," I said finally. "Lots of embarrassing, extremely personal stuff. It's uneven. I don't know any of your secrets."

Crunching, I narrowed my eyes at him. "I think it's time you tell me what you did to get fired at your last job. Why the CEO has it in for you so bad. Spill."

He put his sandwich back on the table and leaned back. With a stone-cold poker face firmly in place, he said, "Taggert could honestly say that I personally cost the company between $10 and $40 million."

A flake of salt and vinegar chip got caught in the back of my throat. I coughed for a full minute before I could breathe again. "Holy shit." Forty million dollars?! His eyes skittered around the restaurant, and his fingers drummed on the table. "Well?" I asked.

"Well what?" He poked at his sandwich.

I kicked him under the table. "What was the good reason? At your parents' house, you told me you did a bad thing for a good reason."

To my surprise, he took off his glasses. I'd never seen him do that in conversation before—was it some sort of self-protective mechanism? Maybe he took them off when he wasn't sure he wanted to see the facial response of the person he was talking to. I didn't much care though; I was too busy soaking in every detail of his naked face. There was a freckle high up on the bridge of his nose that was usually hidden by the frames. *That's* my *freckle*, I thought like a madwoman.

"I was so happy when I started at SideDoor," he started. "They hired really smart people, the technology was cutting edge, and the leadership team seemed like rock stars." A twisted half smile formed on his lips. "My first year there, I was especially bowled over by Cole Taggert, the esteemed CEO. He's charismatic. Magnetic. Absolutely brilliant at sales."

He hesitated, twirling the glasses in his hands. "I hero-worshipped him. He led this brilliant company, he seemed to genuinely understand technology, and he was the kind of guy you'd want to hang out with, you know? So many guys in his position are like Zack Morris."

A pink flush crawled up his neck. "I made it my mission in life to become important to the company and to him, in particular. And it worked. By my third year, I was Taggert's right-hand man, his most trusted programmer. He gave me all the big projects, he brought me to meetings with clients and investors. He even mentioned the possibility of making me the chief operating officer."

I almost choked on my chips again. "How on earth did you get from nearly COO to blacklisted?"

Max tapped his glasses absentmindedly against the table, his unfocused gaze past my left shoulder. "Taggert changed. I don't know if the company's success went to his head or if he was dazed by all the dollar signs our investors were waving around or what. All I knew was that he started caring a lot less about the quality of our products and a lot more about how much the sales team could get for them. He stopped rewarding our top-tier tech talent as well. He switched to a churn-and-burn kind of philosophy with our programmers. It was extremely disheartening—and frankly, stupid. Short-sighted. You can't build top-notch products when you have a revolving door of people."

He shrugged. "I'd changed too. No more hero-worship. After spending all that time together, closely collaborating, I considered us more like partners. I felt free to express myself when I disagreed with him—and he didn't like that. Especially not in front of others. We had a couple of meetings where I openly argued with him on the progress of some of our work or on how our teams should be structured. He got visibly angry. After that, I stopped being his right-hand man and there was no more COO talk."

He picked up his bag of chips, eyed them, and put them back on the table. "I didn't really mind that though. While it was kind of cool to be in the room where all the decisions are made, I'm actually happiest in the pit with the team. I like the problem-solving and building things. Debugging, making stuff work.

"But the situation kept devolving." He sighed. "The other programmers still saw me as a leader and came to me with issues and questions. Taggert didn't like how I'd become the voice of his development team, and it was obvious he wasn't going to let the situation stand for long."

Max looked at my face quickly and then away again. "Then…Aria ended our engagement. I was in a dark place for a few months. I didn't want to be a leader. I wanted to work from home and mope."

He fell silent for a moment, as though I might have

something to say. I didn't, except "Go on."

"My little pity party suited Taggert just fine, and we came to a new agreement. I would work remotely for a few months as a resource for the team's junior programmers who needed help, but I wouldn't be actively involved in planning or leading any of SideDoor's ongoing projects. The only downside for me was that I wasn't really intellectually challenged. I'd dutifully put in the nine-to-five day helping the SideDoor programmers, but I was pretty bored."

He shifted his weight in the seat, and his lips twisted mischievously. "I found a solution to the boredom quickly though."

I put down my sandwich, fascinated with his impish expression. "How?"

He looked off into the distance as if picturing a fond memory. "I read a news article one morning about some ransomware attacks."

"Ugh." I shuddered. I lived in fear of those. A ransomware attack was when cyber criminals release a virus on your computer that locked you out of everything. They would let you retrieve control of your system and documents only when you paid a ransom.

He went on. "I challenged myself to come up with a solution to those kinds of attacks. I started coding like a madman. I'd get off work at five, and at 5:01 I'd switch from my SideDoor equipment to my personal equipment and work until three in the morning. I was obsessed." He snorted. "And, in a hugely geeky way, having the time of my life."

He laughed a little. "A lot of people recover from a breakup by throwing themselves into their jobs, and this was my version. It worked too. I was absolutely high on the algorithms, on the creation. When I finally emerged from my cave of code a couple of months later, I felt great about life in general."

I blinked at him, all innocence. "Maybe you should write a self-help book about your approach. Instead of *Dating for Dummies*, it'd be *Healing Heartbreak for Hackers*."

He did one of those fantastic firecracker laughs. "Maybe I should."

"Get back on track," I ordered. "Taggert." This was all fascinating stuff, but time on our lunch was running out and I still didn't understand how he'd ended up blacklisted.

"Patience is not one of your virtues," Max observed. I just raised an eyebrow.

"In August, SideDoor threw its annual anniversary party. I was ready to rejoin the world of the living at that point. The programmers and I were all happy to see each other, and we had some drinks. The only annoying part of the gathering was that Taggert made a few comments about how I'd turned into a stereotypical hermit loser. I didn't appreciate that, and I ended up mouthing off about my personal project a little. I wasn't being a loser; I was being an entrepreneur!"

He looked down at the table and flushed. "A lot of bravado from a man who hadn't worn real pants in months, but he pissed me off."

Hmmm. My brain was whirring, skipping ahead, putting pieces together. I put my sandwich back on the table. "What happened next?"

"A week after the party, Taggert surprised me at home. He showed up with a case of beer and said he wanted to catch up. When we were on friendlier terms, we'd often grab drinks after work, so I thought maybe he'd missed me." The corners of his mouth turned down. "Poor naïve Max. After a couple of beers, Taggert offered to show me some of the new flagship projects SideDoor was working on. Said he had a few questions where he'd love my opinion. I was flattered, and it was kind of nice to feel important again. We logged on to the SideDoor servers from my system."

Oh crap. Yep. This story was going where I'd begun to expect.

Max took a deep breath. "At some point, while I was in the bathroom or talking to the pizza guy, Taggert took the opportunity to transfer my entire personal project over to the SideDoor servers."

"Thief," I breathed.

He closed his eyes and nodded. "Once the work was on SideDoor's servers, it was game over for me. Any code or work I completed on SideDoor's time and equipment was property of the company. I'd been so careful to use only my personal time and my own stuff...but Taggert had my code for days before I realized what had happened."

"Did you confront him?" I asked, eyes wide.

"Oh yeah." Max nodded emphatically. For a moment, he looked like an outraged child on a playground. "That's just cheating! I took a self-righteous march into his office and accused him of theft and of being an asshole. Taggert laughed. He said that I couldn't prove a thing. That the code had been sterilized, and if I accused him of anything, he could simply say that the work I was describing had been a SideDoor project for some time and I was having delusions of grandeur. Oh, and by the way, I was being let go."

Now he lifted his chin. "I couldn't let him get away with it."

I couldn't help it; I started to smile. Max was always so calm. It was hard—but fun—to imagine him sitting down at his computer with righteous fury guiding his fingertips. "I know what you did," I said.

He gave me an acknowledging nod. "I released the code to the public. I made it open source. I also wrote an accompanying press release from Cole Taggert himself, in which he claimed that this next-generation antivirus product should be available to everyone and not sold for profit."

"Taggert got a ton of free publicity and accolades for that," I protested, laughing. "It's the thing everyone mentions when they talk about his reputation! The Robin Hood of software. You actually did him a huge favor."

Max just lifted a shoulder in disdain. "Oh, I'm sure he loves being revered. But he would have loved the money more. A company that was developing a more sophisticated—but very similar—product received $10 million in their first round of venture capital funding. They ended up having four rounds."

Whoa. Uh, yeah. If Taggert could have raised $40 mil in funding to build off of Max's code, I could see why he was still pissed. In fact, I was pretty sure he'd be pissed forever.

He dusted some crumbs from the table, finishing the story. "Since everything was so public, there was no way for Taggert to officially punish me, even though it was obvious I'd done it."

"Do you wish you hadn't?"

"Some days," he admitted. "But it was not his product to sell. It wouldn't surprise me at all if he did unethical shit like that before and probably still does. Someone needed to show him that he can't act however he wants without consequences."

He shook himself a little. "But here we are, a year later. I'm still unemployed with a powerful enemy."

I pushed his ham sandwich closer to his hands. "At least lunch is tasty."

He picked it up and smiled at me. "Quite true. I might be unemployed with a powerful enemy, but I'm also eating a tasty lunch with a beautiful girl. Things could be a lot worse."

Aw. I hid from the compliment by taking the last bite of my lunch, and then changing the subject. I wanted to just sit there and bask in his smiling, flirting presence—but honestly, it was hard to keep fresh concern off my face. His job situation was much more serious than anything I could have imagined. I hadn't really understood the high stakes of Max's interview today; if he didn't get the job with us, he might be out of work for a really long time.

Chapter Twenty

AFTER LUNCH, I had a series of strategy meetings with the developers. As we talked through our team goals for the next year, I tried to keep my mind on task and not get distracted by the ongoing interview in the conference room. Max was just entering the last and most important leg—his hour with Jack Sorenson and Paul.

Paul asked challenging questions in interviews, but he was always fair. Jack, however, could be a bit of a prick. I'd sat in on some interviews where he'd asked bizarre questions for no reason, other than to make the interviewee extremely uncomfortable. There was no need for him to even be part of the interview process since VPs made their own hiring decisions. But he insisted on attending an interview for every senior position. He said it was because he genuinely cared about the quality of the personnel we hired, but I suspected that he really just liked to make people nervous.

I crossed my fingers and hoped that Max remained as unflappable as usual.

As I finished with the team and retreated to my office, Ron from sales appeared with Zack Morris. "Ready to hammer out the terms of our contract with Away-Ho?" Ron asked me with forced cheer. From the strain in his voice, I guessed that Morris was just as charming today as he'd been on Friday.

"Come on in," I invited.

"Let me grab my laptop and another chair." Ron disappeared briefly down the hall. Morris plopped into the seat across from my desk, giving me a long-suffering look as though we'd somehow forced him to do business with us. He didn't say a single word in greeting. I supposed I should have taken the high road with some small talk, but I didn't feel like it today. I just sat in silence and returned his displeased, flat-eyed stare.

His phone beeped loudly, likely announcing an incoming email. He raised it to his face and read something, his lips twitching in a sneering kind of smile. Since he was so inclined, I unlocked my laptop and checked my own email to make sure nothing urgent had arrived in the last few minutes.

The last item in my inbox made my blood run cold. "MAJOR TEASER WARNING!!!" screamed the subject line from the Sex Ghost.

"No!" Luckily, I'd only screamed the word inside of my head; Morris didn't look up. I opened the email and read the horrifying text. *It's your lucky day, FSG fans. In thirty minutes, I'll be sending out a red-hot major teaser for my upcoming Friday night release. You're not going to want to miss this one… I had a real good time in Chicago.*

Oh. Fuck.

Ron dragged a chair through the doorway—and stopped short when he saw my face. "What's wrong, Tess?" he asked. "Disaster protocol for one of our clients?"

I shook my head at him weakly. "Nothing." Just my personal disaster. Max had said that thirty minutes would be plenty of time to stop the teaser…but he was in the middle of a sixty-minute job interview. If he knew anything about interview etiquette, he wouldn't check his phone at all. He probably wouldn't see the warning email until the teaser had already been sent out.

Ron sat down and raised his eyebrows, waiting for me to take charge. But at the moment, I couldn't even remember what the hell Away-Ho did, let alone how to lead the contract discussion. Stalling, I gestured between Ron and Morris. "Why don't you bring me up to speed on everything you two have covered this afternoon?"

Morris rolled his eyes and muttered "fuckin' waste of time" loud enough for us both to hear. To further make his point, he literally tossed his phone on my desk and stared at the ceiling.

Ron began to outline the terms and conditions discussed so far, and I tuned him out. How could I interrupt Max's interview and get him out of there to help me stop the teaser?

You can't. The voice inside my head was loud and bossy. I couldn't hear anything over it even as I watched Ron's lips move. This job interview was Max's big chance. I had no professional reason to burst in and end it. If he was just with Paul, I'd risk an interruption, but there was no way I could do that with our CEO in the room. Jack Sorenson would think it extremely odd, and it would reflect poorly on us both. After his lunchtime confession about SideDoor, I knew Max didn't need anything else reflecting on him poorly.

I would just have to suffer with the teaser being out in the world until he was free. How many people on the FSG's mailing list would watch it immediately anyway? (I conveniently ignored the memory where Max said that the major teaser campaigns always triggered a spike in site traffic.)

The wild roaring in my ears was so loud, I was lucky to catch the end of Ron's summary. "So that's where we are," Ron finished. "If you could provide Zack with an itemized list of project deliverables for him to review, we can start there."

My hands decided to cooperate and pulled up my Away-Ho notes with no involvement from my brain. Muscle memory is a beautiful thing. "Absolutely, Ron." I showed my teeth to Morris. "I have a list of thirty-eight bulleted items for you to review. I'll print us some copies." With a few clicks, I sent the document to the printer just outside my office. As I stood to retrieve them, I caught sight of Morris's phone on my desk, his screen still displaying his email app.

His most recent email—the one he'd been sneer-smiling at—was the major teaser warning from the Sex Ghost.

My hands and face went entirely numb. I stumbled in my boots as I left the room to grab the printouts. Zack Morris was an email subscriber to the FSG. In less than twenty minutes, he could see me engaging in a graphic sex act.

This was so bad I couldn't even think of the right word for it. *Cataclysmic*, maybe? It would be bad enough if someone internal watched it and reported me. But if an external client did? Particularly the very client Jack Sorenson wanted so badly?

Toast. I was toast.

The printouts were warm on my icy hands. I gripped

them so tightly they were already wrinkled by the time I handed copies to Ron and Morris. *Get ahold of yourself.* This was not the end of the world. Maybe the montage wouldn't even show my face. Morris wouldn't know it was me from a tiny excerpt that just showed my ass, right?

Oh God. I wanted to put my face on my desk and cry.

Instead I detached completely. I felt as though I were watching the scene in my office while floating above it. Was this what going into shock felt like? There was the calm, strawberry-blonde woman talking through a detailed list. There was her colleague Ron, typing notes while he listened. There was the asshole client who continually yawned and rolled his eyes while checking his phone every two minutes.

The strawberry blonde finished her explanation and leaned back in her chair. Her eyes caught on the clock. Eight minutes until the major teaser was sent. "What questions do you have?" she asked the client.

Then the office door flew open, Max dashed in, and my body and brain rejoined in a frantic, jarring smack.

Max's mouth dropped open, but he took in the scene quickly. "Sorry I'm late," he said to Ron. To Zack Morris, he extended a hand. "Tess asked me to join the discussion in case you had any follow-up technical questions."

"Great idea!" Ron said enthusiastically. Even Morris looked minutely appreciative. Clearly, the more people who fawned over him, the better.

Max looked up at me, his eyes an insistent dark laser. "In fact, Tess, why don't I sit at your computer just in case I need to look up anything on the servers to answer his questions?"

My heart thudded so hard against my chest that it actually hurt. *He knew.* Max was going to try to stop the teaser. "S-sure," I said, standing so quickly I banged my knee against the desk. I pressed myself against the back wall as Max squeezed into my chair.

Morris sat up straighter in his chair and puffed out his chest. "The first question I have is about number 14."

I made a big performance of raising my printout and poising a pen directly above it. "Go on." Below me, Max was typing frantically. He had two windows open, one accessing a server and one a plain, white text window.

Morris jabbed at his own printout and then lifted his paw and did one of his typical air stabs toward my chest. "This deliverable says that my team would have to be involved in testing. If we're paying you all this money, I don't understand why my team has to do a damn thing."

Easy one. Lots of clients asked about this point, although they were generally less rude. My mouth went on autopilot with my stock response.

Below me, in the text window, Max typed: *I'm in his server, and I found the teaser. I corrupted the file. The Ghost tried to re-upload it, but I kept corrupting it. He's running out of time to make his subscriber deadline. Since he can't get the Chicago montage to work, I'm betting he's trying to find a substitute file or create another teaser.*

It was quite a feat to deliver a speech on dual-team testing with my mouth while reading and deciphering Max's message with my brain. But I pulled it off. I gave Max a small nod to acknowledge that I understood.

Morris harrumphed. He didn't exactly like my explanation, but he didn't dive deeper. "I also have a question about number 29." This one was on pricing, and to my relief, Ron stepped in to field it.

Max elbowed my hip. Hard. I looked down at his latest message. *He's uploading a different file. We need to watch it to make sure you're not in it.*

Max started to double-click on the file, but I smacked his hand so hard Morris gave me strange look before turning back to browbeat Ron. Giving Max a pointed glare, I reached down and muted my computer's speakers. The last thing we needed right now was to blare a bunch of porno sounds through my office.

Max's lips twitched, and he shook his head in apology. Then he double-clicked on the file. *Please don't let it be another montage with me in it. Please. Please don't let Max have cut his interview short only to get rewarded for his trouble by seeing a clip of me having sex with the Ghost.*

For once, my prayers were answered. It wasn't a montage at all. The video featured just one girl, a young brunette gyrating on top of Westley, her mouth open and boobs bouncing. Max fast-forwarded through the whole minute of the file to make sure there were no surprises.

Not you.

Fifteen minutes later, the three of us had fielded four more Morris questions, and he'd grown bored with us. "I'll have my team review the rest and get back to you," he mumbled, staring at his phone.

"I'll walk you out," Ron said.

Max and I watched them leave just as the new email from the Sex Ghost arrived with a link to the poor brunette's teaser. The text of the email had typos. *Hope you all enjoy this sneek peek at one of my Phoenix Foxes, which is the city I'll be releesing at the end of November. The ladies of Chicago didn't want to cooperate in their major teaser—*

"They sure as hell didn't," I muttered.

—but they'll give you a good show when I release all of their videos on Friday night.

"No, they won't," Max said.

I had a sudden thought. "While we're in his server world anyway, should we try to find and delete my whole video?"

"No," he said firmly. "The teasers are stored in an easy-to-access, unsecure location. Probably because they're free and no one has to pay to see them. The rest of his stuff is in more heavily secured and possibly alarmed areas. I want to be methodical and go with my game plan on Friday night."

"Makes sense." Wrung out, I maneuvered around my desk again and flopped in the chair Morris just vacated. I wished I had a bottle of bourbon in my bottom drawer, *Mad Men* style. "I feel really bad for the Phoenix Fox, but, Jesus, I'm grateful it wasn't the montage with me. Thank you so much."

How had I gotten so lucky? If Max had checked his phone during the interview, Jack Sorenson would absolutely hate that. "How did you know the warning was sent?"

"I'd set a special signal," he admitted, his face flushing. "Any email from the Ghost makes my phone vibrate in a particular pattern. I knew the moment the warning arrived. I kept thinking you would make some excuse to pull me out of the interview."

I didn't say anything, but he wouldn't let it go. "Why didn't you come get me?"

"You were in the middle of y-your interview," I stammered. He looked up at me, but his glasses were doing that annoying tilt where I couldn't see his eyes behind the glare.

There was a long pause. "Anyway," Max finally went on. "I improvised. I told them I needed to duck out early because I'd promised to help you with Zack Morris." He laughed. "Which was a lie that became true. I had no idea he was actually in your office until I burst in."

I joined his laughter. That was actually perfect. In my meeting with Paul earlier in the day, I'd mentioned how disrespectful Morris had been on Friday to me and Ron and how well Max had handled his questions. "Nicely done."

Max stood and walked to the door. Pausing with his hand on the knob, he said, "I can't believe you were going to let that teaser be sent out because you didn't want to interrupt the interview."

His warm scrutiny made me feel twitchy. I shrugged, stood, and switched my voice to breezy. "I figured it'd be minimum exposure," I lied. No need for Max to know that Zack Morris was probably watching the Phoenix Fox right now. "Probably not a big deal as long as you could have removed it sometime this afternoon."

He opened his mouth, no doubt to argue with my stupidity, but then he shut it again. "Oh." Good. I didn't want to talk about it. I didn't want to even think about it...about the sacrifice I almost made.

"Thanks again!" I gave him a cheery wave, sat down at my desk, and began to industriously type nonsense into a blank email.

Chapter Twenty-One

"IT'S UNANIMOUS," PAUL announced, standing in my office doorway on Wednesday afternoon.

I smiled up at him from behind my desk. He often started conversations right in the middle. Some days it drove me crazy, but most of the time I liked the puzzle of Paul-speak. Even though I couldn't wait to take over the VP role, sometimes I got a little hitch in my chest when I thought about him leaving for good. I wondered if he'd ever invite me out to coffee or over to his house for dinner once he'd retired.

"What is?"

"The interview team found Max to be the best candidate for the senior programmer position," he said. "I'll be calling his references in the next couple of days, but that's a formality. He was phenomenal in the interview, and more importantly, he's already proven himself to everyone here in the past couple of weeks. The developers worship him. He's dedicated enough to leave his own job interview to help you with a difficult client, for goodness' sake. Personally, I think he's a nice guy and a great fit for the team. We'll get an offer drafted early next week."

Yes! I did an internal fist pump, picturing the look on

Max's face with that offer in hand. Now we just needed to hope Cole Taggert wouldn't find out about it and call Paul.

I bit my lip, wondering how that conversation would go. "Come in and shut the door a minute," I said impulsively.

He closed the door and perched in my visitor's chair. "What's up?"

I took a deep breath, praying this gamble would pay off. Paul may or may not trust Max over Cole Taggert, but he sure as hell should trust me. "I want to tell you something about Max, in case you get a weird phone call."

I summarized the story Max had told me over lunch yesterday, emphasizing his overall brilliance for designing the antivirus software in the first place, while trying to make it clear that Taggert was a grudge-holding thief. Someone who was not to be trusted. "Obviously, I have no idea what Taggert says to the employers when he calls, but I wanted you to know the actual history."

The frown lines on Paul's forehead creased deep. "That's extremely troubling."

Oh shit. Maybe I'd done something terrible here. Maybe Paul didn't buy the fact that Max had developed the anti-ransomware all on his own. Maybe I shouldn't have brought it up at all.

"To think that such an esteemed executive would stoop to theft." Paul shook his head, and I breathed a sigh of relief. I hadn't been wrong to trust him. He had always been a solid judge of character.

"I appreciate the heads-up," he said, standing. "I'm not that surprised about Taggert though. He's still thought of highly in the business community, but in tech circles he's getting a reputation for sloppiness."

I gaped at him, surprised. "Really?" Paul did routinely attend technology conferences around the city and country. We were actually going to one together the following day. I'd forgotten, though, that they could be so valuable in terms of industry gossip.

"Indeed. Word on the street is that SideDoor's last two projects didn't go well because they can't keep top-tier talent," he said.

In the back of my mind, it registered that his comment lined up with what Max had said at lunch about Taggert's churn-and-burn philosophy when it came to programmers. But it was hard to focus on that when Paul had actually just used the phrase "word on the street."

He paused, a hand on the doorknob. "One more thing. You should know that I recommended a slight re-org. Max's position is not going to report to me—or, eventually, to you—anymore."

I shook my head, confused. "Oh?"

"You'll already be managing four teams and sixteen people. I can tell you from experience that you don't need the additional workload of another person's status meetings and performance evals and all that." He looked straight at me. "Also, it's against company policy for someone to date their direct superior," he said bluntly.

I felt my cheeks blaze with heat. "Oh!" I dropped my pen. "We're not—" Wait, were we? Weren't we? How did he know? I let out a horrible little peep of embarrassment and resisted the urge to dive under my desk.

Paul's lips twitched before turning up into a full smile. I

got the distinct impression that he was enjoying my flailing discomfort. "I've known you six years, Tess. And I've never seen you smile at anyone like you do at Max."

He opened the door and stepped into the hallway. Then, for the first time in our professional relationship, he gave me a sweet, conspiratorial wink. "Good talk."

AS THE END of the workday approached, I hung up on Kat and indulged in a long stretch. Apparently, she and my mom just had a long chat about what outfits they were planning to wear for Kat's party on Saturday. My mother had also instructed Kat to appeal to me not to wear anything "too revealing." There was no clearer sign in the universe that my mother was feeling more herself.

I caught a glimpse of my face in the small makeup mirror that hung on the back of my office door. I was grinning like a loon. And no wonder—Max had called me beautiful. We'd stopped the teaser from being released. Max was getting the job. Even my mother was cooperating by recovering. Talk about a good couple of days.

I felt so great that I put on some lipstick, tucked my hair behind my ears, and marched straight over to Max's cube. Maybe I'd been wrong to be so freaked out by whatever was growing between us. Hell, Paul approved.

Luck was on my side yet again. Only Max sat in the cluster of cubes. Furiously typing, he didn't turn as I approached. "I hear you, Boots," he said. "One sec." With a flourish, he finished some command and dozens of lines of text scrolled upward on his screen.

He swiveled in his chair. I liked that his eyes needed a second to rest on my legs before shooting up to my face. "Hey, you."

"Want to go on a real date?" I blurted. We hadn't done that yet. We'd had drinks and sex and breakfast and lunch and whatever it was when he drew me a bath. But we'd never followed a waiter to a table for two and flirted over a menu. Tonight, I wanted to do that with him.

"I know a great place in Greektown," I continued, warming to the idea. "The restaurant has half-price bottles of wine on Wednesdays."

Max cocked his head. "Can we order saganaki?"

I crossed my arms and looked down at him sternly. "As if it's even possible to go out for Greek food without getting a plate of cheese on fire." Inside, giddy bubbles burst in my stomach. We could yell "opa!" and then I'd tell him about his impending job offer.

Behind me, I heard the distinctive *click-click-click* of a short stride in dainty high-heeled shoes. Had Abigail changed her entire look? I'd never seen her in anything but sneakers, which was one reason I always towered over her. I whirled around to take a look.

"Oh, hey!" Not Abigail. Instead, Aria stood there smiling, looking like a little Audrey Hepburn in tiny black pants and a tinier black sweater. A perfectly in fashion black bomber jacket was folded neatly over her arm, and a Tumi laptop bag was slung over her other shoulder. "It's Tess, right?"

It took supreme effort to not let my smile drop right on

the floor. My stomach, however, plummeted. "Yes! Nice to see you again."

She angled her head around me and waved at Max. "You ready? You want an Uber, or should we take the 'L'?" Straightening, she looked up at me. "Trivia night at CJ's pub. The food is terrible, but we can't resist the challenge."

"Fun!" My stomach returned to its proper place in my body and abruptly turned to stone. The leaden feeling spread to my chest.

I glanced back at Max. He'd risen from his chair and was tugging at his hair. "I forgot all about it," he mumbled.

Aria snorted. "You forgot about the bar trivia we've done every Wednesday night for six years?" She nudged me and giggled. "You guys must keep him pretty distracted."

I tried to giggle back but couldn't manage it. A wheeze was all I could do. "We do try."

I lifted my lips again at her and did a sort of good-bye gesture over my shoulder at Max. I couldn't look at him. I was too humiliated. How could I keep forgetting about her? About them?

"Tess, wait," Max called.

Nope. Not interested. "Forgot that I have a call with the West Coast!" I yelled. "You guys have a great night!"

I hightailed it back to my office and dropped into my chair. A minute later, I heard them coming down the hall so I picked up my phone and said, "So true. There are a lot of synergies that we could leverage once we have the bandwidth." Max looked in as they walked by, but I ignored him, babbling into the fake call and twirling a pencil in my hair.

When I knew they were several offices down, I got to my

feet and peered after them. Aria was talking, and he was nodding down at her. Even in her heels, she came up only to his bicep. He was carrying her laptop bag. When they reached the end of the hall, he stepped forward and opened the door for her.

For some reason, that chivalrous image—of him carrying her bag and opening the door for her—stuck with me all night. As I rode home on the Brown Line, it played in my head on a loop. I was so distracted by it that I completely missed my "L" stop. I hadn't done that since college.

SINCE I LIVED at home, I didn't get the typical college experience. By day, I attended classes on campus, and at night I kept an eagle eye on my mother's fragile recovery. At first I thought I'd be envious of the other students because they got to live in dorms and pledge sororities. But when I chatted with them in class, they seemed so young. And while I was jealous of their carefree lives, I also felt a little superior. They had nothing more important to do than text about last night's keg stand; I needed to rush home to count my mother's pills and interrogate Kat's homecoming date. I was too far entrenched in my early-onset adulthood.

In my junior year, I met Daniel.

Things were slightly more stable at home then, but I was always waiting for the other shoe to drop. Things never felt safe. The night before I met Daniel, I'd stayed up until 4:00 a.m. for myriad reasons. Kat's stupid boyfriend had dumped her, and she was a mess. My mom's doctor had recently changed her prescription, and she was suffering from gastrointestinal side effects. I was struggling with my programming classes because it was difficult for me to stay late and get extra help from the TAs.

I fell asleep on the train into the city. I would have missed my stop if a handsome young man hadn't shaken me awake. "Excuse me, but don't you usually exit at the Fullerton stop? We're nearly there."

I jerked straight to my feet, almost spilling the contents of my backpack.

"Don't worry." He smiled at me. "We have time." He had curly light brown hair and brown eyes. He wore faded jeans with a navy fleece, and his skin was slightly ruddy in a way that made you think of skiing and hiking and all sorts of wholesome outdoor activities.

Daniel also went to DePaul, but he was a grad student. I liked him immediately. He was just so...adult. He'd grown up in the north suburbs, and though he was an only child, he was close with his parents and extended family. He already worked as an engineer at a firm downtown, and he was getting his master's degree in applied mathematics. He walked me to class from the train station, listening carefully as I stumbled through my explanation of my studies and my vanilla story of why I lived at home instead of on campus. (I helped my single mother with my teenage sister.)

"I hope this isn't too forward," he said once we'd reached the computer science building. "But I'd love to take you out to dinner this weekend."

I hadn't been on a date before. As in ever. A humiliating fact for a twenty-one-year-old. But I just nodded like I got asked out every single day of the week. "I'd like that."

We became a couple very quickly. Daniel was kind and gentle, and he fussed over me. He loved taking me for dinner and watching my eyes light up when he ordered appetizers or desserts. He found—and paid for—an individual tutor to help me with my classes. The first time we had sex, he lit candles all over his bedroom and carried me through the doorway like I was a princess. He called me "darling" all the time.

Eventually, I trusted him enough to tell him about my mother and what my high school years had been like. When I finished my sad little tale, he'd had tears in his eyes. "I hate that you were so alone." That was the night he told me he loved me for the first time.

Needless to say, my mom and Kat adored him. He became a constant in our home. He brought flowers for all of us for no reason. He helped Kat with her chemistry homework and did small electrical repairs around the apartment for my mom. He'd invade the tiny kitchen with a sack of groceries and a cookbook, and hours later the four of us would be eating coq au vin or something else French and fancy. He stood between my mom and Kat at my college graduation, clapping fiercely as I crossed the stage to get my diploma.

On my twenty-fourth birthday, he took all of us out to dinner at an elegant restaurant that bordered Lincoln Park. Between dinner and dessert, he got down on one knee and proposed to me. When he opened the ring box, my jaw dropped at the size of the square-cut diamond. "Darling, I knew from the moment I saw you sleeping on that train that you were the woman I was supposed to take care of for the rest of my life. Marry me?" The entire restaurant applauded. Kat burst into tears.

Of course I said yes.

Chapter Twenty-Two

On Thursday, I didn't have to face Max and hear about his super-fun trivia night with Aria, because Paul and I attended an offsite technology conference at a venue a few blocks away from our office. I forced myself to listen to the speakers and to schmooze during the networking sessions.

When it ended I walked Paul to his Metra train stop and then turned north, crossing the bridge that would take me to the Merchandise Mart "L" stop. It was just after five, and night was falling. Daylight savings would happen in a few weeks, and then it would look like the middle of the night at this time. But right now, as I paused on the bridge and looked at the Chicago River, it still felt like twilight. I closed my eyes and breathed deeply, enjoying the fresh air after a day of semi-claustrophobic conference rooms.

"I'm not technology-stalking you," a familiar voice said. "I promise. I'm just headed to the Mart for the train and you happened to be on the bridge." Max cleared his throat. "I'm very happy for the coincidence though."

I opened my eyes. He stood a few feet away wearing a navy peacoat and light green scarf. "Oh. Hey," I said flatly. Then, with one last look down at the water and up at the skyscrapers, I walked quickly toward the train station. My boots were flat today, and my stride ate up the ground quickly.

"Slow down," Max called. "We're taking the same train."

Inward groan. He was right. We'd both take the Brown Line to Addison and then walk in opposite directions to our respective apartments. Unless, of course, he had to go take a pottery class or make homemade sushi with Aria. Who knew what shit they were into on Thursday nights. Bowling league, perhaps?

I hustled through the turnstile and up the stairs to the platform without looking behind me to see if Max was following. A train must have just come through, because the platform was almost empty. Quiet enough that I heard his footsteps and his exasperated sigh when he stopped to stand next to me.

"I was disappointed you weren't at the office today," he said. "Because I'd like to revisit that whole 'real date' conversation."

Was he kidding me? For the first time, I turned and made eye contact. "That offer is now permanently off the table," I said firmly.

A Brown Line snaked slowly into the station, and I hurried down the platform to get a space in the first car. Max followed me, his footfalls sounding heavier and angrier than they did a minute ago.

I jumped into the car and got the last seat. Ha! Undeterred, Max grabbed one of the handles hanging from the ceiling and stood right in front of me. "Why?" he demanded.

I glared up at him. Did he want to have this conversation

in a jam-packed train car? "Do you really not know?" I hissed.

He glanced around and lowered his voice to a whisper. "If it's about Aria, I promise you that there's nothing going on there."

I huffed out a sarcastic laugh. "You might not be having sex with her, but what's going on is not nothing." I said it loud enough that the dozen people in hearing distance all glanced over. Max's face flushed scarlet, and his lips thinned.

Ignoring him—which was difficult because he was literally looming over me—I pulled my phone from my coat pocket and answered work emails for several minutes as the train left downtown and entered Lincoln Park. "This discussion is not over, Tess," Max said. "But I'm not having it in front of the Jolly Green Giant."

It was such a bizarre thing to say that I looked up, only to find that Max indeed was standing next to a man dressed in a head-to-toe Jolly Green Giant costume. Max's nostrils were flared and before I knew it, I laughed too. Halloween was tomorrow, and at one of the stops, a large group headed for a costume party had entered the train. We were now riding with several Disney princesses, the gang from *Scooby-Doo*, and the cast of *Stranger Things* too.

Max was eyeing Velma's orange dress and knee socks appreciatively. He cocked his head toward her. "Most guys like Daphne, but not me. I always had a thing for Velma. I think it's her low voice and the way she talks to everyone else like they're stupid. Reminds me of someone I know."

I absolutely hated that I wanted to laugh again. Damn him.

And fine, our conversation was not over. If he needed me to hold up a mirror for him to see what was going on, I could do that. He liked Velma? Perfect. I could certainly talk to him like he was stupid.

At the Addison stop, we pushed past the party-goers and made our way down to the street. The wind had picked up, and I pulled a stocking cap out of my laptop bag to anchor my hair to my head. Before he could defend his beautifully platonic relationship with his ex-fiancée, I said, "Max, do you think that actions or words are more important?"

He narrowed his eyes at me, turning up the collar on his coat. "Is this some sort of test?"

"It's a question."

"Actions," he said. "Always."

"I agree." *You walked right into that one, dumbass.* "So you *say* that you and Aria are not involved, but from what I can see, the two of you spend a huge amount of your free time together. That's an action."

I forced myself to soften my tone. "Maybe you got a little confused because you and I have fun and the sex was pretty good, but it's obvious to me that you're still in love with Aria. No guy chooses to spend all his time with an ex if he's not still in love."

I sniffed. It was the cold night air causing my nose to run and my eyes to stream liquid. Really. "It's fine for you to be in love with her. It's fine for you to spend all your time with her." I swallowed down the bitterness that wanted to creep into my voice. "Honestly, she's probably still in love with you too or she wouldn't spend all her time with you."

I took a step back and looked him straight in the eye.

"But it isn't fine to pursue me when you have a free evening or because you're bored or because you need a distraction or because you want to get back at her or whatever." A muscle in his jaw flicked, but other than that, his face was completely unreadable. I took a loud, shaky breath. "I might come across as a boozy Amazon, as Abigail so charmingly put it, and I've told you over and over that I can take care of myself, which is true. But I do have feelings and I can get hurt, and I don't want you to hurt me."

OK...that wasn't the strong finish I was planning on, particularly since the last sentence came out as a bit of a sob. But at least I'd gotten across the important point. I was sure I'd given him a lot to think about. So I patted him awkwardly on the shoulder and turned east to walk home.

"I don't spend all my time with her because I'm in love with her," he called. I paused, looking up to the heavens. How far in denial was he?

"I spend time with her because I feel sorry for her," he said, his voice lowering to almost a whisper. "I feel guilty."

Huh? I turned back to face him. Why would he feel guilty if Aria dumped him? "I don't get it. I thought she ended your engagement."

The wind gusted around us, and I shivered. "You're freezing. Let's walk," he said, gripping my elbow and steering us north up Ravenswood, toward my apartment.

A Metra train roared by, then another Brown Line. Finally, silence descended, except for the sound of my booted steps on the pavement. "Talk," I warned.

"Aria did end our engagement," he confirmed. "Eighteen months ago."

"Were you surprised? Were you devastated?"

He smirked a little at my eager, bloodthirsty tone. "Surprised, yes. Shocked, actually. We'd dated for so many years, and we acted like an old married couple already."

"Did she explain?"

He nodded. "She said we were too alike. That there was no real spark between us. That we'd mistaken easy friendship and lifestyle compatibility for long-term love. That she still wanted surprises and romance in her life."

I pictured Aria calmly communicating all of that and felt an unexpected surge of respect for her. Of all people, I knew what it was like to want to end an engagement, and I'd had no idea how to do it with any sort of grace or even basic communication.

"Wow. So were you devastated?"

He squinted, thinking. "No. *Devastated* isn't the right word. I think *disoriented* is better. I'd had my whole life figured out, you know? I'd picked a trusted partner, and I felt very settled. So when she gave me her little speech and handed back the ring, I felt like someone shoved me out of a moving car into an unknown place."

He shifted uneasily, his eyes skittering away. "Like I said the other day, I was sad for a while. Angry. Rejection just sucks, you know? I did all the typical post-breakup stuff. I spent days without leaving my apartment, ate crap food, and drank too much. I went out to bars and hooked up with random girls."

He looked down as if expecting me to get feisty. I held up my hands. "No judgment here. All sounds totally normal and justified to me."

He relaxed. "Then one day, about four months after it happened, I had a sort of epiphany."

I snorted. "An epiphany? Do tell."

He gave me a playful shove. "It wasn't earth-shattering. No clouds parted in the sky or anything. It was just a quiet moment where I was drinking a coffee and walking down the street, thinking about the week ahead. I suddenly realized I was totally content. I didn't feel sad or lonely or scared. I felt the same amount of 'happy,' I guess you'd say, as I did when I was engaged. More, actually. Which made me realize that Aria had been right. We weren't in love and meant to be together if I could feel one hundred percent fine without her. Also, I felt this great sense of anticipation, like exciting things were still going to happen to me, that my life wasn't set in stone.

"She was right," he said again, more forcefully this time.

My pulse began to beat faster. He sounded like he was telling the truth. "OK," I said slowly. "Then why the guilt? Why do you feel sorry for her?"

He sighed. "Promise me you'll keep this between us?"

I shrugged, eyes wide. "Of course."

We turned right onto my street. "Six months after she broke it off, Aria came to my apartment crying," he said. "She thought she'd made a mistake in ending things. She said she missed our life together and wanted our future back."

Whoa. Holy shit. It was hard for me to imagine picture-perfect Aria as sniffling and sad. "Were you tempted?" I asked.

"Not even a little bit," he said flatly. "Besides being truly happy on my own, I noticed something very clearly in what Aria said that night. She missed the life we had, the future we'd planned. It was a lot harder to meet new people at this stage in life than she thought, and she was very lonely. She missed being part of a couple."

Ah. "She didn't miss *you*," I murmured.

His lips curved as he looked down at me. "Exactly."

"So what did you say?"

My apartment building was only a block away. Max shortened his stride, walking slower. "I sat her down, got her a glass of wine. Told her that she was right to break off the engagement and that when she was less raw and lonely, she knew that."

His jaw tightened. "She was so vulnerable and sad that night. My heart really did break for her. I mean, I still cared—still care—for her, just not in the romantic way. So I told her that we should still be close friends. That we should still spend time together. Just because we weren't a couple didn't mean we couldn't hang out and do the things we always enjoyed doing together."

Now he stopped walking altogether and put his hands on my shoulders so that we were standing face-to-face outside of my apartment building. "I know how it's looked to you, but all of the time I've spent with her...it's just been a mixture of laziness and me wanting to protect her. Neither of us was dating anyone, so we just fell back into old routines."

He cleared his throat and cupped one hand on the back of my neck. "I told her last night that I was really hoping I'd be less available in the near future."

I hesitated again. "She and I are really different, Max."

"I know." He nodded emphatically. "But that's a good thing. Aria is a great person, but even at the beginning, there wasn't really a fire between us. And let me tell you a few things. I never crossed the city like a maniac to track her down in a bar. I never pulled eyelashes out of her face. I never had dirty dreams about her."

"Really? You did?" I interrupted, grinning. "Tell me about these dreams right now!"

He smiled down at me. "No."

"Why not?" I demanded.

"Punishment," he said loftily. "Because a few minutes ago you said that the sex we had was only 'pretty good.'"

I batted my eyelashes up at him. "If I admit to being a big fat liar, will you tell me about them?"

"Maybe someday," he said. He pulled me toward him, and I let him. "Just so you know, I also never stayed awake late in the night just crafting witty text messages to make Aria laugh. I never put her into a bath with a glass of bourbon." His voice lowered to a whisper. "She never distracted me—never freakin' invaded my thoughts—the way you do."

Oh my. An unfamiliar warmth was spreading in my chest, and it only burned brighter when his lips touched mine. I broke away to deliver a final warning. "I'm a bit of a handful."

Max laughed. And laughed. And laughed. "Is this supposed to be a surprise? Since I've met you, I've become involved in illegal hacking, technology stalking, and ridiculous hijinks at the office." I winced. He certainly hadn't seen me at my most smooth and suave. Behind my back, his arms tightened. "But, as you should have noticed by now, I keep coming back for more. Apparently, I want my hands very, very full. Now shut up."

He kissed me softly, gently, over and over until I was on my tiptoes and my cold hands were stroking his warm neck. It wasn't "invite me upstairs" kissing. It was "I like you so much and I just want to show you" kissing. And I flippin' loved it.

The front door to my building slammed as Roz exited. Max and I broke apart with a breathless laugh.

She did a full-body scan of Max and raised a purple-penciled eyebrow at me. "Well, this is different for you. Mr. Hacker, I presume. Are we removing the revolving door, Tess?"

"Roz," I warned her, but secretly I was a little impressed that she hadn't said "of dick" aloud. "Aren't you late for Bikram yoga?" She sniffed, put her nose in the air, and walked across the street to her favorite studio, Om on the Range.

Max watched her go, bemused. "Your BFF? Can't wait to meet her."

He looked at me over the rims of his glasses and shook a warning finger. "Now go inside and get warm," he mock-ordered. "Think hard about whether you want to make me less available. I don't want to deal with another one of your freak-outs tomorrow." The tone of his voice was teasing, but his gaze was so direct and earnest and open that I broke eye contact, stepped backward, and grabbed my keys.

Because yes—part of me wanted to throw myself into his arms and declare "Mine!" right this second...but there was another voice in my head, a small, insistent one, that asked me what the hell I thought I was doing. *You're not a long-term girl.*

He was quiet, clearly waiting for any kind of response. As always, I defaulted to sass. "Fair enough." I lifted a shoulder. "I'll think about it. Now you go home and get some sleep. I need you well rested and on the top of your game tomorrow night." I winced. "If you can't erase that sex tape, I'll be moving to Timbuktu and this whole conversation is moot anyway."

He snorted. "Did you actually just use the word *moot*? That's ridiculous." He leaned down again and gave me a last soft, lingering kiss. When he pulled away, I actually clutched at his shoulder for balance. Now *that* was ridiculous.

Chapter Twenty-Three

THE HOURS OF Friday, October 31, passed in excruciating slowness. I hid in my office most of the day—a horrible preview of what life would be like if Max couldn't get my video deleted from the Sex Ghost site.

My only distraction in the afternoon was an email from my mother requesting help with her insurance paperwork for her hospital stay and new medication. Unfortunately, she'd scanned all the documents funny, and for the life of me, I couldn't get the forms to align properly on my computer screen. "Can you just bring the actual paperwork to Kat's party tomorrow?" I replied.

To which she'd snapped, "Fine." (OK, it was over email, so I was inferring the snap.)

Employees with kids left in the early afternoon, no doubt to begin the trick or treating extravaganza. Paul waved as he walked by, clutching an ancient VHS copy of the *It's the Great Pumpkin, Charlie Brown* under his arm. I stared after him, amused, wondering how many VCRs were still in his house and if the youngest members of our programming team would even know what a VHS was.

Abigail stuck her head into my office as the clock finally, finally approached five. "Want to come to a costume party tonight?" she asked. "I'm dressing up as Alex from *A Clockwork Orange.*"

I groaned. "Of course you are, you little hipster."

She gave me the finger. "What are your Halloween plans then?"

To my dismay, my face began to get hot. "I, uh, sort of have a date." I mean, if you count going over to your new love interest's apartment to cheer him on as he deletes a video of you having sex with another guy as a date.

"Realllllllly," Abigail drawled. "Instead of partying in some slutty costume at a bar, *you* are going on date?"

I couldn't help myself. "There will still be a slutty costume involved."

"Blech." Abigail gagged. "Sorry I asked." Rolling her eyes, she headed out for the night.

Hmmm. I looked down at my plain, navy suit. I wasn't due over at Max's for several hours. A silly idea popped so fast into my head that I gasped and laughed aloud. Oh, this was going to be good.

I KNOCKED ON the door to Max's apartment with a giggle in my throat.

My long, black trench coat covered me from shoulders to calves, and I had the all-important accessories to my costume hidden behind my back. I just needed two minutes alone in his bathroom to put it all together. He was going to *love* it.

But then Max opened the door and said, "I'm so sorry about this. I had no idea they were coming over."

They? "What?" I asked. Uh, now was not a great time for me to be meeting new people. Not unless they were judges of the Most Ridiculous Scantily Clad Costume Contest.

Max closed his eyes briefly. "My sisters are here. They wanted to meet you and share details about the great shellfish retaliation before they head out to their Halloween party."

Hmmm. It wasn't great timing, but the idea of meeting some of Max's family was pretty alluring. As long as they got gone well before midnight, aka "sex tape eradication time."

"Can I take your coat?" he asked.

"Nope!" I said quickly. "I'm a little cold, actually."

He frowned. "You could borrow a sweatshirt."

Yes, I could. But a sweatshirt would not cover my slightly bare butt cheeks, which were hanging out of the bustier I was wearing. "I'll just keep my coat on."

Max shrugged. "OK. They're in the kitchen." He led the way down the hall. When I was sure he wasn't looking back, I threw the hat, sword, and cape into his bathroom. Hopefully, neither of his sisters would have to pee before they left. If they did, they'd think their brother had gotten into some weird cosplay.

Max's sisters were sitting at the breakfast bar, drinking wine. They were both dark-haired and wearing matching red lipstick. One of them had brown eyes and the other had blue, and they were both dressed as the bride from Tarantino's *Kill Bill.* "I like it," I announced, waving my hands at the yellow tracksuit Uma Thurman had made so famous. "You're totally embracing the revenge theme."

"Thanks," said the one with blue eyes. "I'm Ashley."

"Sarah," said the other. She turned to Max. "Where are

your manners? Didn't you offer to take her coat?"

Oh, for God's sake. "He did! I was cold!" My face was so warm it had to be pink, and I knew there was a thin layer of sweat on my forehead. But there was nothing to be done about my obvious lie except go for a quick subject change. "I'm Tess." I plunked my elbows on the counter. "So, has Dickhead Andrew started opening all his windows yet?"

Both girls pealed with laughter. "Yes! We've been watching. He opened them on Tuesday morning. And we drove past his place on the way here. He still has his windows wide open, and it's barely forty degrees outside."

I nodded sagely. "That's the first stage. When he still has hope. In two days, that will be gone and I predict he'll either check into a hotel or arrange to have his place fumigated."

Ashley beamed at me. "This was the best idea. You have to hear how we broke in!"

Max groaned and covered his ears. "I want plausible deniability."

I grinned at him. He was pretty dang cute in exasperated big brother mode. "I don't," I said, pouring both sisters more cabernet. "Tell me everything."

Thirty minutes later the wine was gone. After we gleefully laughed over every hidden piece of shellfish in Andrew's apartment, Sarah and Ashley moved on to peppering me relentlessly with questions about my best and worst experiences using Tinder and Bumble and other dating apps. Finally, I held up my hands in surrender. "Ladies, I'm an old-fashioned girl. I've had better luck meeting guys in bars." I winked at them. "I'm just classy that way."

Max shook his head disapprovingly at all of us, but there

was a twinkle in his eye. "This conversation has devolved quickly."

Sarah tsk-tsked. "Sorry. Since it's your apartment and all, I suppose we could raise the level of discourse." She looked back at me. "Max told me you're in technology, like him, but you specialize in disaster recovery. That's a pretty unusual niche. How did you land there?"

Great question and an easy answer. "I'm a strong believer in the inevitability of disasters."

Both of his sisters blinked at me. "Ouch," said Ashley. "You must have a pretty pessimistic world view then."

I shook my head quickly. People always misunderstood. I wasn't some Debbie Downer. It was just that disasters could be separated into the event itself and what came next.

"No," Max said before I could explain. "She's just also a strong believer in surviving them."

And...that was exactly right. I turned to stare at him, open-mouthed. "Yes," I said slowly. "The incident itself is one thing. The fallout, or the outcome, is another. One you can't manage, but the other you absolutely can."

A small smile turned Max's lips slightly upward, and his eyes did my favorite crinkle at the corners. "You like to manage the hell out of them," he said softly.

How did he understand me like this after only a few weeks?

One of the sisters cleared her throat and said, "Well." I realized that Max and I had been gazing at each other for a weirdly long time. "I think we should get to our party," Sarah said, a laugh in her voice. "Ash, let's leave these two crazy kids alone."

Max's cell phone rang, and he glanced down at the display. "It's Mom," he said to his sisters.

"Tell her we said hi!" Ashley said, popping off the stool. "Tess can walk us out."

Max nodded and ambled away with his cell phone, already distracted. "What? Mom, just turn off your lights if the trick or treaters are bothering you," he grumbled.

I followed the girls down the hall. As they opened the coat closet, Sarah winked at me. "What have you done to my brother?" she teased. "Holy wow."

I crossed my arms over my chest and swallowed. "What do you mean?"

She slipped a leather coat over her tracksuit and raised an eyebrow. "He's smitten! The body language! He angles himself toward you at all times, like he's the sunflower and you're the sun."

I took a step back as a mixture of giddiness and fear spiked through my veins. "That's...quite an analogy."

Ashley gave her sister a playful shove and shook her head at me. "Don't mind her. She's a frustrated English major. She's not wrong though. I never saw him like this with Aria. Not once in all those years."

Before I could process that, she leaned forward and lowered her voice. "Question. Are you naked under that trench coat?"

Busted. I didn't know whether to laugh or lie. Instead, I just stood up taller and kept a straight face. "Not entirely."

Both of them burst into giggles. "I like you," Sarah announced. And then, with a flurry of hugs and promises to text me about the ongoing shellfish revenge, Max's sisters chattered away into the night. For a moment after they left, I just leaned against the front door and breathed in and out.

Down the hall, Max was wandering around the kitchen, still on the phone. "Put the bowl of candy on the front porch then," he suggested, rubbing his eyes.

I went into the bathroom, closed the door, and finally took off my coat. When I caught sight of myself in the mirror, I cackled. I looked truly absurd. Sexy and outrageous in the most cheesy Halloween-y way. The orange-brown fur bustier shoved my breasts almost to my chin. The belt, with its holster and sword, sat nicely at my hips and matched my big brown boots. I grabbed the black cape from the floor and tied it around my neck.

The most important flourish was the black swashbuckling hat with the orange feather. I plopped it on my head and cocked it to a rakish angle. I contemplated drawing some whiskers, but I was already too warm. If I put eyeliner on my face, it would smear in a matter of minutes.

Putting my ear to the door, I waited until I heard Max say, "Bye, Mom," and then gave it another thirty seconds for good measure.

"Tess?" he called. "You want a glass of wine? I can open another bottle, since my sisters didn't leave us any of the first."

Licking my lips, I left the bathroom and marched down the hall. My boots made a very loud thunk with every step. Max's back was to me as I entered the kitchen. "Sure," I breathed. "Wine sounds good."

He turned to face me, his lips forming a response. I had the pleasure of seeing every one of his facial muscles freeze.

The bottle of wine in his hands slipped down several inches.

Thrilled, I did a slow turn, allowing the cape to drift off my semi-exposed bottom. I ended my twirl by pulling out my sword with one hand and bowing to him, taking off my hat with the other.

"You're...you're..." he stuttered.

"Sexy Puss in Boots," I supplied helpfully.

He was silent for another thirty seconds as his navy gaze roved over every inch of me. Finally, a wheeze escaped his lips and he leaned against the counter. "I don't know whether to laugh or carry you into the bedroom," he managed.

I sauntered up to him, took the wine bottle from his shaky hands, and poured myself a glass. "Laugh now, bedroom later?" I suggested.

He did laugh then, one of his firecracker bursts that transitioned into the low chuckle and back again. "Woman, you're going to kill me." He sounded so happy and desperately turned on that I decided in that instant never to be anything else for Halloween. His response had been one hundred percent worth sweating in my coat for an hour.

Max cleared his throat—but kept staring at all my exposed skin. "You're going to need to cover yourself while I'm working or I'll never be able to concentrate."

I gave him a kiss on the cheek, super satisfied with my entrance. He hissed as my lips brushed his face and my breasts pressed against his chest.

"No worries. I just wanted your initial reaction. I'll change into some of your sweats or pajama pants." Something cozy would be the best attire since I'd probably be pacing up and down like a madwoman while he battled my cyber fight.

"Oh," he said, sounding disappointed.

I bit back a triumphant smirk. "We can negotiate later though. I'm sure I could be convinced to put the costume back on."

"Deal," he said quickly. Then he continued to stare at me, standing stock-still, until I left the kitchen and sashayed into his bedroom to change.

Chapter Twenty-Four

Of course, a few hours later, my silly costume was the very furthest thing from my mind. In ten minutes, the FSG's Chicago videos would be live to the world. As the seconds on the website's countdown clock plummeted, I started to twitch.

Max sat at an elaborate workstation in the corner of his living room. At least three laptops surrounded him, and they were plugged into larger monitors that shone down on his face, illuminating the lenses of his glasses. Except for the clickety-clack of his keystrokes, he'd been completely silent for the last forty minutes. "Getting prepared," was the only thing he'd grunted when I'd begged for a status update.

I knew he wished I would just sit calmly. Instead I was bouncing off the goddamn walls. One minute I wanted to do shots of whatever booze Max had in the house. The next I was absolutely positive I'd vomit up anything I drank. The more fidgety I got, the stiller Max sat. He looked positively rigid in his sensible, ergonomic chair. Maybe he was even more nervous than me.

Three minutes on the countdown clock. "Do you need a shoulder massage?" I asked, hopping on the balls of my feet. I pictured him as the boxer and me as the crusty old dude giving him a pep talk. Maybe I should go grab a towel from the bathroom and hang it over my shoulders. I could dab perspiration out of his eyes. Of course, right now I was the one who was sweating.

"No," he said curtly.

I popped to the kitchen and pulled open his fridge door. "How about an energy drink?" He didn't answer, probably because he already knew what I'd discovered; he didn't have any energy drinks.

Heck, why not throw caution to the wind? Maybe he needed to be uncharacteristically hardcore tonight. "Do you want some cocaine?" I trilled. I was pretty sure I still had the numbers of a few dealers in my phone. You met all types at Fizz.

"Tess!" His voice was like an ice pick. "What I need is for you to sit down and shut up. Can you do that?"

If forced, I supposed so. I lowered myself onto the sofa. Now that I was motionless, the roiling in my stomach was even more noticeable. I hated every piece of this. I hated how random strangers were about to watch me having sex. I hated how everything was out of my control.

And most of all: "I hate that you're going to see it," I said to Max, the small tremble in my voice surprising us both. But seriously, what girl would want a new boyfriend to view graphic footage of an old one-night stand? Ugh. Quickly, I forced myself to lighten the mood. "At least my ass looked really good five years ago. So enjoy that."

He swiveled and smiled at me. Kindly. "Boots," he said gently. "It's not like I'm going to settle in with popcorn, sweetheart. Once I verify it's you, I'll just be focusing on the file's metadata and the server's configuration and security properties."

I took a deep breath and looked out the window. For the first time, I wondered about all the other Chicago victims of the FSG. Were they crouched over their computers, terrified of what would be released in less than a minute? Or were they happily oblivious tonight, completely unaware that tomorrow some sexist asshole might tag them as a whore on social media and that life as they knew it would change forever?

"Max," I said suddenly. "Do my video first. Obliterate. Make it disappear. All that. But if you have time and you see the other Chicago videos on the server…can you get rid of them too?" I swallowed. "No one deserves this—"

"I was already planning on doing that," he cut me off with a grin and a gleam in his eye.

Oh.

As the countdown timer hit the ten-second mark, I watched Max do an exaggerated arm stretch and knuckle-cracking routine. Five seconds. "Do not ask questions. Do not say a word. Got it?" His voice was low and commanding and… Yowza.

"Got it," I answered. How inappropriate of me, in this moment, to hope he'd use that tone of voice in bed later.

The timer on the website went off with pipsqueak ding. "Here we go," Max said.

I shut my eyes and put my head between my knees. I was so anxious that the skin on my arms and chest was blotchy, hot and pink. But my bare feet were freezing cold. I felt nauseated and jittery, like I'd drank an enormous pot of acidic coffee on an empty stomach.

Please, Max.

I don't know how long I sat like that, bent in half, almost praying to the man across the room. My ears were hypersensitive to every noise he made. I could tell when he leaned forward in his chair—was it good or bad? A few times I heard him jab the same key in a row—was that the backspace, and if so, what he was deleting? I wanted to ask him how long it would take, if things were looking better or worse than he expected. But I didn't. Partly out of respect for him and partly out of fear for the possible answers.

From time to time, he murmured. It was so quiet it was almost under his breath, so I held mine and angled my head up to catch the words. Almost immediately, he said, "There, there you are. Can't hide anymore." Which sounded promising until he went dead silent again.

Every second seemed like an hour, so I wasn't sure how much later it was when he scared me to death by saying in his normal speaking voice, "Holy Christ. You dumb motherfucker."

That sounded like good news, right? Unless he was talking to himself. What was going on?! But I forced myself to keep my mouth shut as I looked at the clock—12:16 a.m. How many guys had watched me in the past sixteen minutes? *Oh please God, let no one who knows me have watched it. Or, OK, fine. If someone who knows me did watch it, please let it be someone who doesn't post something about me on social media and link to it. That's not too much to ask, is it, Lord?*

At 12:38, Max swiveled around and said, "Done."

I shot to my feet. "Done? What do you mean *done*?"

He took his glasses off, rubbed the bridge of his nose, and then slid them back on. "Your video is no longer on the site."

"Really?" I screeched. "Oh my God."

He looked at me with an air of suppressed excitement. "Because of the preparations I'd made in advance, I was able to remove your video from the site within forty-five seconds of it posting."

My thudding heart slowed. "Forty-five seconds? You mean, no one really could have seen anything at all? Oh my God. Max. That's incredible. You're incredible." I sank back down onto the sofa cushions, my lungs and muscles recovering from the emotional wringer. "The other Chicago recordings? Is that what were you doing the rest of the time?"

He took a deep breath, his expression inscrutable. "I was pretty sure I'd be able to delete your video from the offshore server easily. But I assumed that the Sex Ghost would have his own copy or copies, and when he saw it wasn't on the site anymore, he'd upload it again. So I was using the attributes of the file to modify a program I wrote over the past few weeks. Basically, the program was written to recognize your video, corrupt it, and notify me for as many times as he tried to post it. I figured it would be such a pain in the ass that he'd eventually stop trying."

I processed everything he said and swallowed hard. "You are so smart."

He took another deep breath, his eyes gleaming. "And then something even better happened."

I hopped to my feet again. "What? What?"

"He must have noticed right away that your file was gone," Max said. "He was probably monitoring all of the files closely because of what happened with the teaser. Maybe he figured it was a weird system glitch with that particular set of recordings. Anyway, he logged on and tried to upload the file again."

"And? And?" Oh yeah, totally shrieking now.

Max stood too. For the first time, I noticed his hands were shaking. "I'm trying to figure out the best way to explain…um…he clearly didn't expect someone like me, because he logged on to the server without any, ah, protection." He looked at me, a little dazed. "It was an open connection. I was able to slide right into his own machine, his own servers, all of his backups. His whole damn system, Tess."

"What did you do?" I whispered, my eyes locked with his.

In an instant, his face transformed from one of wondrous disbelief to one of pure, cocky, badassery. "I annihilated it."

Oh my. The confident tone of voice. The smirk on his lips. The way his shirt was rolled up his forearms. The flood of relief and victory in my veins. I licked my lips and walked toward him.

He watched me move closer. I wondered if my pupils had fully eradicated the bright amber of my eyes, making them look black. "Explain the annihilation," I ordered.

A flash of teeth. "I deleted every video or picture file he had. Everything from Chicago—and every other city. Everything was axed from the offshore servers, everything disappeared off his main computer, every file off of every server he was connected to—vanished. And I was just getting warmed up."

Was this the first time in the history of the world that a woman had become completely aroused by a discussion of the deletion of digital files? I made a mental note to Google it tomorrow.

"So you're telling me that the Ghost lost all of his files? That no one can watch them? That he can't repost them?" If I was understanding correctly, Max was a hero.

He moved his head from side to side. "I think so. If he was smart enough to have an unconnected backup location then maybe not. But since I took a virtual snapshot of his entire system and copied it to mine, I'll figure it out. And if he posts videos again, I'll keep taking them down and corrupting their replacements. As an afterthought, I put a kind of GPS tracker on every piece of his equipment I could remotely access. Won't be useful if all the equipment is stationary, but if there were some laptops or phones, we may be able to track his movements."

"Wow." I was too high-pitched and breathy. I sounded like an airhead pinup girl from the '50s. But apparently the vigilante hacking was an aphrodisiac for Max too, because he was looking at my lips and chest and breathing hard.

I wanted him quick and hard and immediately. I put my hands to his shoulders and pushed down until he was seated in his desk chair again. His eyes were blazing behind his glasses, and I was pretty sure he was going to like what I had in mind.

Standing between his knees, I shimmied out of the pajama pants I was wearing and pulled the long-sleeved thermal shirt over my head. "I know I said I'd put on the costume, but—"

"Later," he interrupted, his voice raspy and with that edge of command I'd found so attractive when he started his work. "Get up here."

He didn't have to ask me twice. The chair was wide enough that I could climb on board, my knees on either side of his thighs. His mouth was on my breasts and his hands gripping my ass before I had even caught my balance. "Oh," I moaned, not caring that I was loud. Or that we were partially silhouetted in his window. I might not want to be on the internet, but it didn't bug me if a few folks on the street below caught a dimly lit show.

"I want your mouth," he said, releasing my nipple. I bent down to press my lips to his. We were starving for one another, and the kisses were ravenous and wild. After long minutes of the kind of kissing I'd dream about for the rest of my life, he continued the assault on my neck and I carefully removed his glasses. I wanted more, more, more of him. How had I let days go by without this?

The scruff of his face brushed against my sensitive skin, and I hoped that it would leave marks. When I looked in the mirror tomorrow, I wanted to see evidence of his claim to me. And I wanted to brand him as mine too; I bit his bottom lip hard enough for him to gasp. He returned the favor by pinching my bottom so tightly I squeaked.

His hands were everywhere. Down the muscles of my back, unfastening my bra, sliding under my panties. I yanked his shirt over his head and rubbed myself shamelessly against his wiry body. "Jesus, Tess," he growled.

I raised myself higher on my knees and fumbled with the button on his pants. "Help," I begged. "Get these off. I want you inside."

With a strangled moan, he anchored me to him by fisting my hair and kissing me until I was panting and sobbing. Then he shoved me to one side of the chair and somehow got his pants off his hips. "Good, good," I encouraged.

He laughed. "You still have your underwear on, you know."

I pushed back and smiled down at him. "They're pretty flimsy."

Max's eyes narrowed. Without looking away, he ripped my silky panties right off my hip. "Very efficient," I congratulated, reaching down to grip his length.

He closed his eyes and let out a harsh sigh. "I've never wanted anyone like this," he bit out. "Like I want you."

I wanted to laugh and dance and cry all at the same time. "Same," I assured him.

Then I rose again, guided him inside me, and sat. We both moaned as he filled me. And oh my…it was so good. I rode him, up and down. He put his hands on my hips to guide the rhythm. And there was that deep kissing, broken up by wonderful interludes on my nipples and neck. When we were both close, he moved his hand exactly where I needed it, and I broke over him, with him, screaming and quivering.

Chapter Twenty-Five

THE ALARM ON my phone went off at 8:00 a.m. on Saturday morning. If my body weren't so blissed out from multiple orgasms, I probably would have thrown it across the room. Instead, I just flicked it off and cheerfully swung my legs over the side of the bed.

Max raised his head, blinking. "Who are you and what have you done with Tess?"

I giggled. Me! Giggling before noon on a Saturday. Unprecedented. "Kat's going-away brunch is today. I have all sorts of sisterly duties to attend to."

He lay back down and burrowed under the covers. "Note taken. Tess is allowed to be disturbed from weekend sleep for Stan's Donuts and for her sister. Period."

I agreed with a vehement nod. "All other causes are suspect." Bounding into his bathroom, I made myself walk-of-shame presentable. It was kind of nice how his apartment was only four blocks from mine. Sleepovers were going to be so convenient.

I pulled on my trench coat and propped the Puss in Boots hat on Max's kitchen counter to make him laugh later as he drank coffee. Actually, on that note, I took two minutes to figure out his coffeemaker and started it. Now when he got up for the day, there'd be a full pot waiting. I stuffed the rest of my silly costume back in my bag. That outfit was definitely going to make a reappearance, but when Max least suspected it.

I poked my head into the bedroom one last time before I left. He was on his side, facing the door, eyes closed. For having spent most of the night intertwined, the urge to touch him in some way right this second was surprisingly strong. But I didn't want to wake him.

"Kiss me good-bye," he said grumpily, without opening his eyes.

My face split into the world's sappiest grin, and I obeyed. It was a sweet, soft, chaste, close-mouthed kiss, but my pulse still sped off like a racehorse. I gave in to the need to stroke the back of his head, feel his hair on my fingers, the warmth of his neck against my hand.

His eyes opened as I finally pulled away. All grumpiness had vanished. His lips were curved and his gaze looked as warm and dreamy as mine felt. Good God, if I had seen two people looking at each other like this on the street, I would have wanted to punch them in their dopey faces.

He tugged my ponytail and then let his hand drift to the base of my spine. During the night, he'd often traced his fingers over the design of my tattoo. "Have fun today. I know how important she is to you."

My breath caught in my throat. I loved how he understood. I'd never said to him, "Kat is a huge part of my world, and I'm so happy for her but semi-devastated that she's moving," but with his intelligent and sympathetic eyes on my face right now, it was clear he knew anyway.

"Would you want to come?" The words popped out on their own, surprising me almost as much as they did him. As his sleepy eyes sharpened, I backtracked immediately. "Never mind. I'm sure you're bus—"

"I'd love to."

WE'D DECIDED TO hold Kat's farewell brunch in a private room at an Italian restaurant on the north side of the city. After a quick stop at my apartment to shower and put on a knee-length and long-sleeved purple dress, I gathered up a bunch of Kat in Chicago photos I'd printed and stopped by the florist for the arrangements I'd ordered to decorate the room.

I arrived at the restaurant before anyone else and took twenty minutes to arrange the flowers and photos. When my mom and Kat walked in the room together, Kat's eyes filled. Poor Kat was such a crier. She'd probably be weeping all day. She threw her arms around me. "It looks wonderful in here."

Even my mother smiled and nodded. "I like your dress." Would wonders never cease! I'd worn heels instead of my signature boots today, so maybe that's what she actually liked.

I examined her critically. She was a bit thinner than normal, but she had a lot more color in her cheeks than when I'd last seen her in the hospital. Her eyes were clear, so either she hadn't been crying or she'd invested heavily in Visine. Best of all, she seemed calm, not tense as if she were holding it together under duress. Good. Dr. G and the miracle of chemistry had obviously turned her in the right direction.

As Kat wandered around the room, cooing at the flowers, my mom pulled a manila envelope out of her bag. "The insurance paperwork," she said quietly.

"Ah." I grabbed it and stuffed it in my purse while Kat was distracted. "I'll look at it tonight."

She joined Kat to sip mimosas and laugh over the different pictures. How often would I actually see my mother once Kat was in San Francisco? I saw her monthly now because Kat always organized some sort of meal or outing and guilted us both into attending. But once our intrepid peacekeeper was on the West Coast, would either of us make the effort? I honestly didn't know.

A gaggle of Kat's sorority sisters showed up next, and I schmoozed with them until I could hand them off to my mother. A bunch of Kat's coworkers appeared, followed by a few of her male friends who'd been in love with her for years. Poor saps. I directed them to the bar immediately. And finally...Max walked in. He wore dark jeans and a navy sweater that matched his eyes. His hair was still slightly wet from the shower.

He came straight over, kissed me on the cheek, and rested his hand on my lower back. "H-hi," I said. I'd never liked it before when a guy had been proprietary with body language. But with Max, everything was different.

"Hi yourself," he said, grinning widely.

"Put that smile away," I mock-scolded. "Don't you know that this is a going-away brunch? A sad occasion. I can't allow someone as happy-looking as you to attend."

Max's grin got even bigger. "My apologies. It's just that I had the most incredible night."

Scenes from the two of us in his bed danced through my mind. The way he'd kissed me until I was trembling and begging. How he'd looked at me like I was a goddess when I rolled on top of him. How I'd woken up in the night to find him holding my hand.

Now I was smiling almost as big as he was. "Oh yeah?"

Now he smirked. "Yeah, I took down the servers of an internet asshole." He blinked innocently. "What did you think I was referring to?"

Jesus, that sexy, nerdy confidence. I was a goner.

He gave a lingering look to my purple dress and heels. "I'll always like you in the boots the best, but you're beautiful like this too."

My heartbeat tripped, and I smiled at him so hard that my eyes vanished into happy crinkles.

Which brought Kat to my side approximately one second later, her own eyes bright and expectant. "Kat, this is Max. Max, Kat." I chewed on my lip. Should I have introduced him with some sort of label? Like "my friend?" Or "my coworker?" Those didn't sound right, but we weren't at "boyfriend" yet, were we? "The guy I'm sleeping with" was factually accurate but tacky and...less than what we were.

"This is a surprise!" Kat exclaimed. "But Tess *was* all blushing and bouncing about you when we had breakfast last weekend."

Max's lips twitched as he glanced over at me. "Is that a fact?"

"No," I retorted. "I was blotchy because I was hot and

antsy because I was hungry. It didn't have anything to do with you at all."

"Fair enough." He winked at me and turned back to Kat, who was looking back and forth between our faces like she was watching a tennis match. "Congrats on your new job! I've heard that Starcross is an amazing place to work."

The maître d' pulled me aside to confirm the brunch's schedule. The mingling and mimosas would conclude in five minutes, and then we'd all sit down for a family-style brunch. A few of the guests would give toasts halfway through the meal. Finally, the waiters would serve dessert and I promised we'd vacate their precious private room by 1:00.

When I turned around, Max was trapped with my mother, the poor guy. God only knew what kind of questions she was asking him. Probably something along the lines of: "You seem like such a nice boy; what are you doing with my hurricane of a daughter?" Hopefully, she wasn't telling humiliating Tess stories, like the time we were all out for Easter brunch and I tripped and fell into the buffet's carving station.

Luckily, the waiters began urging the guests to sit at the long table, and I grabbed Max's hand to make sure he sat next to me. Kat sat at the head of the table on the other end, with my mom at her side. Good; no more interrogation. As soon as everyone was seated, I stood again and tapped my champagne glass with a spoon.

"Thank you, everyone, for coming this morning," I said. I looked around the table and dropped my voice to conspiratorial whisper. "Does anyone but me feel like this is a terrible idea though? Does anyone think that Kat should just forget the whole thing and stay in Chicago?"

Everyone laughed and hooted. A few of her glum admirers piped up a loud "yes," which got more chuckles. "Good, good. Glad I'm not alone," I said. I swallowed hard. I needed to keep this short and sweet or I would lose it. Raising my glass, I said. "You are beloved, baby sister. We are so proud of you and happy for you, but we will miss you every day."

Kat nodded furiously, tears flooding her face.

"To Kat!" I finished. The table echoed my sentiment, and I sat down, ready to eat.

"You were so good," Max said, sounding impressed. "Were you nervous?"

"Not a bit," I said honestly. Given the subject matter, I'd had a lump in my throat—but no nerves. Public speaking had never bothered me. It was private conversation I was bad at.

Brunch was actually quite lovely. The food was delicious, Kat looked happy, and every couple of minutes, Max would squeeze my knee under the table.

One of Kat's coworkers was giving a long-winded toast when my phone began to buzz. I was going to send it to voice mail, but I saw it was Paul. Shit. Paul was very respectful of weekends. He wouldn't call unless it was something important. There must have been a disaster happening to one of our clients.

I stood up, phone in hand. "Work," I whispered to Max, and he nodded. I left the private room and walked to the front of the restaurant.

"Hello?"

"Tess, it's Paul. I apologize for bothering you on a Saturday." His tone of voice scared me right away. During a disaster, he always sounded hyper, speaking quickly and in short bursts. But right now, his tone was low and slow and sad.

"What's wrong?" Oh God, maybe this wasn't about work at all. Maybe something bad had happened to someone in his family and he was calling me because he wouldn't be in the office. I hoped it wasn't one of the grandkids.

"I have bad news. Cole Taggert made his phone call about Max, but he didn't call me." Paul paused, allowing my scrambled brain to catch up.

Shit. I'd been right in the first place. He *was* calling about a disaster, just a different type than I expected.

"He called Jack." I closed my eyes. *Checkmate, Cole Taggert.* Sorenson probably started drooling the moment he heard Taggert's voice.

Paul went on. "I just got off the phone with him. Not only is Max to be withdrawn from the applicant pool for the senior programmer position, we're also terminating his temporary contract, effective immediately."

I winced, audibly. Paul heard my whimper of protest and spoke louder. "I tried, Tess. I really did. But Taggert is a powerful man, and knowing Jack, he was thrilled to be able to do him a favor." He sighed. "I might have had more pull in the past, but with my retirement just a couple of months away, I'm a lame duck now. I would have pushed even harder if I thought I had a realistic chance at convincing him."

I believed him. I knew Paul enough to realize he would

have argued, and I'd been around Jack Sorenson enough to know that he'd ignore anything he didn't want to hear.

"I'm calling because I wanted your input on how to tell Max," Paul went on. "He can't come into the office on Monday, so it has to be this weekend. Would you prefer that I call him? Or do you want to let him know?"

Ugh. I wanted to take the coward's way out and make Paul do it and plead ignorance to the whole damn thing. But I couldn't. I knew about it now, and there was no way I could walk back into the party, sit down next to him, and pretend things were fine. "I'll do it." My voice was hoarse.

I walked over to the bar and jabbed my finger at a bottle of bourbon until the bartender got out a tumbler and started pouring. "Double," I mouthed. The minute the glass hit the bar, I snatched it and downed it, almost all in one gulp.

"I'm so sorry, Tess," Paul finished.

Not as sorry as I was.

Chapter Twenty-Six

WITH ANOTHER DOUBLE bourbon in hand, I went back into the private room. No one was seated at the table anymore. People were standing and chatting in small groups, balancing drinks and their dessert plates.

Should I just go straight to Max and tell him about the work situation bluntly, like pulling off a Band-Aid? Or would it be better to wait until we were alone later and ease into it? I honestly didn't know. Max and I were so new. I didn't know the best way to deliver bad news to him yet.

Kat bounded up and gave me a huge hug. I let her squeeze me, breathing in the scent of her hair. Kat still used the same shampoo as when she was a teenager. Sometimes when she hugged me and pulled away, I'd jerk back when I saw her face. Part of me still expected her to be fourteen years old. "This was so wonderful," she said in my ear. "Thank you."

"Anytime," I managed. "I'll throw you a party anytime you come back to visit. So you should visit a lot."

She laugh-sobbed. "I will, I promise." We clung to one another for a long minute, until it got sappy and embarrassing. Over Kat's shoulder, my mother watched us, giving no clue what she was thinking.

Clearing her throat, Kat took a step back and swiped at her tear-stricken face. "I'm such a mess. Do you have makeup in your purse? The college girls want to take a picture."

"Of course." I pointed to the door of the private room, grateful for the pedestrian subject change. Between Paul's call and the bourbon and Kat's hug, I was on the verge of crying too. "It's out by the coat check."

"Hey, I loved meeting Max. He's great." Kat waggled an eyebrow. "Are you changing your ways? Is it serious?"

"Oh, I don't know." Really, I didn't. Did I want it to be serious? Maybe. But we were just starting and I was about to fire him. I couldn't really explain all that to Kat though, so I hedged. "It's not really my modus operandi to get serious," I said lightly.

Her face tightened, then fell. "I guess I feel sorry for him then."

Huh? "Why?"

She widened her eyes and cocked her jaw. "Why? Good God, Tess, he's Daniel 2.0. You'll crush him."

As the shockwave of her words hit me, she was pulled into a sea of sorority girl good-bye hugs. I backed myself slowly into a corner of the room and drank my bourbon. She couldn't be right. Max wasn't anything like Daniel. But the moment that sentence hit my brain, I was bombarded by an onslaught of comparisons.

The way Daniel's brow had furrowed when he was deep in thought over one of his calculations. The way Max rolled up his sleeves and leaned forward until the glare from the computer screen reflected in his glasses.

How Max carried Aria's bags and opened doors. In the years I'd dated Daniel, I hadn't opened a single door when I was with him. He even opened the passenger car door for me every time. He made sure I was the first person on and off the elevator.

Daniel had prided himself on taking care of me. He cooked, he fussed, he pampered. In my mind's eye, I saw Max drawing me a bath.

Regardless of what happened later, for a long time I saw Daniel as a knight in shining armor, swooping in to rescue me when I was downtrodden and weary. And duh. Max was a rescuing knight as well, saving me and all the other Sex Ghost victims from the consequences of our sex tapes.

Oh no. No, no, no.

IN THE MONTHS leading up to my wedding, I lost a bunch of weight for the first and only time in my life. I wasn't trying to look my best for photographs or fit into a smaller-sized white dress. I just couldn't eat.

Which was odd because Kat was happily off to college and thriving at Northwestern. She made a ton of friends easily and still found time to call me and Daniel every day. Her favorite topic of conversation was the stunning Monique Lhuillier dress she would wear as my maid of honor. She emailed Daniel her calculus homework so he could review it before she turned it in.

I loved my first job after graduation. I was working as a systems analyst for a large consulting firm and learning more about technology and corporate culture every day. It was a "work hard, play hard" environment, and I soaked up the intense and competitive atmosphere. I was already trying to figure out which technology niche I wanted to pursue and how I wanted to shape my long-term career.

Despite loving my job, along with losing my appetite, I also stopped sleeping. Sometimes I fell asleep at 10:00, but I'd wake at 3:00 a.m. for the day. Or I might never fall asleep at all. I'd just lie there, listening to Daniel's deep breaths and counting down the hours until I needed to get up and shower.

When I think back to that time now, everything is blurry except the arguments. Daniel and I had never argued in the course of our entire relationship—except for those last few months. Because of that, it was easy for him to brush them off. "You're hungry, stressed, and exhausted," he'd say, walking away.

But I couldn't brush them off or blame them on the fact that I was tired. Why did he get irritated when I wanted to go out with my coworkers for happy hour? Casual friendships were something I'd been denied as a teenager, and I wanted to make up for lost time. Except Daniel couldn't understand why I wanted to laugh over a martini with coworkers instead of coming home to make dinner with my fiancé.

Then one day my boss asked if I wanted to be transferred to one of the most coveted teams in the company. It was an exciting opportunity, but I had to be able to travel from Monday through Friday, three weeks out of the month. I'd burst through the door of our apartment that evening, so exhilarated I could barely talk. In my entire life, I'd barely left Chicago. Now I was going to be given the chance to see cities all over the country.

At first, I thought Daniel was just as happy as I was. He popped the cork on a bottle of champagne and toasted me and my boss, for "recognizing brilliance." But then he said, "How did they take it when you turned down the offer?" Stunned, I said I didn't turn them down. Daniel gave me a look of pure disbelief. "You want to start our married life living so much apart?"

I turned down the offer the next day.

Finally, a month before the wedding, I found him poring over real estate listings for the North Shore. "I don't want to leave the city," I'd protested immediately.

"Not right away," he soothed. "Not for a year or so." He gestured around his one-bedroom condo. "But when we're ready for children, we'll need a real house."

I'd been holding a smoothie, one of the few things I was able to ingest in those months. The instant he said *children*, my stomach closed and I threw the cup in the garbage. He wanted children in a year? I wasn't even twenty-five. I was just starting my career. Goddamn it, I'd just finished raising a child.

By the time my wedding weekend rolled around, I'd lost almost thirty pounds. Everyone told me how beautiful I looked. Well, everyone except my mother. She'd been conspicuously absent during a lot of my engagement, and even when she was around, she usually talked to Kat or Daniel instead of me.

At the rehearsal dinner, Daniel gave a speech to thank

everyone for coming, to celebrate along with him and his "darling angel." I actually didn't know who he was referring to at first. Maybe I wasn't quite sure who exactly I was at that point in time, but I did know I wasn't a darling angel. I was the girl who'd just lied to his face and told him I was drinking a club soda when it was actually a vodka soda. My fourth of the evening. While I couldn't get food down my throat, alcohol slid down just fine.

As the night went on, more and more of Daniel's parents' friends came over to say hi and congratulate us. They joked that soon we'd be neighbors up in Lake Forest or some other hallowed suburb.

Somewhere after that fourth vodka soda, everything that had been fuzzy and blurry in my sleep-deprived mind became suddenly clear. The girl Daniel fell in love with was not the girl I actually was inside. The girl inside wanted to start screaming and never stop. The girl inside wanted to stay out all night and go dancing. The girl inside wanted to work hard and go for every single promotion and not think about having kids for a damn decade. The girl inside didn't want to be taken care of anymore.

But my fiancé didn't know the girl inside, and she was too much of a chickenshit to introduce herself.

Daniel and I were sleeping in separate rooms at the wedding hotel that night. He dropped me at my door and reminded me that he and his mother would be by at 8:00 a.m. to pick me up for my salon appointments. "I've got a key to your room, just in case you oversleep." Of course he did. It was just like Daniel to plan for every possible eventuality. "I love you, darling." He kissed me good night for the last time.

After his footsteps receded down the hall, I went back to the hotel bar and ordered another vodka soda. The bar was mostly empty, and I didn't recognize any of the few late-night drinkers. I didn't have a plan. I was just drunk and desperate.

When the semi-sleazy-looking guy with longish, blond hair offered to buy me a drink, I said, "Yes, please." When he asked me up to his hotel room an hour later, I said, "Let's go to mine instead." I purposefully didn't lock the dead bolt.

On the morning of our wedding, Daniel and his mother found me naked in bed with a guy who turned out to be one of Daniel's cousins. His mother was apoplectic, but I think Daniel would have forgiven me if I'd offered the tiniest excuse. I didn't.

I'll never forget the look on his face that morning. Or the look on Kat's when she learned what I'd done.

I'll never forget how haggard and old Daniel turned in the following weeks as I moved out of his apartment.

I'll never forget how he quit his job and left Chicago because he "couldn't exist in the same city with me."

I'll never forget how I annihilated the one person in my life who had always been kind to me.

"WHAT'S THE MATTER?" Max's voice snapped me out of my reverie, and my memories of Daniel's face were replaced by Max's look of concern. "Why are you standing in the corner drinking bourbon like it's water?"

I glanced around the room. The last brunch guests were filing out, helpfully guided by the waiters leading them to the coat check. My mother was the only other person still in here. She was gathering up flower arrangements on the other side of the room.

"Tess?" Max tried again. "Want me to take you home? What's wrong?"

He was looking down at me with real worry. Something inside snapped.

"Nothing!" I scooted away from him so he couldn't touch me. My voice was sharp and cold. "I need some space, that's all."

He shook his head, looking confused. Ignoring my comment completely, he said, "Are you upset about Kat? Or is it something else?"

"I'm not upset," I lied. "I just told you that I need space. From you. We're not...compatible."

Max went completely still. "What?"

"You're the kind of person who wants to form a life around someone," I explained, my eyes sliding away from his. "I'm the kind of person who makes lives explode." Yep, I was doing this. "I'm the type of person who fucks her fiancé's cousin the night before her wedding."

Max recoiled as though I'd physically hit him. The corners of his mouth turned down, probably in disgust.

"Yes!" I nodded. "That is the correct response to the kind of things I've done. I can't even help you at work anymore. Paul called me. Taggert reached out to Jack Sorenson and you can't have the job. I failed there too."

He mumbled something like, "That's not your fault,"

but I could tell he was still hung up on the fucking-the-cousin thing. Well, good. He should be.

"Paul said you can't even contract for us anymore," I babbled. "Effective immediately, your temp employment with us is over. Which is probably good. You know, so we won't see each other at the office."

Max's mouth dropped open. I'd never heard him yell before. "Do you realize that you're acting batshit crazy?"

I seized on that. "Yes! I am batshit crazy. Nothing you should be around. Ever."

I waited for him to take my words to heart and storm out, but Max stood frozen in place, his mouth still agape. "Tess, I literally have no idea what to say or do right now."

Those words almost broke me. They were so honest, and he sounded bewildered. Angry as well, of course, but mostly bewildered. Kind of similar to the way Daniel had stared at me from the doorway the morning of our wedding. More shocked and heartbroken than angry.

See? Max was already looking at me the same way Daniel had and we'd just begun. This was clearly for the best. I couldn't bear the idea of hurting him someday like I'd hurt Daniel. I literally felt nauseous at the idea of putting him through that kind of pain.

"I don't know what to do," he whispered again, his words an angry plea.

I swallowed and jutted out my chin. Pointed at the door, just in case there was any confusion. "Leave."

So, he did.

He tore his gaze from my face and strode to the door without looking back. His footsteps echoed in my ears. I felt them in my chest; they pounded right in time with my bleeding heart.

And the moment he crossed the threshold and vanished, Kat burst back into the room, clutching the sheaf of insurance paperwork from my mother's hospital stay.

Chapter Twenty-Seven

"WHAT THE HELL is this?" she shrieked. She actually shrieked. My mother and I both flinched and took full steps back. Kat rarely got angry, but when she did...she burned.

She stomped toward my mother, the hand with the papers outstretched. "You were in the hospital? When I thought you were with Wendy?"

My mom's face crumpled, and she sank into the nearest chair without answering. I didn't remember a time in our family's life when Kat screamed at her, and I bet she couldn't either. In high school, I'd done pretty much all of the disciplining, and they'd always been so close. It was jarring for *me* to hear Kat take that tone with her; to my mother, it probably felt like a physical knife in her throat.

For a moment, her trembling lips parted as though about to speak, but no words came out. Where could she start after so many years of intentional silence?

Kat rounded on me then, her eyes huge and wild. "The paperwork was in your purse. You knew she was in the hospital! Why did you lie to me about this?"

Because that's what I do, I almost blurted. *That's what I've always done.* Instead, I licked my lips and fumbled for an excuse. "I didn't want you to worry. You have so much on your plate with the move—"

"Bullshit," she howled. She shook the papers in the air. "It says she was hospitalized for severe depression. That she wasn't able to function at home. That kind of thing doesn't spring up out of thin air."

She looked at my mother, who was now bent over in the chair, her elbows on her knees and her face in her hands. Her shoulders were shaking. Kat's furious expression changed to one of terror.

But when she turned to me again, the fear transitioned straight back to anger. "How long has this been going on? How long has she been sick?"

Oh boy. Kat was going to freak out. But there was no sense in telling partial truths now. She'd only figure it out herself when she was calmer, and then she'd be even angrier. I sighed and did the math in my head. "More than fifteen years."

The hand with the papers dropped to her side, and Kat's face went white. She swayed on her feet. I reached to try to steady her, but she shoved me away.

"It's episodic!" I quickly amended. "She has bad streaks and good ones. She's been mostly good, mostly stable for a whole decade now."

Still ashen, Kat dropped into a chair at the other end of the table from my mother. Almost a full minute passed before she spoke again. "So it wasn't migraines all those years when I was little." Her voice had almost no inflection at all.

I imitated it with my response. "Correct."

Kat turned her back on me and switched chairs so that

she was right next to my mother, who still sat with her face in her hands. "Mom," Kat said gently. She tugged on my mom's wrists until my mom straightened and opened her eyes.

Shame was clear on her face. After all these years, she was still so humiliated by a condition she had no control over. Even though we butted heads constantly, her embarrassment broke my heart.

"Why didn't you ever tell me?" Kat whispered. "I don't want to be angry with you, but I feel so…betrayed. We talk about everything. Or I thought we did. Why would you not share this huge, important, life-impacting, horrible thing with me?" Fat tears plopped out of her eyes and trailed over her bright pink cheeks. Kat was one of those super-annoying girls who looked pretty when she cried. "Did you think I couldn't handle it?"

My mom shook her head furiously and wiped the tears from Kat's face. "No, my beautiful girl. You can handle anything." She cleared her throat. "It was purely selfish of me to keep it from you. I didn't want you to know."

"But why?" Kat pleaded.

My mom closed her eyes. Her voice was so hoarse. "Because I wanted one daughter to think of me as purely 'Mom.' Someone whose love for me wouldn't be complicated and diminished by my illness." She tucked Kat's hair behind her ear. "Someone who still looked at me like a role model. Someone to think I was strong."

Drops of water landed on my hands and ran between my fingers. Oh. Tears. My face was completely wet.

Kat nodded thoughtfully to show she was listening. Then

her eyes crinkled tenderly at the corners, and she gave my mother's shoulders a little shake. "And do you think that I suddenly feel differently toward you now that I know about this?" She raised her voice. "Of course not! Mom! There is nothing that would change the way I look at you or how I feel about you. If anything, I love you even more and think of you as even stronger now that I know what you've been dealing with all this time."

My mom gripped Kat's shoulders, and they clumsily collapsed into a weeping hug. I took a long, shaky breath and finished my bourbon. Good. This was good. *No more secrets.* I'd always known that Kat's love wouldn't change one whit if she knew about my mother's illness. Thank goodness my mother finally realized this too. And if seeing them cling to each other in their little lovefest made me feel like a third wheel...well, I was used to it.

An anxious waiter appeared in the doorway. "Ah, we're going to need this room."

"Ten more minutes." I stared him down until he left.

My mom released Kat and pulled back to look at her tenderly. "I've imagined telling you everything for years, but I was just scared. Thank you for not being angry with me."

Kat managed a watery smile. "Of course I'm not angry with you."

I let out a sigh of relief and rotated my neck. One crisis averted. Now we could move on—

At the table, Kat stood and marched toward me with her hands on her hips. "But I am livid with you, Tess."

I almost laughed. Of course. I wasn't going to get off easy. Kat needed someone to blame for all these years of being in the dark, and it wouldn't be my frail mother.

She advanced on me. "There's no excuse for *you*. You should have told me about this years ago. I get that I was a kid when it all started, but I haven't been a kid for a long time. You had no right to keep this from me! This is my family, for Christ's sake! How could you?"

There were so many things I almost said. That I didn't tell her because my mother always asked me not to. That most of the time I actually did still think of her as a kid. That I wanted to protect her.

But I knew that none of these answers would placate her. She wanted to lash out. I was feeling guilty about this and so, so awful about Max…I deserved a little wrath right now. I could be her target. So I just shrugged and looked at the floor.

"What the fuck is wrong with you, Tess?" I almost flinched again; Kat never used the f-word. "I love you, but you can be so goddamn hurtful. You honestly make the worst emotional decisions of anyone I've ever met."

Her words pierced me like an arrow to naked skin and vulnerable organs. The day's events had stripped me of any armor, so I just absorbed the pain. She wasn't just speaking of my reticence about my mother's condition. I knew my sister.

"Kat, no—" My mother softly tried to interrupt.

I waved her off. "She's talking about Daniel too."

Kat's eyes blazed. "So what if I am? That was the last time we all cried so much, right? And again, it was because of something Tess did." My mother drew in a sharp breath, but I held my ground. The words hurt—but she wasn't wrong.

"Kat," I tried softly. "I told you at the time and I'll tell you again now. I'm *so sorry* that you were hurt so much when Daniel and I split up. It was incredibly unfair—"

"I'm not just upset for myself!" she yelled. "I'm not that shallow. Jesus, Tess. Do you have any idea what it's like watching the person you love most in the world blow up her life? And for no reason!" I let out a helpless wheeze of air. She'd loved Daniel so much. I could never make her understand.

Her lips curled into a thoughtful sneer. "Sometimes I feel like you're the emotional equivalent of someone going around accidentally killing people with her car...you don't mean to do it, but it's negligent homicide just the same." She shook her head, looking self-righteous and contemptuous. "To yourself and others, you're just a life-ruiner—"

"Katharine, that is enough!" My mother's voice cracked through the air like a whip.

Kat and I both gaped at her. Kat probably because my mother had never yelled at her and me because...uh...it almost sounded like she was defending me. That couldn't be right.

She pushed herself out of her chair so that she was standing too. "Tess's behavior at the wedding...well..."

"Holy shit," I exclaimed. We were really going to do this, huh? Seven years later, my mom was finally going to talk to me about Daniel? We'd never discussed it before. Never. When everything erupted on my wedding day, she'd cooperated with Daniel's fuming mother to shut everything down, but she never talked to me about it. She never even cared enough to ask why I'd ruined it all.

Until now, apparently. "*You* want to talk about Daniel now?" I gripped my hands into fists because they were shaking. "You finally want to ask why I slept with his cousin?"

"Heavens, no. I know why you did that." After all these years, my mother could still shock me. Kat gasped.

"Oh really?" I asked, sarcasm and skepticism dripping from the words. She knew nothing about me, then or now.

My mother walked to me and looked me straight in the eye. For just a moment, it was less like looking at an older version of Kat and more like looking in a mirror. "You did what you did because you knew that marrying Daniel would have been a huge mistake."

Kat let out a murmur of protest, and my mom half turned to give her an emphatic head shake. "He didn't love the real Tess, sweetheart. He loved the Tess she'd had to be for all those years taking care of us."

She turned back to face me. "You didn't want to go from dutiful daughter and half mother to Kat to being a dutiful wife to Daniel. You wanted to be a rising star at work. You wanted to go a bit wild." She cleared her throat and raised an eyebrow. "While that streak has gone on longer and been more extreme than I personally like, you deserved it."

Reeling, I didn't even pull away when she tentatively reached out, put her hand on my shoulder. "You deserved to be an individual. To grow into your own woman instead of being defined by everything that had happened and by everyone around you."

She tucked my hair behind one ear, just like she'd done with Kat. "The thing with Daniel's cousin…well. Tess, you did the right thing in a terribly wrong way."

More tears fell from my eyes to the floor. The shock of her words, the shock that she was dead-on right, had numbed me a little, but my body was apparently reacting in all sorts of ways.

Kat walked slowly back to the table and plopped down hard onto one of the chairs as though my mother's words had vanquished her ability to stand. I followed and dropped onto the chair next to her.

The anxious waiter stuck his head back in the room. "Ten more minutes!" I barked. It looked like he might protest, but confronted with three weeping women, he fled.

My mom sighed and sat down as well. "I never should have let your engagement get as far as it did. I knew you were miserable. You'd never have gotten so skinny otherwise," she said wryly, and I almost smiled.

"I should have made you face it, but I was in denial too." She gestured between herself and Kat. "Daniel was so good to Kat and me that I wanted him to be right for you. But deep down, I knew he wasn't." She looked down at the table, avoiding eye contact. "During your engagement, you lost weight and stopped sleeping. I had one of my worst depressive episodes."

What? My eyes popped to her face. She just smiled sadly. "Thankfully, I got myself out of that one."

I closed my eyes and scrunched up my face. "The morning after the non-wedding, I cooked myself a full pan of scrambled eggs and ate the entire thing. That night, I slept eight straight hours."

She sob-laughed. "Your body knew it was the right thing,

even if your heart and mind were torn."

The room was silent for a long minute before my mom spoke again. She sounded exhausted. "We should have had this conversation a long time ago, girls. That's my fault, and I'm sorry."

The radiator in the corner of the room hissed on, flooding the space with warm, stuffy heat. "It's not all your fault," I heard myself say, as if from a great distance. "We're both bad at this kind of stuff."

"You really, really are," Kat muttered. "Both of you. Just awful."

I hiccupped a laugh and risked a look at her face. The rage was gone, replaced by a wide-eyed and wary look. I certainly couldn't blame her. My mom and I had put on quite a show today. Strangely united, we'd given her a lot to process.

I had so much to pore over myself. To think, all this time there'd been someone who understood. And for that someone to be my mother. I pictured my brain exploding.

The waiter stuck his head in the room again, a look of resolve on his face. A look that quickly disappeared as the three of us yelled in unison, "Ten more minutes!"

Chapter Twenty-Eight

THE NEXT DAY, Kat left for California. The three of us spent the morning shoving boxes into her U-Haul. We worked mostly in silence, speaking only of traffic and routes and the best cities for her to stop at during her cross-country journey.

When she was finally fully loaded and ready to go, my mother ran to the nearest Starbucks to get her a coffee for the road. Kat jiggled her keys and swallowed. "I'm sorry I said those things yesterday."

"You don't have to apologize." I sighed. "After Daniel, you were the one I hurt the most by doing what I did, and I should have explained myself a long time ago."

"Yes, you should have," she said bluntly. "Don't treat me like a child anymore, OK?"

"I'll try not to," I promised.

"And I'll try not to be such a brat." Her voice was teasing, but there was also sincerity in it. I bent over and hugged her tightly. Part of me wished we'd never had yesterday's confrontation; what if it changed things between us? But the bigger part knew it was long overdue and that all relationships changed.

Mom returned and handed Kat her venti latte. "Don't

drive for more than five hours at a time," she warned.

"I won't, I promise." Kat took a deep breath. "I'm leaving now," she said firmly, "before we all start bawling again."

"Call me tonight," my mother and I said in unison.

I savored her laugh. Kat's laugh sounded different over the phone. It lacked all the depth and richness it carried in person. "I will call you both." Tears were in her voice, so I practically tossed her into the cab of the truck. She was right. We were ten seconds from another sob fest.

My mother and I watched the truck disappear down Fullerton, headed for 90 West. When it was out of sight, I blew out a long breath. Now I just had to make it back to my apartment before collapsing. After yesterday's meltdown, I'd drank two glasses of red wine on an empty stomach before crawling into bed, and the resulting hangover was screaming in my temples and gut.

I'd pushed everything Max-related into a deep, dark pit in the center of my chest, but shit wasn't going to stay there. Between Kat's departure and the Max fiasco, I had a solid Sunday afternoon of crying planned.

"Take some Advil, for God's sake, Tess. I can almost see your headache." My mother handed me a couple of pills and a bottle of water.

Too tired to argue with her, I gulped them down. "I'll call you tomorrow," I said dutifully. I doubted that either of us would want to chat, but I'd need to check that Kat's physical departure hadn't triggered another depressive episode.

"I'll drive you home now," she said. She was using her no-nonsense tone, and if I refused, it would definitely lead to a fight. I was too weary for a fight today. Plus, a warm ride in her car sounded a lot easier than navigating the CTA right now. So I just shrugged and got in.

When we pulled up to my apartment building, she parked and turned off the engine. "Oh. Uh, you don't have to come up," I said. I really, really didn't want company today. Especially hers. I was still too overwhelmed by everything that had happened the day before. "It's super messy."

"So what else is new?" she shot back. "I'm coming up. I want to talk."

"Fine." I got out, resisting the urge to slam the car door. She didn't deserve a Tess tantrum, but God, I just wanted to be alone.

I plopped on my sofa as soon as we entered my apartment. I hadn't been expecting guests; I had no refreshments to offer. Undaunted, she looked through my kitchen cupboards until she found my ancient teapot and got it going on the stove. "I don't have any tea," I called rudely.

She opened her bag and pulled out a box of her favorite honey vanilla chamomile blend. "I brought my own."

Foiled again. I waited in silence until the pot began to whistle and she poured two mugs. I almost resisted out of spite when she handed me one, but damned if a hot cup of tea didn't actually sound perfect right now.

"What did you want to talk about?" I finally asked, curiosity triumphing over my annoyance. I couldn't remember the last time my mom had initiated a Talk with me. Yesterday we'd both been forced into one by circumstance. Good God, I hoped she didn't think that was the new normal.

"Some of your behavior," she said primly.

Some of my behavior? Like I was a bratty teenager? Unbelievable. I squinted at her, the weight of sadness on my chest transitioning into a flare of anger.

She ignored my expression and went on. "Your little outburst at the end of the brunch yesterday. How you sent Max packing for no reason."

I glared at her and scooted a few inches farther away. "It wasn't for 'no reason.' You saw what I did to Daniel. Maybe you understood why I did it, but it was still a terrible thing to do. I hurt him so badly. Kat was right. Max is just like Daniel. I can't hurt him like that."

She leaned back against the sofa cushion and steepled her fingers in her lap. She opened and closed her mouth a few times, as though she was choosing her words carefully. "With all due respect to Kat, I spoke to Max, and I don't think he's much like Daniel at all."

Before I could protest, she held up an imperious finger and went on. "Sure, they're both kind and intelligent—unlike every other guy you've introduced us to in seven years," she said dryly. "You can forgive Kat for making too basic of a connection."

I exhaled loudly through my nose, shaking my head quickly. Mom was definitely wrong.

"Listen," Mom insisted. "Apart from being nice and smart, Max in no way reminded me of Daniel." She held up her hand and began ticking off points on her fingers. "Daniel was, in a wonderful way, simple. He cared intensely about his work and his family, but didn't have a lot left over for anything else."

I stopped shaking my head. She had a point. Daniel would talk enthusiastically for hours about anything related to his job, and he knew every single birthday, hobby, hope, and dream of every member of his extended family. But he tended to tune out when I rhapsodized about one of my favorite mystery novels or when I wondered aloud about how the hundreds of emerging tech companies would change the Chicago business landscape.

"Max seems more complex to me," she continued. "While he clearly loves his family and his IT work, I talked to him for fifteen minutes and our conversation went in a lot of different tangents. He was enthusiastic and interested in everything." Memories of Max reciting the history of bourbon and the hundreds of books on his Kindle popped into my head, unbidden.

She smiled, her lips smirking a bit. "Max also seems a touch more wicked."

"Mother!" I exclaimed, heat streaking up my neck and onto my cheeks. Maybe we were bonding, but we were not going to compare the men sexually.

Of course, now that the thought was in my head, I couldn't help it. Daniel hadn't been a prude or anything, but sex with him had been more about comfort than excitement. More gentle enjoyment than frantic pleasure. He was always tender and reverential.

I'd only had sex with Max a couple of times, but I'd, uh, describe it very differently.

"I wasn't speaking about the bedroom," my mom said, fully smirking now as she clearly understood the turn of my thoughts. "I just meant that he seems a little spicy, a little edgy with his humor. He's quick, he's witty, he likes to banter. Which you absolutely need to keep you interested."

I felt disoriented again. All these years, I'd felt unseen by my mother. But she'd been paying close attention.

"Finally," she said, pointing hard at me, "the biggest difference is how they each see you. Daniel imagined you as a delicate flower who wanted to be worshipped and cared for. Someone who wanted the difficult decisions made for her. Someone who was looking for a champion." Guilt swamped me for the thousandth time. He wasn't entirely wrong; that's how I was when he first met me.

Again, my mother followed my thoughts. "You were that way for six months tops, Tess. After that, you struggled. You tried—in ways that were too small, unfortunately—to show Daniel your real self. But he wasn't interested in changing his fantasy for the reality. He didn't want to see that you didn't need a champion."

Her tone brightened. "But Max seems to see you for exactly who you are. I suspect he's encountered you at less than your best already—" uh, yeah, multiple times "—and he was still looking at you yesterday like you were the sun."

In my head, I heard Max's voice from Fizz. Y*ou charge around the office in those goddamn boots, and I can't take my eyes off you. I sit in meetings and watch everyone get nervous when you zero in on them with your smart-ass mouth. You are the most independent woman I've ever met, and it turns me on like I've never been turned on in my entire fucking life.* I'd remember that little speech until I was dead in the grave. It was the best thing I'd ever heard in my entire life.

Daniel would have disliked the boots. He hated the rare

occasions when my smart-ass mouth appeared around him.

Before I could reconcile all of this, my mom's voice got louder. "One other thing, Tess. I understand the guilt. But you didn't *kill* Daniel. He had a bad year or two." Her tone turned sarcastic, maybe a little bitter. "We've all had bad years." She brushed her hands together briskly. "He survived. He's probably very happy by now with someone much more suited to him."

She took a deep, bracing breath before pulling me into her arms for a full-on hug. I turned stiff as a tree trunk, my eyes as wide as saucers. We hadn't hugged in years. But she didn't pull away. "It's time to let all that go," she whispered. "It's in the past, and the only person you're hurting now is yourself."

"You sound like my therapist." I sniffled, still rigid against her.

There was a long pause. "I didn't know you were seeing a therapist," she said. "How long?"

"Off and on since the wedding," I said.

I felt her nod against the top of my head. "Good." Gradually, I softened against her until my head was on her shoulder, and I just closed my eyes and breathed in and out. We sat like this for a long, long time.

"Do you think that maybe we could go together sometime?" My mom's voice was quiet and hesitant. "To therapy, I mean. I've wanted to do that with you for years. To try to heal from everything that happened while you were in high school. You were put in an atrocious position. I know there's resentment on both sides... We've never recovered. But I very much want to."

If she could be this brave and plainspoken, so could I. "Me too."

Something she'd said yesterday to Kat had been niggling on the edge of my mind and conscience. "You said one of the reasons you didn't ever want to tell Kat about...stuff...was that you wanted one daughter whose love for you wasn't complicated and diminished."

She nodded again. I cleared my throat. "It's true that...ah...things got complicated. But..." Jesus fucking Christ, I hated these true confessions. This month really was going to be the death of me. I forced it out anyway. "My love for you was never diminished though."

She squeezed me tighter, and I was beyond grateful that she didn't say anything in response. A little unnerved, however, to realize it was because she was holding back sobs.

I needed to lighten the mood ASAP. "I'd say we should take a selfie of us hugging on my couch and send it to Kat, but I think she'd be so shocked she'd drive off the road."

She snorted and then smiled ruefully. "You know, she'd probably think it was worth it for her to move to San Francisco just to get us talking like this again."

"Then don't ever tell her," I said quickly.

"I'm not stupid." My mom sniffed. "Between the two of us, we'll concoct some sort of plan to get her back here in a few years."

"Deal." We smiled at each other until I felt uncomfortable again and had to deflect. "Well, Mom," I said breezily. "After such a cathartic scene, I feel like that uplifting Carly Simon song from *Working Girl* should be playing in the background."

Immediately, she held up her phone. "'Let the River Run'? I have it on iTunes. Should I put it on?"

Terrified she was serious, I leapt back a foot before I saw that her shoulders were shaking with repressed laughter. I'd truly forgotten how funny she could be. Before I knew it, I was giggling too.

Chapter Twenty-Nine

THERE WAS SO much whispering and so many puzzled looks among the programmers about Max's abrupt departure that I finally called Abigail into my office on Monday afternoon and told her that what she'd originally predicted had come true. Max was mysteriously blacklisted in the tech community and it had ruined his chances at our company. I really wanted to blab the whole story about Taggert, but it wasn't my tale to tell. I'd already told Paul and it hadn't helped one bit.

"This is so shitty!" She ran her fingers through her hair until it stood out from the sides of her head in purple spikes. "Ridiculously unfair!"

"Yeah." I swallowed hard. What else was there to say? It *was* shitty and unfair and our efforts had failed. She looked so outraged that I quickly went on before she organized some sort of developer walkout. "Paul tried to fight it. You can't be mad at him. He was overruled by Jack."

I lifted my hands in a pathetic shrug. "Max probably wouldn't want any more gossip spreading around, OK? I just wanted to let you know what happened so you guys didn't think he made some sort of coding error or upset anyone here."

She snorted. "Max doesn't make coding errors, Tess. He ran circles around everyone here, and we have a pretty sharp team. Plus, he's about the nicest person I've ever met. Who would he upset?" With one of her trademark eye rolls, she left my office.

He'd upset me plenty. Just by existing.

Ugh. This hollowed-out feeling would eventually disappear, right? The leaden, suffocating feeling on my chest had to evaporate soon, didn't it? I'd only known the guy for a month. It would be completely ridiculous to keep feeling like the world had ended. I knew that. I wasn't some sixteen-year-old dealing with her first bad breakup.

But I was having a hard time eating. I woke every night around 3:00 a.m. and stared at my dark ceiling until the alarm went off.

Jack Sorenson was correct in that signing Away-Ho brought a lot of new business through the door. But despite the increased workload caused by the influx of new clients, the week dragged on. Paul was in a bad mood on Tuesday because the Cubs were definitively not going to the World Series this year. On Wednesday, Kat arrived in San Francisco and sent me dozens of photos of her minuscule new apartment. By Friday, the photos included new faces. Kat had always made friends quickly.

I called my mother every day to make sure that Kat's departure hadn't sent her into another downward spiral. She didn't appreciate my heightened vigilance. "I'm not the one speaking in a monotone like a depressed serial killer, you know."

The only thing that made me feel even the tiniest bit better was the world's reaction to the mysterious vanishing of the Fucking Sex Ghost's site. Micki, Joe, and Toby sent me links to a bunch of online speculation from the Ghost's newsletter recipients. Theories ranged from "the dude probably got arrested" to "some bitch put him in the ground, yo."

Toby followed up with a group text. *Did you get the Ghost locked up?*

To which Joe responded: *Nah. Tessie totally murdered him.* Thumbs-up emoji.

I stalked the Facebook group of the FSG's victims and felt warm inside when I read their happy, relieved posts. One of his California victims wrote, "For the first time I can go on a date with someone new and not be terrified that he's going to Google me and see me with my ex on the Ghost's site!"

One of the Texas girls responded, "Yes! Except for me it's a job interview!"

The same woman who had written the *New York Post* editorial that I'd read in Natasha Long's office wrote a follow-up letter. "My sources say that it wasn't a legal action that got the site taken down. And there's no way in hell the Ghost took it down on his own. So, with no proof, I'm going to choose to believe that this was the victims of NCP's answer to the #metoo movement. I'm choosing to picture some glorious vigilante who did the right thing. I'll never know how it happened, but all I can say is thank you. Thank you to the Ghost killer."

#ghostkiller even trended on Twitter for a day or two.

I wondered if Max was following all of this too. I hoped

so. He didn't get much else out of his association with me. At least he deserved to feel like the hero he was.

On Friday afternoon, Jack Sorenson officially offered me the VP position. As soon as I verbally accepted, Paul sent out his official "I'm retiring" email to the entire staff. While I'd known it was coming, seeing the details of his departure in black and white made me more emotional than I would have expected. First Kat, now Paul. Two of the closest people in my life, leaving my day-to-day world. Biting my lip, I reached around to trace the anchor on my lower back.

In Paul's email, he said he knew the transition would be seamless because I was his successor. It put a lump in my throat—one I quickly had to swallow as dozens of staff stopped by my office to congratulate me.

It should have been one of my favorite workdays of all time. But all I could think about was how much better it would be if Max were still here. How he'd lean on my office wall and congratulate me with a wide grin. How he'd looked across the conference table in the meeting with Away-Ho and said, "She's the boss."

I stayed at the office late, plowing through work that didn't need to be done until next week. But why leave early? I wasn't hungry for dinner. Kat was gone, and I wasn't feeling up to a night at Fizz, trading quips with Micki, Joe, and the guys. When I heard the vacuum cleaners from the cleaning crew, I reluctantly got to my feet. A bottle of wine and whatever looked good on Netflix—it'd probably be my new Friday night routine, at least until it didn't hurt as much to breathe or move or think.

I left the office and skidded to the Merchandise Mart

train station as quickly as I could. The temperature had dropped steeply this week as though the Chicago winter had woken up early in a pissy mood and said, "It's November now, bitches. Brace yourselves." I hated when the temp dipped below thirty degrees in November. When you knew warm weather wouldn't arrive until late May, the early cold just made the winter seem endless.

Waiting on the train platform for the "L" with the wind howling through was pure torture. The inch of bare skin between the bottom of my skirt and the top of my boots was going to be raw and chapped. No more skirts or dresses for a while. The train finally roared in and I hopped on, shivering. I found a seat, but the train grew more and more crowded as we headed north. Soon, a guy was standing right over me, just the way Max had stood the night he finally told me the story about Aria.

I closed my eyes. Max. If I ever wanted to eat or sleep again, maybe I needed to stop pushing him out of my head. Because when my guard was down, usually after a couple drinks while I stared at the ceiling, all I did was think about him. His face, his voice, his hands. Every word he'd ever said to me, and how they made me feel. How I constantly wanted to impress him. How he made me want to be the best possible Tess. How I wanted him texting me, insulting me with that twinkle in his eye, feeding me donuts, staring at my face while I came, putting me in a bath when I cried. How I wanted to do all of that back to him times infinity. How I wanted him—

Actually, that was it in a nutshell. I just wanted him. In my life, in my world, in my head, in my bed. He was my new green eggs and ham.

But how could I convince him of that when I'd acted like such a bitchy nutcase? He hadn't so much as butt-dialed me since Kat's brunch, and I couldn't blame him.

As the train approached my stop, a series of get-Max-back ideas danced through my mind. Maybe I could wear the Puss in Boots outfit over to his house and try to lure him back through sex? Hmm. That would be easiest on me, and Max did like the costume. But sex had never been the problem with us. My gut told me it was too flippant of an approach. I couldn't erase what I'd said and done with a manipulative bout of sex. Even if it would be fun.

Maybe I could write him a letter? A long one that described everything that happened with Daniel and the life-hangover it'd left me with. One that tried to explain how I'd gotten confused and pushed him away. Was that too old-fashioned? Or maybe just too chickenshit?

Probably. If I really wanted him, I'd need to be an actual grown-up. I'd need to invite him out, pray to God he accepted, and then explain in person. After that, the ball would be in his court. Could he forgive me for freaking out? Would he want to try dating me? My stomach roiled. It was a perfect setup for a stinging rejection.

But...he was worth the risk. Even if he gave me the verbal equivalent of a slap in the face.

I descended the "L" station stairs, took a deep breath, and pulled my phone out of my pocket. Crap. My phone was completely dead. In all the fuss of my promotion announcement, I hadn't plugged it in today. Oh well. I could use the walk home to rehearse my "I'm sorry and I swear on all the French fries and bourbon in the world that I won't push you away again" speech.

I was so focused on putting words together in my mind that the cold walk home took no time at all. But as I approached my building, I saw a truly bizarre sight. Roz was pacing the block...dressed in black leather?

When she saw me, she broke out in a full-on sprint before I could protest. "Where have you been? Why is your phone off?" she screeched. "Mohawk's going crazy looking for you!"

"What?" I said. "Why? Is Micki OK? And what are you wearing?"

She shooed me emphatically through the front door and up the stairs to my apartment. "Plug your phone in! Call her back! Now!"

I wanted to demand answers, but she was already half wheezing with excitement. "Down, girl," I ordered, pushing her gently into a chair. "I've had a hell of a past month. I am not starting November with one of Tess and Roz's Excellent Adventures at the ER."

As soon as I got the phone plugged in, I dialed Fizz. Micki picked up on the first ring. "Holy shit, Tess." Micki's voice was hushed and the background was quiet. She couldn't be tending bar. "I'm in my office. The Ghost is here. At Fizz!"

I froze. "What?"

"He's asking around about you! He asked me about a tall woman with reddish-blond hair who hangs out here a lot. This is nuts!"

Nuts? Actually...no. I'd spent a lot of time thinking

about the FSG's victims and how they were reacting to the site vanishing, but I'd strangely spent almost no time considering the actual Ghost's reaction. And I should have. After all, Max and I had demolished the man's livelihood and celebrity in one fell swoop.

She lowered her voice to a whisper, sounding worried. "Listen, he's putting on the charm to anyone who talks to him, but he looks angry to me. He's barely drinking, and he's not looking for a hookup." She paused. "I was so shocked to see him in person that I just walked away when he asked about you. Luckily, Joe also pretended not to know who he was talking about, so the others followed his lead. But there was a lot of confused eye contact among them, and I think the Ghost knew they were lying."

My mind was racing. Somehow dear old Westley knew the site crash was related to me. Maybe he'd run some analytics software on his servers and had seen that my video was the very first thing deleted before Max started wreaking the rest of his havoc? But what was the connection to Fizz?

"Of course, it's Joe's fault that he's here in the first place," Micki muttered.

I snapped back to attention. "What do you mean?"

"The idiot posted something on Twitter. Something like 'I know the #ghostkiller. Chicago ladies don't stand for that kind of shit.'" She huffed. "I made him delete it, but it was up for a full day before I saw it."

Now that made sense. If Westley was searching for clues and saw that post, the next step would have been to examine Joe's social media. He'd posted dozens of pictures of us at Fizz over the years. Westley would have recognized me and put two and two together.

Adrenaline coursed through my veins. *Yes!* This was going to be a kick-ass Friday after all.

"So don't come in tonight. We can beat Joe up together tomorrow. If the Ghost asks me about you again, I'm going to say that you left the neighborhood," Micki went on. "Hopefully, he'll just leave."

"No!" I exclaimed. "Tell him I'm on my way. Micki, do not let him leave before I get there." Sure, I'd already taken away his money and his fame. But that wasn't nearly enough.

Roz did a fist pump, and I suddenly understood her outfit. I covered the phone's mouthpiece and gave her a once-over. "Are you trying to look like Black Widow from the Avengers?"

She nodded briskly. "And I'm totally pulling it off."

Actually, she really was. Scar Jo at seventy would have nothing on Roz. But before I could verbally agree, Micki shouted, "Do not come in, Tess! That is a terrible idea. I don't want you to get hurt, and I don't want trouble in my bar."

"Trust me," I soothed. "Neither of those things is going to happen. I'll be there in fifteen minutes."

As soon as I hung up on Micki, Roz leapt to her feet again. "We just need to stop at my apartment and get my gun out of the safe."

"Forget it," I said sternly. "You know how I feel about you and that fucking firearm." Her elderly age was not the sole reason every resident of our building treated Roz with respect. Everyone lived in fear of the armed and nearsighted vigilante on the second floor.

Disappointment shaded her features, but she quickly rebounded. "My Taser then."

"Jesus Christ." I pointed her at the chair again and dialed Natasha Long's cell phone. Since it'd been printed on her business cards, I figured it was fair game to call even after hours on a Friday. That's what having a lawyer on retainer was for, right? (Did I have her on retainer? I didn't remember, and I didn't care.) Hopefully, she didn't have fancy plans tonight. I let it ring through to voice mail. Undaunted, I kept calling back again and again. Usually people intuit an emergency after such behavior and will eventually pick up.

On my fourth straight call she answered, her voice tense. "Yes?"

"So sorry to bother you, Ms. Long. It's Tess Greene." I was a little out of breath from all the excitement. I hadn't anticipated a face-to-face encounter with my nemesis when I'd chosen my tightest pencil skirt this morning. "I know where the Sex Ghost is. He's here in Chicago, at a bar on the north side." I rattled off Fizz's address. "Can you help me with the whole bench warrant thing? He can be arrested, yes?"

I heard her excuse herself and the sound of a chair backing away from a table. I'd caught her on a night out after all. She must have stepped out from the restaurant to the street because I heard an ambulance going by.

"I can help," she said simply. If I weren't mistaken, there was a note of excitement in her voice. "I'll call my contacts at police headquarters immediately and get the ball moving. Since it's not an emergency, it may take a few minutes though. How can you be sure he'll stay at the bar?"

I'm quite certain the smile on my face at the moment would have scared any living man. Maybe even a few dead ones. "Oh, he'll stay."

Chapter Thirty

ROZ TRIED TO make me put on a black leather ensemble too but let me off the hook when I admitted that I didn't want to be compared to her and found lacking. I did change into jeans and put on a fresh coat of bright red lipstick though.

Westley was easy to spot at Fizz. He sat stiffly at the bar, nursing some sort of clear drink, and he constantly scanned the room. The dumbass actually rested his eyes on my face for a moment before continuing his scan.

Five, four, three, two, one. His gaze popped back to me. I cocked my head and nodded at him in recognition. He launched himself off his stool in my direction.

Behind the bar, Micki straightened like a soldier. I gave her a reassuring wave. At my side, Roz bounced on the balls of her feet. "Go sit down," I whispered. She looked so disappointed to be cut out of the action I threw her a bone. "I'll signal you if I need backup, OK?" She nodded importantly and marched to a table at the corner. I hoped to God she wouldn't tase somebody by accident. Or on purpose.

Striding toward me, Westley's facial expression underwent a metamorphosis. Sitting at the bar, he'd tried for a casually pleasant look. But Micki had read him right. An undercurrent of anger had tensed his jaw and temple too much for him to look casual or pleasant.

Now though, as he headed straight for me, he forced the tension away, melted his features into the cocky, flirty guy who'd hit on me five years back. Man, that was a long time ago. It seemed like a different life. Hell, it kind of was.

As he approached, he held up his arms as if to give me a hug. "Do you remember me? It's been a minute. It's so great to see you, pretty girl," he exclaimed, looking at me from head to toe. "Don't you clean up nice! I almost didn't recognize you."

I sidestepped his arms. I didn't want him to touch me for one second. Beneath my cool exterior and exultation at being the bringer of the Sex Ghost's legal doom was a burning, molten layer of pure fire at how he'd used me and all the other poor girls on his site. And wow. That anger wanted a chance to come out and play before the cops arrived. "Hello, Westley."

Beaming, he put a hand over his heart in a sort of "aw shucks" gesture. "You do remember me!" He pointed toward the bar. "Can I buy you a drink?"

I was tempted if only to have something to throw in his face. "No thanks," I said. "Being drunk would definitely make it easier to spend time in your presence, but I can get my own."

His eyebrows shot up and then down, as though he didn't know if I was joking or how he should respond. Finally, he arranged his lips in a mock pout. "I seem to remember you having fun." His expression tried for jovial, but his voice was icy.

I snorted. "We have different definitions of fun then. Because for me, having unenjoyable sex only to find out that it was posted on the internet years later without my permission is not my idea of fun."

I gave him a cheeky grin and spoke in a whisper I was positive no one else in the bar could hear. "For fun, I like to play with servers. Offshore ones are my fav."

His eyes narrowed. "You did do it then, didn't you?" If I were the type of girl to shiver at the sound of a pathetic man's rage, I would have done it then.

Instead I marched myself to the bar, and Micki handed me a bourbon without being asked. "Thanks," I mumbled to her without moving my lips. "Cops'll be here soon. I'll get him outside when I know they're coming." Her lips turned up in an approving grin, and she moved to the other end of the bar, whistling.

A few stools down, Joe looked between Westley and me, eyes narrowed. "You all right, GK?"

My lips twitched at the new nickname. Ghost Killer. I liked it much better than Tessie, but it was a little inaccurate. Tomorrow I'd have to tell him that I'd only hired the Ghost Killer. It didn't have quite the same ring to it. "I'm fine."

I watched Westley in the mirror behind the bar. He looked furious, but he took a deep breath and pasted on that same fake smile and walked over to stand behind me. He tried to order a drink, but Micki ignored him. Finally, he perched next to me and met my eyes in the mirror. When he spoke, his lips were so close to my ear I could feel his disgusting breath. "Look, we can fix this. Now that I know you are…" he paused, obviously unsure how to give a compliment to a woman "…a person to take seriously." He cleared his throat. "My bad, OK?"

I flicked my eyes over his face dismissively. "Yes, Westley. It was definitely 'your bad.'" I've always hated that expression. I took a swallow of my bourbon and grinned at Micki's back. She'd given me a free double of Woodford Reserve.

"So, listen," Westley said, vibrating on the stool next to me. I marveled at how diminished he was since I'd seen him last. He couldn't sit still, and there was a layer of sweat on his pale face. Either he was financially devastated by the loss of his seedy livelihood or he had substance abuse issues. Probably both. "How 'bout we come to some sort of arrangement? Like a partnership?"

Oh, I just couldn't resist. I licked my lips and cooed at him. "You mean, you would want me for a real partner?" My voice was ridiculously breathy and high. He didn't seem to notice. He just nodded quickly. I batted my eyelashes. "So I would make money too whenever you record girls and put them on the internet?"

He bobbed his head up and down. "That's right! You give me back my videos and remove all the viruses or whatever's all over my system and I'll share the profits of my business with you."

My phone buzzed in my pocket. I glanced down at it surreptitiously. It was a text from Natasha Long. *Two cop cars and myself en route. ETA five minutes.* Perfect.

Westley was too busing waxing on about our future partnership to even notice that he'd lost my focus. "What do you say, Good Time? Fifty/fifty, OK?" God, he was stupid. Did he actually think I'd want to be referred to by his sex tape name for me?

"Why don't we talk about it a little more outside?" I suggested in my baby-doll voice.

He held out his arm. "Lead the way." He opened the front door for me, and we stood on the sidewalk. This stretch of Ashland was always busy during the day because of all the auto repair and other small businesses. At night, though, Fizz was the only bar on the block and it was much quieter.

Westley opened his backpack and showed me the laptop inside. "OK, partner. What do we need to do to fix my system and get back online? We're losing money every second the site is down."

I couldn't even pretend anymore. My eyes and voice went back to normal. "Fuck you." I laughed. "As if I would ever be party to such a shitty and hurtful and criminal enterprise. Do you have any idea of the pain you've caused people? The lives you've derailed, maybe permanently?"

Oh, I wished every single one of his victims were here with us right now. There were more than seventy recordings on the site when Max took it down. I pictured seventy angry women on this dark street all bearing down on him. It was a beautiful image.

Westley's face went still and cold. He took a step closer and shook a finger in my face. "Listen, bitch, I didn't force anyone to have sex with me. And I didn't force anyone to make a recording. All of the women made that choice on their own. All I did was share them." He grunted and shrugged. "If you girls don't want the consequences, you should make better decisions."

I wanted to kill him. Put my fingers around his throat and squeeze until his eyes bulged and his face turned purple. If those cops didn't show up soon and I had to listen to any more of his victim-blaming, I was going to give in to my baser instincts.

I threw back the rest of my bourbon with one hand and waved my other around his movie-star face. "What a waste of good genes you are."

Westley caught my hand by the wrist and squeezed. Hard. I didn't let myself wince or flinch. "You better fix my system or you'll be sorry you ever met me."

Ha! I leaned forward. "Never going to happen, Tough Guy, and I was sorry thirty minutes after you bought me a drink."

His handsome face darkened and folded in on itself, and he showed his teeth. This was the real Westley, the ugly one he'd never video. He kept squeezing my wrist as hard as he could. It hurt like a mother and I'd have a monster bruise tomorrow, but I didn't lose my smirk. The cops would arrive any minute, and they'd pull up to see the elusive perp in person, manhandling one of his victims. This couldn't be going more perfectly if I'd had weeks to plan it. But then…

"Let her go."

Westley and I both froze.

I whipped my head toward the familiar, beloved voice. Max stood on the corner, breathing hard and sweating, as though he'd been running like a maniac. I almost laughed. He'd put remote GPS trackers on as much of the Sex Ghost's equipment as he could. The laptop Westley was carrying must have been emitting a signal. What must Max have thought when he saw it pinging from Fizz?

"I said, let her go," Max said through clenched teeth.

Westley shook my enclosed fist at him. "Not a chance in hell. This whore stole something from me, and I'm not letting her go until I get it back."

"Don't worry, Max," I said, giggling. Giddy because I was so happy to see his face, even if it was tight and anxious. Even though he probably would have shown up to be a white knight for anyone, not just me. "I'm totally fine."

Max glared at me, and I suddenly realized there was a fair bit of fear mixed into his mad. "You're not fine! You're alone with this asshole and he's got a grip on you. He could drag you into a car or down a side street. This situation is the polar opposite of fine!"

OK, that was a touch dramatic, but he didn't know about my friends inside or the lawyer or the cops arriving soon. Out of context, perhaps my situation did seem dangerous.

Max wasn't finished. "Hasn't he hurt you enough?" he demanded. "You're always going on and on about how you can take care of yourself, and then I find you like this?"

Westley seemed to like that I was getting harangued. "Stupid bitch," he added.

I'd had enough of them both. With my free hand, I smashed my empty bourbon glass on the sidewalk. The sound surprised Westley enough that he loosened his grip on my wrist and I was able to yank it away. Quickly turning so that my ass was to Westley's front, I raised my knee and brought the heel of my big, black boot down as hard as I could on his toes. I crushed those suckers. One or two might even have broken.

Westley grunted and leaned forward. I whirled again to face him, grabbed his shoulders and kneed him the balls. There was a month of emotion built up in that knee, and he went down howling. Excellent. It wasn't the first time I'd used the sequence of moves I'd learned in self-defense, but it was certainly the most satisfying.

As I straightened and smoothed my shirt, I heard one of the best sounds of all time. Max's firecracker laugh. Again and again he laughed, eventually leaning against Fizz's brick exterior for breath and balance.

When he finally got himself under control, he gasped. "And to think, I was coming to save you."

That wasn't really funny. I frowned. "You already did," I reminded him. "The night you shut him down. If not for you, my life would have been over. I would have lost my job. I would have been an embarrassment to everyone I know. You absolutely did save me."

He shrugged, a twinkle in his eye glinting behind the lens of his glasses. He pointed down at Westley, who lay curled on his side, twitching. "I had something more physical in mind."

"Do you want to hit him?" I asked helpfully. "The cops are still a few blocks away. You can probably fit in one good sucker punch." For some reason, that set him off on another peal of laughter. I reveled in it. The sound bubbled over me and washed away all the ugliness of the night.

The door to Fizz opened, and Roz poked her head outside. "Oh." She looked down at Westley's crumpled form. "Nice. Guess you don't need my Taser then." She looked up at me hopefully. "Unless you want me to give him one quick zap?"

"No," I said firmly. "But thanks."

She waggled an eyebrow at Max. "The hacker's here too. Interesting." She squinted down the street where two cop cars were one block south, waiting at a red light. "I'll go tell Mohawk that everything's fine."

Seconds later, the police cars pulled over, and Natasha Long jumped out of the passenger side of the one in front. "Are you all right, Tess? What happened?"

I cleared my throat. "He said I was going to be sorry we'd ever met. He called me a stupid bitch. He grabbed my wrist and squeezed." I held up both wrists. For once, my fair skin was doing me a favor. A hideous bruise was already forming on my left wrist, and you could see how swollen it was compared to my right. "I stepped on his foot and kneed him in the crotch to defend myself."

Natasha took over then, reminding the men with her about the outstanding John Doe warrant. Westley was shoved into the back of the second squad car, and the officers took his laptop into custody.

Before she climbed back in the first car, Natasha pulled me aside. "We'll take it from here, Tess, although you will be called in to make a statement at some point. I've already notified the attorneys in the other Sex Ghost cases. How did you know he was here?"

I decided to ignore Max's GPS trackers and go with only my story. "The bartender is a friend of mine, and some of the regulars are on the Sex Ghost mailing list. They're how I found out about the whole thing a month ago, and they called when they recognized him tonight."

She patted my arm and gave me a wide smile. "You've given me my most exciting case in a while."

I laughed. "Glad to help."

I watched the cars drive south and disappear. I wanted to do a little dance, imagining Westley in lockup tonight. And I would—later.

But right now, Max stood five feet away from me.

Chapter Thirty-One

MAX WAS STARING at my face, an inscrutable look on his own. Should I invite him into Fizz to get a drink? But it was loud in there, and I was sure Micki and Joe would want the whole Sex Ghost scoop. Frankly, I was done with Westley for the night. Hopefully, for life.

"Walk me home?" I finally said.

Max shrugged. "Sure."

Stalling, I sent a quick text to Roz and Micki, letting them know that I was heading home. Max just walked next to me, not saying a word.

Talk, Tess. I opened my mouth, but the words I really wanted to say didn't come out. Apparently, I needed to ease in with some small talk. "Everyone really missed you at the office this week," I said truthfully. "I'm so sorry that didn't work out."

"It's fine," he said, surprising me. "You guys were great, and the last couple of weeks have really got me thinking about what I should do next."

"Oh?" We turned the corner and ambled slowly in the direction of my apartment building. A stiff breeze was blowing, but I couldn't feel the cold. I had way too much adrenaline in my system, partly from the Westley encounter but more from Max.

"The past year I've been focused on finding a full-time job like the one I lost," he explained. "But contracting is actually a really good solution for me. I'd never thought of it before you, but I have a lot of contacts who can bring me in to less-scrutinized, under-the-radar kinds of temp positions. I can pay the bills that way and keep learning different stuff and meeting new people. If it leads to something permanent, great. If not, it keeps me solvent and my mind active. Who knows? Maybe I'll be struck with inspiration and come up with another product to develop, like the ransomware. Or maybe I'll pursue a second option."

"Second option?"

He grinned down at me. "Did you know that the FBI has an enormous cyber-crime division?"

I hadn't been wrong at all about Max. He was definitely a knight. "The Ghost Killer has a taste for taking down online villains, eh?" I asked, delighted.

"Maybe a little." He paused a moment. "What do you think?"

Exactly what I had thought from the moment he'd saved me. "You're a hero. It's a great idea."

We walked another block in silence. I could see my apartment building in the distance and dreaded our approach. What if he deposited me at the door and walked away before I could get the damn words out?

Max started chuckling. "I still can't believe you dropped him on the ground like that. You did it so easily! It was incredible." He gave me a sideways glance, eyes mischievous. "Frankly, you terrify me."

I wasn't going to get a better opening than that.

"You terrify me too." Ugh, my voice was actually shaking.

He stopped walking altogether, leaving me no choice but to stop too. I could feel his gaze, but my own was now refusing to leave the ground. "Explain that to me," he said softly. His voice was so kind I almost lost my breath.

I didn't know how to begin. What if I started in the wrong place or said the exact wrong thing? How could I explain that my scrambled brain had mixed up the past and present? He waited a full minute while I stared at the ground in silence.

Maybe saying nothing was the only wrong thing.

"M-my fiancé, Daniel, was a wonderful man," I stammered. "He was kind to me and my family. I leaned on him when I was in danger of falling over." Yuck, could I get more dramatic? What was I, the star of a soap opera? Puke.

But Max just nodded. "Go on."

"I freaked out at the brunch because Kat compared you to Daniel," I said quickly, aware that I was jumping around chronologically and hoping he'd follow. "Even though he was wonderful, he didn't really know me. The real me. At all. I figured out too late that marrying him would have meant choosing him over me and the life I wanted to lead. And I couldn't do that… I chose myself. To get out of the wedding, I did something horrible." I figured I didn't quite need to mention the cousin again. That little tidbit was probably burned in Max's brain for all of eternity.

"Ending the relationship was the right thing to do. He didn't know me and I wasn't in love with him. But I've never forgotten how hurtful I was." Here was the crux of it. Could I make him understand? "I freaked out because I didn't want to hurt you like that."

With the words out, I finally managed to look up from the pavement and at his face. To my dismay, he looked crushed. Damn it! What had I said wrong?

Max took off his glasses. "Ah. So you feel the same way about me that you felt about him? You care, but not in the right way." He did a strange raspy cough. "You don't think you'd ever fall—"

"Oh!" I exclaimed, finally getting it. "No! Max! That's the whole thing. It's completely different." I babbled. "I'm half in love with you already."

Oh boy. Now I shut up fast. My face felt like someone had taken a flamethrower to it. I peeped at Max out of the corner of my eye. He was looking away as well, but there was a definite smile on his lips.

"I suck at this," I mumbled. But I cleared my throat, determined that he'd understand. "When Kat compared you to Daniel, I freaked out because I remembered how I'd had to make a choice between being myself and being with the man in my life. But that was stupid. You and Daniel are only similar on the surface. With you, I didn't have to choose. You knew—and liked—the actual me."

I sighed, miserably, thinking of the last week and how much I'd missed him and how awful I'd felt every single moment. It was time to grovel. "Once I figured it out, I wanted to erase everything I said. I still can't believe how I acted. I was so wrong! So wrong to push you away. So wrong and sorry—"

"Tess." He put a finger on my lips. It felt so good to have him touching me again that all the words vanished from my mouth and I pushed my face harder against his finger. He dropped it—but only to gently cup his hand around the back of my neck.

He stared down at me, his eyes crinkled at the corners. I was glad he wasn't wearing his glasses. There were no barriers between us. "I'm not one to judge actions in old relationships. I was making a huge mistake myself. A mistake of...passivity. If it weren't for Aria being brave, I'd be married to her right now."

Wow. I hadn't thought about it like that before. I needed to send that woman flowers or something. He leaned down so that our noses rubbed. "Do you know, the night we first met, I went home and thought 'What if I'd met that girl'—you—'after I was already married?'"

He stood up straight, widening his eyes for effect. "It was the first time I realized what a near miss I'd had." He lowered his voice to a whisper. "What if, Tess? What if I'd never gotten to feel the way I do..." He leaned down again, pausing with his lips an inch above my own. "Right now." And then he was kissing me. In seconds, I was on my tiptoes with my arms around his neck. He tasted so good—like relief and joy, passion and hope. I was ready to kiss him for hours, maybe days.

But he pulled away and looked down at me. "I think I know why you chose an anchor for your tattoo."

I blinked at the non sequitur. He'd been wondering about the meaning of my tattoo? I certainly hadn't expected him to give it much thought. But that was Max. His brain never stopped working. For some reason, I was lucky enough to have it focused on me. "Oh yeah?"

His gaze was direct and loving. "An anchor is a symbol for strength and stability. It's something that holds you in place. It provides the means to hold on, no matter how rough things get."

I nodded, holding my breath. When I'd explained the anchor symbolism, in almost the exact same way, to Daniel all those years ago, he'd immediately seized me to him. "Oh, darling," he said. "I understand. You've been looking for an anchor. From now on, I'm it." It had been such a lovely sentiment and so heartfelt that I'd never corrected him. Never told him he was dead wrong.

Max went on. "Obviously, I don't know everything about you. Yet. But...you're the anchor. Right? You got it as a reminder to yourself that you have the strength to hold everything in place."

To my horror, my eyes flooded with tears. Because yes. That was exactly right.

"In your nonsensical speech at the brunch, you said that I was the kind of person who wants to build a life around someone. That's inaccurate, Boots. I want to build a life *with* someone, not around them."

He looked away, a telltale flush blooming on his cheeks. "I know we're in early days yet, but a woman who prides herself on her strength is exactly the kind of person I want to build a life with."

Exhilarated butterflies swam into my stomach and began to do backflips. I was a little afraid that a loud giggle-scream would erupt from my mouth at any moment. I'd met him as the "Good Time" and I'd certainly lived up to my Disaster Girl moniker, and yet Max still saw me as the anchor, my own most treasured self-image. How much luckier could I get?

Max was right. We were in early days. But it was incredibly easy to envision a future that involved him. More nights laughing together. Those "real dates" we'd never been on. Getting to know his quirks and kinks. Watching him battle Roz for the best dirty one-liners. Lazy Saturday mornings intertwined in bed. Coming home after a long day to vent about work issues. Taking him with me on a visit out to see Kat. Charming his parents and big brothers while being a questionable influence on the dating of his younger sisters. Cheering on his brilliance as he demolished other internet assholes.

He cleared his throat in an embarrassed sort of way, and I realized I hadn't spoken in quite some time. "Well, OK," I said nonchalantly. "If you want to work on the other half, I guess I'm up for it."

His brow crinkled in confusion. "The other half?"

"Yeah," I said, in my best smart-ass tone. "Like I said, I'm only half in love with you right now. If you want to try for the other half, you can." I knew my wide, vulnerable eyes didn't match the cocky voice or words, but with Max, that was OK.

A wide grin covered his face, and he nodded briskly. "Let's go upstairs and I'll get to work."

The End

If you enjoyed *Disaster Girl*, don't forget to leave a review!

Join Tule Publishing's newsletter for more great reads and weekly deals.

Acknowledgements

This book is my favorite thing that I've ever written. But it took a lot of help to get the story that was in my head onto the page.

Thanks to Julie Sturgeon, who gave me confidence in this book when I most needed it and for doing an incredible job editing, as always. Thanks to Janna Bonikowski, my agent, for being so patient with my revisions and for being a true partner in the publishing process. Thanks to Nathalie Holberg and Ruth Vincent, the two best critique partners in the world, who read early drafts and provided so much valuable input and support.

I wanted to write this story because of Tess. I had her voice in my head from the very beginning and I hope I was able to do her justice. Basically, I wanted to see my friends on the page. The women I know are independent, self-confident badasses. They inspire me every day and I'm so lucky to know them.

About the Author

There are only three things Michelle Dayton loves more than sexy and suspenseful novels: her family, the city of Chicago, and Mr. Darcy. Michelle dreams of a year of world travel – as long as the trip would include weeks and weeks of beach time. As a bourbon lover and unabashed wine snob, Michelle thinks heaven is discussing a good book over an adult beverage.

Thank you for reading

Disaster Girl

If you enjoyed this book, you can find more from all our great authors at TulePublishing.com, or from your favorite online retailer.

Made in the USA
Middletown, DE
06 June 2021